INDIA BLACK

INDIA BLACK

Carol K. Carr

BERKLEY PRIME CRIME, NEW YORK

THE BERKLEY PUBLISHING GROUP
Published by the Penguin Group
Penguin Group (USA) Inc.
375 Hudson Street, New York, New York 10014, USA
Penguin Group (Canada), 90 Eglinton Avenue East, Suite 700, Toronto, Ontario M4P 2Y3, Canada
(a division of Pearson Penguin Canada Inc.)
Penguin Books Ltd., 80 Strand, London WC2R 0RL, England
Penguin Group Ireland, 25 St. Stephen's Green, Dublin 2, Ireland (a division of Penguin Books Ltd.)
Penguin Group (Australia), 250 Camberwell Road, Camberwell, Victoria 3124, Australia
(a division of Pearson Australia Group Pty. Ltd.)
Penguin Books India Pvt. Ltd., 11 Community Centre, Panchsheel Park, New Delhi—110 017, India
Penguin Group (NZ), 67 Apollo Drive, Rosedale, North Shore 0632, New Zealand
(a division of Pearson New Zealand Ltd.)
Penguin Books (South Africa) (Pty.) Ltd., 24 Sturdee Avenue, Rosebank, Johannesburg 2196,
South Africa

Penguin Books Ltd., Registered Offices: 80 Strand, London WC2R 0RL, England

This book is an original publication of The Berkley Publishing Group.

This is a work of fiction. Names, characters, places, and incidents either are the product of the author's imagination or are used fictitiously, and any resemblance to actual persons, living or dead, business establishments, events, or locales is entirely coincidental. The publisher does not have any control over and does not assume any responsibility for author or third-party websites or their content.

FIRST EDITION: January 2011

Library of Congress Cataloging-in-Publication Data

Carr, Carol K.
  India Black / Carol K. Carr—1st ed.
    p. cm.
  ISBN 978-0-425-23866-0
1. Brothels—England—London—Fiction. 2. International relations—Fiction. 3. London (England)—History—1800–1950—Fiction. I. Title.
  PS3603.A7726I53 2011
813'.6—dc22   2010029315

PRINTED IN THE UNITED STATES OF AMERICA

10 9 8 7 6 5 4 3 2 1

INDIA BLACK

PREFACE

My name is India Black. I am a whore.

If those words made you blush, if your hand fluttered to your cheek or you harrumphed disapprovingly into your beard, then you should return this volume to the shelf, cast a cold glance at the proprietor as you leave, and hasten home feeling proper and virtuous. You can go to Evensong tonight with a clear conscience. However, if my admission caused a frisson of excitement in your drab world, if you felt a stirring in your trousers or beneath your skirts when you read my words, then I must caution you that you will be disappointed in the story contained in this volume. No doubt you're hoping to read in these pages the narrative of a young woman's schooling in the arts of love or perhaps a detailed description of some of my more memorable artistic performances. As for the former, there's enough of that kind of shoddy chronicle available, most of it written by men masquerading as "Maggie" or "Eunice," and therefore not only fictitious but asinine to boot. As for the latter, I'd be the first to admit that I was a tireless entertainer in the boudoir, but that's another story for another time and will cost you more money than this volume when I get around to writing it down.

But you are a *whore*, you say. There must be *some* sex involved in this chronicle. Indeed, I am a whore, and well versed in the skills of my profession. It is to that profession that I owe my involvement in the affair hereafter described. But if you want sex, you'll have to pay for it. I'm out of the game myself these days, but I can set you up with a nice girl, any night after seven, at the Lotus House on St. Alban's Street. You'll have to go elsewhere if your taste runs to men, boys, or ruminants.

Well, if you haven't already shelved this book on account of the dearth of depravity and vice you were hoping to find in it, presumably you're still interested in learning what a whore has to contribute to the literary scene. I have written a true account of how I met our esteemed prime minister, Benjamin Disraeli (the old queen himself), of my encounter with the tsar's intelligence agents in London, and of my pursuit of these same Russian spies across England to the Channel and beyond. Some of you may be disinclined to believe the veracity of what you read in these pages. "Pshaw," you say. "How did a London trollop become embroiled in such weighty affairs? The idea is preposterous."

Now you may think it highly implausible that the government of Great Britain would stoop to enlisting the services of a whore, no matter how serious the predicament in which it finds itself. But if you ponder the topic awhile, as I did, you'll realize that there's a natural affinity between politicians and whores, having, as they do, certain similarities that breed a type of professional courtesy, if you will. For example, we share the same line of work: we each provide a service in exchange for something else. In my case, it's money, and for politicians, it's votes. We each exercise our charm and wile to convince our customers to pay us or vote for us, for we're in competition with others who can provide the same services. And we'll both do just about anything, as long as the price is right. Frankly, I think it's a damned slur against the tarts to consign them to the social rubbish heap just for earning a living while praising the politicos as selfless public servants. At least bints aren't hypocritical: you'll never hear one of them blathering on sanctimoniously that they do what they do for the benefit of the British public.

That's all I've got to say about the subject. Every word in this volume is the gospel truth. You can put your money on the counter and buy the book, or you can go to the devil. It's all the same to me.

ONE

The day that Bowser kicked it was a bleak winter Sunday like any other in the year of our Lord, eighteen hundred and seventy-six. The fog had set in early that afternoon and a fine mist was falling, muffling the sound of the church bells around the city. The whores were all asleep in their beds upstairs, their customers having departed early to share the comforts of hearth and family, a joint of mutton, and the Book of Common Prayer. Or, if they were young blades, they had trundled off to their soft feather mattresses to sleep off a night of debauchery while I counted their sovereigns.

That was my usual occupation on Sundays: tallying the preceding night's receipts over a glass of whisky or a pot of steaming Earl Grey and some of the petrified horse droppings Mrs. Drinkwater, my cook, so charitably called her muffins. There was very little custom on Sundays, save for Bowser, and he'd been here so often that I no longer felt obliged to chat him up when he arrived. This Sunday was no different from the others. I'd yawned my way out of bed shortly after noon, put on a dressing gown and slippers, and conducted the customary post-Saturday-night inspection of the premises to determine if any object had been stolen, vandalized or destroyed, or if anyone had passed out on the sofa in the salon and needed to be ejected.

I'd christened my establishment "Lotus House," an obvious reference to the poem by Mr. Tennyson; a fact which eludes all of my bints but is recognized by a fair number of my clientele. I cater to gentleman, you see. No butchers, navvies or sailors (naval officers excepted, of course) allowed through my door. Only junior ministers, high-ranking civil servants, minor aristocracy and military officers visit my premises, but since most of them are Lord Somebody's son and heir, I'm wagering that my stock will continue to rise where it counts.

A plain establishment offering watered whisky and slovenly girls won't do for the bloods who frequent my place of business. Lotus House is both elegant and comfortable, more akin to a gentleman's club than his home, for who wants to play slap and tickle with a whore in a room that reminds you of your own parlor and your sweet, insipid little wife? So you'll find only plain wallpaper and tasteful carpets in Lotus House. No flocked velvet paper in viridian and orange, no stuffed birds in cages, no ungainly wooden monstrosities that resemble devices of torture more than pieces of furniture. The only concession to the particular business conducted in Lotus House is in the selection of pictures upon the wall. Imagine that the Earl of Rochester's talents had been those of the visual arts and not the verbal, and you'll have a fair idea of the kind of thing that adorns my establishment. It's not my taste at all; the pictures are only there to stimulate the customers, for one thing I learned at an early age is that a stimulated gentleman is a profligate gentleman.

I keep a stock of fine wines and brandies and a humidor of Cuban cigars, and my bints are lovely, stupid and discreet, just the way the toffs like them. I take great pride in my business and in Lotus House, lavishing all my attention on them, leaving very little time for my own amusements. But being the madam instead of the worker bee suits me.

I gave up the game years ago, preferring to herd my own flock of tarts than waste my youth and good looks servicing an assortment of randy gentleman. I'm a damned handsome woman, if I do say so myself. My figure attracts attention, being both lithe and buxom. I've a cloud of raven hair, eyes of cobalt blue, and a creamy English complexion (thanks to my self-discipline; I don't indulge in laudanum, tobacco or opium, like most London whores).

It can be hellish out there, competing against the other abbesses for the quality customer. There isn't a madam in London who wouldn't poison your reputation to make a few pence, spreading rumors of diseased, loquacious or kleptomaniacal bints at your establishment. Still, I wouldn't trade Lotus House for the world. There may be easier ways of earning a sou: I could allow some pedigreed ass to keep me in French perfume and silk gowns, tucked away in a cozy pied-à-terre in St. John's Wood, and driving a four-in-hand along Rotten Row. But I like my freedom. There is not enough money in this fair isle to entice me to flutter my lashes and drop my knickers for a pompous peer who smells of horses and hasn't got the brains God gave a goose. Owning Lotus House ensures that I am my own woman. I give the orders and keep the profits, and no one dangles me like a puppet on his purse strings. Besides, you might say that Lotus House is my patrimony, having been acquired by me as it has, and as it's unlikely I'll ever see anything else resembling an inheritance, I'm rather attached to the premises.

This morning, all was well. No bloodstains on the Turkey carpet, the pictures on the wall still hung true, and none of the wineglasses had ended up in the fireplace. There was the usual pall of cigar smoke, bay rum, stale cognac and cheap perfume, but I flung open the windows in the salon and waited for the stench to be replaced by the acrid fumes of a winter afternoon in London.

I rapped on the door to the kitchen, stuck my head into the darkness and bellowed, "Tea." I was not surprised to hear the sound of breaking glass, followed by an oath from Mrs. Drinkwater (a most inappropriately named woman). I resolved to conduct an inventory of the cooking sherry in the coming week.

The study, a pleasant room facing St. Alban's Street, smelled less offensive than the salon. I only entertain the gentlemen here for a few minutes after they arrive, jollying along the repeat customers before summoning their usual bints and sizing up the new clients before introducing them to "a nice girl who'll just suit you." Then I gently shepherd them out the door into the salon, where I ply them with free booze and decent cigars while they dandle the girls on their knees and leer at each other through their whiskers until they're ready to stagger upstairs.

I was gratified to see that Mrs. Drinkwater had completed her duties in my study before wading into the liquor supply. A seacoal fire burned in the grate, the lamps had been lighted and their wicks freshly trimmed, and last night's empty glasses had been removed. I lit a taper from the fire and used it to ignite a saucer of incense. The scent of sandalwood filled the air, eliminating the faint odor of smoke that clung to the cushions. Mrs. Drinkwater had placed the morning papers in a neat pile in the center of my desk, and I glanced through them idly while I waited for my tea.

The headlines were depressingly familiar: The Russians were rattling sabres, backing their lapdogs, the Serbs, in their fight against the crumbling, decadent Ottoman Empire, and threatening to march on Constantinople. Dizzy, the novelist turned present prime minister, had dusted off a rusty rapier himself and was waving it rabidly, uttering dire warnings that Constantinople was the key to India and England must do whatever necessary to prevent the Russian Bear from occupying the city. Gladstone, the former prime minister turned evangelist, was on the sidelines, scrawling religious screeds against the Mussulman massacres of Christians (ignoring the tit-for-tat massacres of Mussulmans by the Christians), and sniffing around No. 10 Downing Street like a lion smelling zebra on the African breeze, waiting for Dizzy to make the fatal misstep of backing the bloody Turks (Mussulmans, by God) against the Russians (nominally Christians, but not really our type).

Bloody politics and politicians. I had very few rules here at Lotus House, but one of them was that gentleman were forbidden to flog their favorite horses while they were under my roof. Discussions inevitably led to arguments, which usually led to two portly gents with red faces and bristling whiskers glaring balefully at each other as they circled the room, while the other customers lined the wall and cheered them on, the girls squealed with excitement, and I calculated the loss of revenue with a sinking heart.

I tossed the papers in a heap on the floor and crossed the room to the Chinese screen in the corner, which hid from view a heavy iron safe. I'd just extracted the bag of gold coins when I heard the clatter of crockery as Mrs. Drinkwater lurched into the room, her pink face ("Heat," she says; "Drink," I reply) screwed tight and her lips pursed in concentration as she strained to balance the tea tray. She's rather unsteady on her pins ("Age," she says; "Drink," I reply), and the china rattled ominously as she weaved her way across the room. She deposited the tray on the desk with a thump, huffing like a dray horse released from the harness. I winced as the Limoges bounced.

"Here's your tea, then," she announced breathlessly. "Will you be wanting anything else?"

"Lunch?"

Mrs. Drinkwater released the agonized sigh of a martyred saint. "You'll be dining in, then?"

"Yes."

"Will there be any guests?"

"I'll be dining alone."

I was treated to another wheezing bellow of affliction.

"That will be all, Mrs. Drinkwater," I said.

She gave a half bow that threatened to send her arse-over-heels, and then tacked unsteadily out of my study. I poured a cup of tea and pondered, not for the first time, why I employed such a drunken, ill-bred creature. I know the reason, of course. Lotus House, as fine an establishment as it is, is still a brothel, after all, and it's damned hard to find a cook who's willing to work among a gaggle of half-naked women and drunken roisterers. Mrs. Drinkwater, occasionally surly and inevitably intoxicated, was the best of a bad lot.

I poured a cup of tea, hefted one of the cook's scones, debated its relative worth as paperweight or weapon, and returned it to the plate untouched. The bag of coins jingled merrily as I picked it up. There's no sound I like better in the world than that of sovereigns cascading onto the leather blotter on my desk. I raked my fingers through the gold pieces and contemplated them with pleasure. Last night had been exceptionally lucrative. A troop of cavalry officers, home from India a fortnight before they'd been scheduled to dock, had descended on Lotus House like a plague of locusts. They'd drunk the house dry in under an hour and I'd had to send Mrs. Drinkwater to knock up the owner of the nearest wine shop to replenish my stores, but it had been worth it.

I stacked the coins in a row of small golden towers and settled myself at my desk to review the month's expenses. Casks of sherry, cases of whisky, Madeira and brandy, gallons of porter, ale and rum. A quarter of beef and two of mutton; bushels of potatoes, wheels of cheddar, slabs of butter; dozens of loaves of bread; not to mention sugar, coffee and tea. Those damned whores were eating (and drinking) me out of house and home. I could of course stop feeding them and let them fend for themselves on their earnings, but they'd be thin, ragged and diseased in a fortnight. It was better to keep them here, where I could keep an eye on them, and see that they stayed fresh and plump for the customers. My plan worked admirably, but at the rate my trollops were going through supplies, I'd have to raise rates again this year, and how the gentlemen would grumble, until I fetched a young filly in her petticoats to sit upon their knee and tickle their chins, and then no price was too dear.

I was totting up the charges and wincing at the image of my pile of golden sovereigns disappearing into the pockets of the greedy tradesmen when my roving eye detected an entry that made me look twice, then roar for Mrs. Drinkwater to fetch me Clara.

I read the entry again, just to be sure I wasn't imagining it. Two pounds for pineapples. *Pineapples?*

Clara Swansdown, formerly Bridget Brodie of Ballykelly, all flaming red hair, pale skin and freckles, came bustling in, eyes still filmy with sleep, fumbling for the sash of her dressing gown. "God's truth, that old crone give me such a fright I nearly wet meself. Whatever's the matter? The Queen ain't dead, is she?"

I brandished my pen at her accusingly. "Pineapples?" I asked.

She scratched her bum through her dressing gown and looked abashed. "Oh. I reckon I should have told you about that 'fore I sent out for 'em. Tubby Farquhar asked for 'em special."

"Got a thing for fruit, does he?"

Clara nodded vigorously. "He do indeed. He was stationed in Montevideo for a spell and he got right fond of 'em."

"I see. No doubt pineapples are quite common in Montevideo. Probably lying about all over the place. Have to hire a gang of little brown boys to remove the damned things from the polo field so as not to cripple the ponies."

Clara looked doubtful. "I don't think Tubby plays polo."

"Nor do I suppose he's ever bought his own pineapples. They may be thick on the ground in Montevideo, but they're a luxury in London. I expect Tubby sends out the servants to do that sort of thing and has no more idea what a pineapple costs than why fleas fart."

"Fleas fart?"

I could see that Clara was losing the thread of the conversation. "Do *you* have any idea how much a pineapple costs in London?"

"No, ma'am."

I consulted my records. "Two quid."

Clara's mouth fell open. "Blimey. That's robbery."

"Indeed. I don't mind making allowances for some of our oldest customers. I'll even go so far as to cut my profit margin a bit for them and indulge some of their little fancies at my expense. But Tubby Farquhar is hardly a valued customer, at least not yet. If he wants pineapples . . ."

"Oh, he does. He was stationed in . . ."

"Yes, I know. Montevideo. As I was saying, if he wants pineapples, he shall have them. But he must pay for them. Do you understand?"

Clara nodded. "Yes, ma'am. I'll get the two pounds from him when he comes in on Tuesday."

I shook my head. "Clara, my dear, there's a lot you must learn. Tell Tubby the pineapples cost two and six. Keep a shilling for yourself, and bring the rest to me."

Clara's eyes were the size of my tea saucer. "Oh, ma'am, that's genius, that is."

You can see why I'm the abbess and Clara's the bint. She's a nice girl, Clara, but as thick as two planks, which is one of the reasons I employ her.

"That's all, Clara. You may go now." She was at the door when my curiosity got the better of me. "A moment, Clara." She turned back into the room. "What exactly do you and Tubby Farquar do with those pineapples?"

"Well, ma'am, it's like this . . ."

I never did hear what Tubby and Clara were up to with the tropical fruit, because at that moment the door burst open and a garish figure reeled in, squealing like a stuck pig, and hurled itself into my arms. The casual observer might have thought the Prince of Wales, undergoing an unfortunate experiment with his mustache and dressed in a confusing array of corsets and trousers, had finally succumbed to venereal disease and gone barking mad, had wandered into the Lotus House and was now running amuck through the halls. But I recognized the face of Arabella Cloud, one of my newest employees, and the favorite of Bowser, my regular Sunday afternoon customer.

"Good God, Arabella. What's happened?"

Tears streaked her face and slid down into the wispy mustache pasted to her upper lip. "It's Bowser, ma'am. He's dead."

TWO

Bowser was indeed deceased, though it took some minutes to ascertain that fact, as I had to paw through a lace ruff the size of a barrel hoop to get at the pulse of the corpulent gentleman who lay sprawled across the four-poster in Arabella's room.

I pressed my fingers into Bowser's fleshy wattle, all the while issuing helpful advice like, "Breathe, you bloody bastard," and, "Don't die here, you thumping great whale," but my admonitions had no effect. Bowser remained dead.

Bowser was a regular customer; a stout, tweedy old cove with a blue-veined nose who worked in the War Office. I called him Bowser because he panted a great deal, had the mournful eyes of a spaniel chastised for soiling the carpet and had a distressing tendency to hump the leg of any available female. He always arrived on Sunday afternoon, dressed in a sober dark suit and a top hat, and carrying under his arm the black leather case that signified the senior British civil servant. Come straight from the office, he'd told me years ago. It was the only time he could get any work done, without the ceaseless interruptions he had to endure Monday through Friday. Lotus House was his bit of fun. Bowser would settle in the salon with a drink and a cheroot, and Arabella would come tripping downstairs with a rakish air, brandishing a fake mustache and whiskers and bleating, "Hello, Mama, dear." After a few draughts of brandy and soda, and a few minutes winking at Arabella and addressing her as "Dear boy," Bowser would toddle up the stairs and down the hall to Arabella's room, where he'd shed his suit and combinations, dress up as Queen Victoria in her mourning clothes (did she ever wear anything else?) and stimulate himself while he flogged Arabella and castigated her for her wanton ways and losses at the gaming tables. In this game, I've seen and done most everything (although every whore has at least one thing she won't do), but even I found Bowser's penchant for dressing up as our sovereign while a tart masqueraded as the wicked Prince Bertie a tad peculiar. However, he paid handsomely for the privilege, and who am I to judge my fellow man? What the prince consort would have thought of this little pantomime, I shudder to think, though I'm of the opinion it's a good thing Albert died when he did; otherwise, he'd be remembered (despite Vicky's attempts at beatification) as a pious prig with a thick accent. But I digress.

I closed the protruding brown eyes (not out of respect, but because their bulbous stare looked vaguely accusing), gently disengaged the riding crop from the spastic grip of the corpse, and said: "Tell me what happened, Arabella."

Arabella was sniffling in the corner. She had Slavic cheekbones and breasts like the Caucasus, and as she had a flair for accents, excelled at playing Polish émigrés and impoverished Russian princesses. She wore a nifty set of trousers, too, and had become a favorite of Bowser's shortly after she'd arrived on the steps of Lotus House six months ago.

Arabella's great white bosom heaved. One side of her mustache had begun to droop. "Lord, I don't know. One minute, he was shaming me for losing a hundred pounds at vingt-et-un and rogering Nellie Clifden on the grounds of Kensington Palace, and the next he was flat on the floor, flailing around like a dying goose and shouting for Mabel."

"Mabel?"

"Mrs. Bowser, I reckon."

The mention of the wife made me blanch. It was bad enough that a government bureaucrat had kicked the bucket in my establishment, which meant God knows what by way of interference and investigation into my affairs, but the poor sod also had a wife who'd have to hear the news somehow. Luckily, that was no concern of mine. For that matter, neither was the government's loss. My only concern was getting Bowser out of the house.

"Listen to me, Arabella. If word of this gets out, I'll be ruined."

Arabella swiped at a tear that was trickling through the powder on her cheek and nodded dumbly.

"You don't want to have to find another house, do you?"

"No, ma'am."

"Good. Then see that you keep quiet and don't say a word to any of the girls." Bints are prone to gossip, and I knew that if one word escaped Arabella's lips, the news that India Black had lost a customer would be all over London by teatime. It wouldn't take long for some enterprising competitor of mine to whisper a word into the ear of the nearest peeler, and I'd have a serious problem. I needed to get Bowser (God rest his soul—somewhere else, of course) out of here as quickly as possible.

"Dry your eyes, Arabella, and fetch Mrs. Drinkwater."

By the time Arabella had returned with the cook in tow, I'd succeeded in stripping the heavy black bombazine gown from the old codger and was removing a petticoat the size of a schooner's sail from the limp body. Mrs. Drinkwater teetered over to help, and between us we peeled off the rest of Bowser's costume until he lay stark naked on the carpet, then dressed him again in his own clothes. It was a bit like playing with a large, albeit cold and clammy, doll. Mrs. Drinkwater proved to be of considerable assistance in the matter, perhaps because she was oblivious to the indecency of the occasion, being blind drunk, though she wheezed and huffed like a bellows, all the while moaning about "the sort of work a respectable woman is required to do in this establishment."

"What do we do now?" asked Arabella, when Bowser once again looked the dignified civil servant.

"Roll him up in the carpet and shove him under the bed," I said. "We'll move him after dark."

"Move him where?"

"Down by the river. Someone will find his body by morning."

Arabella recoiled in horror. "And what am I supposed to do until dark? I'm not staying here with a corpse under my bed."

"You can stay in Nancy's old room."

"Why can't we move the old geezer up to Nancy's room, and I can have my own room back?"

Bints are so thoughtless. "Because Nancy's room is on the

third floor, and I don't fancy hauling Bowser up and down stairs a dozen times today. He stays here."

Bowser made an unwieldy bundle, stuffed into the carpet like a sausage in its casing. We pushed and shoved (with Mrs. Drinkwater exhaling copious clouds of gin-scented breath) until we'd managed to wedge our visitor under the four-poster. We emerged, huffing like we'd run the length of Great Russell Street with a bobby on our heels.

"Weighs a bloody ton," Mrs. Drinkwater said, between gasps. "We'll be lucky to get him down the stairs without dying ourselves." The same thought had occurred to me.

I was pondering my predicament when the bell rang to announce a visitor to Lotus House. The three of us froze, Mrs. Drinkwater wheezing faintly and all of us gaping and looking guilty as hell, rather like a bad painting by Edwin Landseer entitled *The Quarry Hears the Pursuit*, or some such rot. I regained my composure first and poked Mrs. Drinkwater in the ribs.

"Go answer the door," I said. It seemed the sensible thing to do. I didn't think the local plod would be on the doorstep, as there wasn't any reason yet for anyone to be suspicious, and it might be a paying customer.

Mrs. Drinkwater lurched off, mumbling something about fair wages for additional and extraordinary duties, which I ignored. Arabella and I waited for a considerable period of time while the cook plodded down the staircase. I heard the front door open and the murmur of low voices, then the ponderous tread of Mrs. Drinkwater ascending the stairs.

"Well?" I demanded in a whisper, when she'd reeled into the bedroom.

"It's Reverend Calthorp, ma'am. He was hoping for a word with the young ladies."

I groaned. I've no objections to clergy as a rule; some of my best customers are members of the cloth. But Reverend Charles Calthorp was no customer. He was a Low Church do-gooder of Gladstone's ilk who'd committed his life to helping those less fortunate than himself, whether they wanted his assistance or not, and he'd decided that the girls in my house were ripe for conversion. He spent a good deal of time loitering about the place on Sunday afternoons, passing out tracts, staring at the décolletage surrounding him and blushing like a maiden aunt at the mention of unmentionables.

"Bloody hell," I muttered. "Why me, Lord?" But as no answer was forthcoming from the Deity, I had to take matters into my own hands. "Show him into the salon, and give him a glass of sherry," I instructed Mrs. Drinkwater. "Not the good stuff," I added, as she exited. Calthorp wouldn't know the difference between amontillado and giraffe piss.

I recinched my dressing grown and trotted off down the hall to find Mary, whose dewy, blond, virginal façade concealed a veteran *fille de joie* overly fond of the essence of juniper berry and laudanum. Her bedroom smelled like a gin palace and was dark as a tomb, the curtains drawn against the grey English sky. She was sleeping soundly, wrapped in a cocoon of quilts, snoring louder than a company of the Queen's Own Highlanders.

I nudged her, none too gently, in the ribs. "Wake up, Mary. You've got a visitor."

She stirred, mumbled, then burrowed farther into the pillows.

I prodded the bundled bedclothes with more force. "Come on, you lazy cow. He's waiting."

"I ain't got no customers on the Sabbath." Her voice was muffled by goose down. "Who is it?"

"Calthorp."

Mary bolted upright, and the bed erupted, quilts ballooning into the air and tiny feathers wafting to the floor. "*He* ain't no customer," she said, nose quivering indignantly. "You've got a nerve, waking me up so I can entertain Charles Calthorp. Go spin the plates for him yourself."

Ungrateful wench. Disrespectful, too. I should turn her out on the doorstep, but I needed a favor.

"I'd ask one of the other girls, but nobody is as good as you at handling him."

It was true. Mary was a vicar's daughter and had a great deal of experience at fending off the inquisitive paws of prebenderies and curates. And, being a vicar's daughter, she can spout Old Testament claptrap with the best of them.

"Keep him occupied for an hour, and I'll send Mrs. Drinkwater for a bottle of the finest for you."

I left Mary happily contemplating an evening spent with her favorite companion, and headed back down the passage to Arabella's room. I stopped short at the sight of the slight figure standing hesitantly in the hall outside Arabella's door, hand reaching for the knob.

My heart gave a lurch. "Reverend Calthorp," I sang out, a bit shrilly.

The figure started. "Miss Black," Calthorp said, gesturing vaguely at the door to Arabella's room. "I was told you were in here."

Damn Mrs. Drinkwater. "You're mistaken, sir. I asked that you be shown into the salon. Won't you accompany me there now?"

He bowed stiffly. He looked the very image of the impoverished clergyman, in his ill-fitting suit of rusty black broadcloth and his seedy white collar, sleek brown hair brushed back over a high forehead, his brown eyes vague and doe-like behind gold-rimmed glasses.

We traipsed downstairs, me leading the way and sashaying my hips for the good vicar's benefit and praying Mary wouldn't take too long with her toilette. Mrs. Drinkwater had preceded us into the salon with a silver tray in her hands bearing a cordial glass and a decanter of the swill I offer the non-regulars, and was gazing round her with an air of bewilderment. Her face cleared when I ushered Calthorp into the room. She plonked the tray on a side table and sloshed a little of the sherry into the glass.

"Wondered where you'd got to," she said to Calthorp, handing him the glass. "Here you are, Your Grace."

Calthorp coloured at the elevation in rank. "Just plain 'Reverend Calthorp' will do, Mrs. Drinkwater." He took the glass, nodded his thanks and seated himself on the sofa, after a careful inspection of the cushions and the antimacassars.

"I was hoping I'd find you in, Miss Black."

I was at the window, staring at the leaden sky and calculating the hours until dusk. "I don't provide services myself, Mr. Calthorp. It'll have to be one of the girls."

He blushed a fiery red, extracted a large, threadbare handkerchief from his breast pocket and mopped his brow. "I'd no intention of availing myself of your 'services,' as you so delicately phrased it, as I'm sure you well know."

"Church need a new steeple, then?" My anxiety about the lifeless Bowser made me snappish. I made an attempt to rein in my irritation and be polite: even a Calthorp could turn into a customer. There may be men who pant after tarts for the purpose of saving their soul (that great booby Gladstone likes to prowl the

cobbles for that very purpose, or so he says, but we all know better), but I've yet to meet any.

Calthorp had recovered himself. "I have come to ask you for
money, Mrs. Black, but not for something trivial." Here he stole
a glance around the room, making sure I noted him gazing at
the Turkey carpet, the crystal glasses on the bar, the silver candle-
sticks. "I've no doubt you could easily afford to share generously
with those in need, should you so choose."

"Charity begins at home, Reverend. I'm doing my bit to keep
myself out of the parish workhouse, so as not to burden the well-
to-do members of your flock."

He brightened considerably. "Why, that's the very thing I've
come about. Seeing that these young women have some alternative to the life they live now; a way to earn a wage and support
themselves so they needn't debase themselves as, as . . . " Here
he coughed delicately, though he needn't have concerned himself
with my feelings.

"Sluts?" I suggested. "Whores, prostitutes, bints?"

No actor was ever more punctual. Calthorp blushed, right on
cue.

It is wearying to converse with a young man with an exaggerated sense of modesty. I'd be here all day, trying to winkle out
what Calthorp wanted, while he tried to avoid calling attention
to the fact that he was talking to a madam about prostitution. I
had other things on my mind, such as disposing of that oversize
corpse laid out in Arabella's room.

"What is it you've come about, Mr. Calthorp?" I asked.

He composed himself, not without difficulty, and without
meeting my eye, launched into a hurried exposition of his scheme
for the bints, which amounted to finding a place for them with

dressmakers, milliners and seamstresses and such, serving as apprentices to the trade while earning a small wage. This would provide them a living and allow them to enter the "society of decent citizens" (as Calthorp called it—I could have disillusioned him on that score, as dozens of those "decent citizens" regularly passed through the doors of Lotus House).

Most reformers are well-intentioned idiots, and Calthorp was a prime example of the species. My girls made more in a night at Lotus House than they could make in a month as a dressmaker's apprentice, which is why so many of those very seamstresses and dressmakers moonlighted on the side as whores ("dollymops," they're called). Not to mention that a bint's work involved no more than lying on her back (or in other positions) for a few hours each night, instead of working fourteen hours a day to deliver a dress to an arrogant biddy who would never, under any circumstances, admit a former whore to "decent society." Ah, well. It's not my allotted purpose in life to correct the Calthorps of this world; better to let them blunder along in their righteous idealism, having meetings, drinking tea and writing tracts: it gives them something to do.

Mary came flouncing in then and I escaped from Calthorp, leaving him earnestly expostulating his grand plan to her while she listened sympathetically and stroked his knee from time to time, to soothe him. I made a discreet little tippling motion to Mary to remind her of her reward and retreated to my study.

I spent the rest of the afternoon and the early evening hours pacing a slow circle in the carpet. The body upstairs exerted an unsettling influence on me. I had the oddest feeling that Lotus

House was being watched, yet each time I drew aside the curtains and peered into the street, I saw nothing unusual. Still, I couldn't shake the feeling that an unknown watcher waited outside. The fog thickened throughout the day, until visibility was restricted to only a few feet. The conditions were perfect for moving a corpse, but they also provided ample cover for anyone to observe the removal in secrecy.

I was much too nervous to eat anything, but I fortified myself for the night's work with copious amounts of tea and the odd whisky and soda, and whiled away the hours behind the closed door of the study, leafing through the papers and eyeing the clock on the mantle. At last, the damned thing struck eleven, with a soft whirring of chimes, and I gathered a cloak, pinned on a hat and slipped out the back door into the alley.

Under less trying circumstances, I'd have sent one of the girls to fetch a cart and horse from the ostler down the lane, but I trusted no one else with this errand. The mist that had been falling most of the day still drifted down in a gauzy veil, and one of the city's famous fogs had risen, so that walking through the streets felt like walking through a cloud. The moisture beaded on my cloak and dripped off my hat. The flaring gas lamps made a valiant, but feeble, effort to cut the gloom, but their light was limited to the few square feet below their posts, and great black shadows engulfed the distances between them.

I walked briskly, keeping a wary eye. I was known in this street, but that was no guarantee against a knock on the head, or worse. It's a shame, isn't it, when a mostly law-abiding citizen and woman of property doesn't feel safe to walk the streets of London? And after all the publicity that little snoop Dickens had brought to the needy and the homeless, not to mention the criminal class. You think something would have been done by now about the crime rate and the appalling condition of the poor, but the politicians kept waving their Union Jacks, fretting over Ireland, swilling champagne and stuffing themselves with oysters, and couldn't be bothered. In these circumstances, the astute madam entertained no illusions about the police being within a thousand yards of the neighborhood, and protected herself. An acquaintance of mine had provided me (at an exorbitant price, I might add) with a fine Webley British Bulldog, along with a number of lessons in its use, conducted in the forest a few miles from London and prying eyes. You may think the .442 caliber of the Bulldog to be too much to handle for a woman of my size, but I'm wiry (not to mention stubborn), and I had conquered the massive kick of the firearm. It is amazing what a woman can do if only she ignores what men tell her she can't. If I do say so myself (and I seldom refrain from doing so), I'm a deuced fine shot, and if anyone feels inclined to meddle with me, he can expect some hot lead for his hubris. Consequently, while I was cautious, I was not frightened. The cold weight of my pistol in my purse comforted me.

I traversed a lonely stretch of pavement lined with shops that sold used clothing, mutton pies, secondhand furniture, and cheap tobacco, all shuttered for the night, with the faint glow of candles or lamps from the living quarters above leaking feebly into the street. The sidewalks were piled with rubbish, and the air smelled of horse dung, soot and grease. Most of the citizenry had retired for the night, but occasionally a shadow crossed a lighted window or a dim figure passed by on the opposite side of the street, appearing and disappearing like a conjurer's phantom through the swirling mist. In the distance, a dog barked once, sharply, then fell silent. My footsteps echoed on the pavement.

I turned north into Pagan Alley and saw the dark silhouette of the steeple of a church outlined indistinctly against the faint orange glow of the city. Water had pooled among the uneven cobblestones so that I had to lift my skirts and thread my way carefully through the filthy puddles. The odor was nauseating: putrefying vegetables and excrement, the decomposing carcasses of rats (and only rats, I hoped) and rancid ale. The buildings on either side of the lane rose ominously overhead, rendering the alley perilously dark and desolate. But I was not alone.

On either side of the narrow passage, shapeless forms huddled in doorways or clustered together in an attempt to stay warm. Some of the figures stirred as I walked past; one or two stretched out a beseeching hand, as if by some instinct they realized the steps that passed belonged not to another unfortunate creature, but to someone who might part with a shilling or two (quite mistaken on that point, I assure you). My progress had slowed to a crawl; I had to inch forward to avoid stepping on any of the alley's inhabitants, and I was sure that I was drawing close to my destination, though it was difficult to tell in the mist and smoke and darkness.

Behind me, a boot scraped the stones; there was a scuffling noise, a crash and a venomous oath split the air. I whirled round at the commotion, but it was impossible to see down the length of the alley. Around me, the sober sleepers bolted upright, while the drunks whimpered and moaned and thrashed about.

"Oi!" said a rough voice. "Watch where you're walkin', you great oaf."

I heard a low murmur; the rough voice swore, grumbled and subsided. The alley's inhabitants remained poised for a moment, sniffing the air, debating whether the ruckus heralded the arrival of the peelers to roust them out of their night's accommodations, then hearing nothing further, as one body they turned in unison and resumed their slumbers.

I waited breathlessly for a moment, my eyes searching futilely through the inky blackness. Trying to dispose of a dead body and trawling through one of London's most dangerous neighborhoods at midnight had made me a trifle jumpy. But there was nothing to see and nothing more to be heard, and so I turned to resume my slow journey through the passage.

A hand encircled my wrist, and a foul, gin-scented breath gusted around my face. "This ain't no place for a lady to be at this time o' night." A soft laugh echoed off the glistening walls. "'Course, you bein' no lady, you got no cause for concern."

"Vincent, you little blighter," I hissed, extracting my wrist from his grasp.

"What brings you out on a night like this, India?"

"I've a job for you. Is there somewhere we can talk privately?"

Vincent took possession of my wrist again and drew me along in his wake, stepping with caution among the sleeping figures until we reached the end of the alley and saw the dark bulk of St. Margaret's looming before us.

"This way," said Vincent, leading me past the entrance to the church and around the side to a set of stairs that disappeared into the gloom below street level. "Wait here," my guide instructed me, and I heard him descend as cautiously as a cat, feeling his way down the steps. After a few moments, a sullen yellow glow filled the landing at the bottom of the stairs, and Vincent appeared with a bull's-eye lantern in his hand, beckoning me to join him. He cracked open the door that led into the cellar of the church, and I followed him into a dank, airless passage that Vincent had adopted as his own. The light from the lantern revealed a roll of damp blankets, the end of a loaf of bread, a dried scrap of cheese, and a half-empty bottle of gin.

"Very cozy," I said.

"It'll do when my reg'lar lodgings at the Ritz ain't available."

Vincent set the bull's-eye on the floor and sank gracefully to a sitting position on the bedroll. "'Ave a seat, m' dear," he offered, like a gentleman, nudging the blanket beside him, "and tell me why you've walked out on such a night."

The floor was streaked with grime, and the passage smelled of must and mildew. I'd no intention of getting my taffeta anywhere near the floor, nor the blanket, either, which was likely home to a colony of fleas. "Thank you, no. I'll only be a minute."

Vincent shrugged. "Suit yourself." He picked up a piece of wood and a knife, and began slowly planing its surface, affecting a cool disinterest in the purpose of my journey. In the lamplight, he looked all of ten years old, which he might well have been, though I believed him to be fourteen, at least, if not older; the lack of fresh air and decent food, sleeping rough and fighting to survive the streets of London tended to stunt the growth of most street urchins. The do-gooders were forever trying to whip up sympathy for the poor, rescuing some innocent with the face of an angel from the streets, washing his face, dressing him in a set of stiff new clothes, teaching him how to say the Lord's Prayer and showing him off as the very model of an enlightened attitude toward the poverty-stricken. But the do-gooders would have taken one look at Vincent, averted their eyes and scuttled past.

He wasn't cherubic, or handsome, sweet, kind or humble. He was toad-faced, quarrelsome and cunning, with the heart of a mercenary. His voice could crack windows, and he could drink a

navvy under the table. There wasn't a dirtier boy in London, and
that's saying something, that is. In summer, he attracted more
flies than a Cairo camel market, and in winter you could just tolerate being in the same room with him provided the fire was low
and the window cracked open. He was an incorrigible little snoop,
as skilled as any of Her Majesty's spies at ferreting out useful bits
of information, and not at all reluctant to use what he'd learned
to his advantage. If you wanted to know which bint had a history
of relieving her clients of their valuables or attempting to extort
money from their gentlemen callers, Vincent knew. I always vetted my girls with him; he was as good as an employment agency
at winnowing the wheat from the chaff.

Further to his credit, he had his own code of ethics, which was
unusual in a boy of the streets: he discharged with alacrity any
commission he was given, gave value for the money received, only
blackmailed those who deserved it and was as silent and inscru-
table as the Sphinx about his activities. Consequently, I trusted
him, which was why I was here now.

"I need a horse and cart," I said.

"Tonight?" Vincent tested the blade of the knife with his
thumb. "That'll cost you."

I opened my purse and fished out a handful of coins. "Bring it
down the alley behind the house. Be quiet about it."

"Got the landlord after you, have you?" There was a glint of
humour in the boy's eye. His attention remained fixed on the
knife and the piece of wood in his hands. "Doin' a runner in the
middle of the night?"

"I've a parcel to deliver," I said shortly.

He glanced up at me, a half smile on his face. "Delivered where?
Wapping Stairs? Blackfriars? Or am I to catch the tide?"

"I'll want the parcel found," I said. "But not anywhere near Lotus House. And there must be nothing to connect it with me. Can you do it?"

"'Course I can. Though I must say I'm surprised at you, India. This ain't your style. Ain't your style at all."

"I didn't help him along, Vincent. The old gent died of a heart attack."

"That's a great relief to me, India. My faith in human nature is restored. Why do you want the body found?"

"There's a wife."

"Ah. It will cost you more if you want me to keep it quiet that India Black 'as the milk o' human kindness flowin' through her veins."

I snapped shut my purse. "Cheeky sod. How long will it take you to get the cart?"

"I'll 'ave to call in a favor," he said. "Say an hour or two."

"I'll be waiting for you. Knock quietly at the kitchen door. Mrs. Drinkwater will let you in." I nudged the crust of bread on the floor with my toe. "When did you last eat a proper meal, Vincent?"

He scratched his head, making a show of thinking. I'd no doubt he knew exactly when he'd consumed his last meal. "What day is it?"

"Sunday."

"Then 'twas Friday mornin'. I stole a bun from the baker's."

I found another coin in my purse and handed it to him. "Get yourself something. You've a long night of work ahead of you."

"I'm touched, India."

"Don't be. I can't have you fainting while you're hauling my body away."

He touched his forehead mockingly. "Then I'm at your service. Shall I walk you 'ome?"

I hesitated, remembering the scrape of boot leather in the alley. But dawn was just a few hours away, and there was no time to lose. "I'll be careful, Vincent. You go after the cart."

Vincent extinguished the bull's-eye, and we groped our way out of the cellar and up the stairs. I breathed deeply of the night air. Foul as it was, it smelled much better than Vincent's hiding place, the odor of which had reminded me of the monkey cage at the Regent's Park Zoo. Outside the church, we parted, with Vincent disappearing quickly into the mist-shrouded darkness on his errand and me turning resolutely toward Lotus House. I chose a different route than I had come, however. The thought of returning through the cramped blackness of the alley, with its silent forms sleeping restlessly in the doorways, did not appeal. My route took me along broader streets, which were better lit, but these thoroughfares were just as devoid of human presence (well, they would be, as in the distance the bells of St. Margaret's tolled midnight. I legged it home, striding along like a champion sprinter, head swiveling to peer into each shadowy doorway and alley that I passed, ears pricked to catch the slightest sound in that damp, suffocated world. I kept my hand in my purse, fingers curled around the grip of my pistol.

I couldn't account for my apprehension; I was a sensible woman, born and bred on these streets, and I knew my way around the neighborhood. There were places in London where even I wouldn't set foot, but for the most part, I felt safe here in my own patch. But as I walked along, my scalp was bristling and a shiver was playing up and down my spine. I attributed it to the stress and anxiety of the day: Bowser's death, leaving him rolled up under the bed for the afternoon while Calthorp and Mary sang hymns in the parlor, my midnight ramble through the streets in search of Vincent. The nagging feeling of being watched, and that footfall in the alley behind me.

I was glad to turn the corner into St. Alban's Street and see the dim yellow glow of a lamp burning behind the curtains of my study. The remainder of Lotus House was dark. Mrs. Drinkwater was no doubt snoring in the kitchen, and the girls had all gone to bed long ago. I lifted the latch of the gate and strode up the brick path to the front steps, fumbling for my key. The door swung open on oiled hinges, and I gained the safety of the front hall, locking the door behind me and taking my first easy breath since leaving the house hours before.

There was nothing to do now but wait for Vincent. Mrs. Drinkwater was asleep in the kitchen with her head on the deal table, and I briefly considered waking her to make me a cup of tea, but instead I poured myself a restorative glass of whisky and drank it in one long gulp, standing in my cloak and bonnet in the study with the water dripping onto the floor. Feeling somewhat refreshed, I topped up the glass, removed my wet outer garments and collapsed into my chair. The clock ticked soothingly, the whisky burned delightfully as it slid down my throat, and for the first time since Arabella had come stumbling into my study with the news that Bowser had crossed the River Jordan on my premises, I felt relaxed, if not wholly content. There was still the body to dispose of, after all.

There was an hour or more before Vincent was due to arrive; I had just time enough for a quick nap. I struggled upright and unlaced my boots, fingers fumbling at the laces. I tugged them off and let them lie where they fell, then got up to extinguish the lamp. The curtains were drawn, and the room was inky as a tomb. I felt my way to the window to open the draperies, so that the faintest light of dawn would be noticeable, hoping Vincent would arrive long before daybreak.

Tomorrow the street would be full of hawkers, plying their trade in oranges and buns, tea and scones and pies. Tradesmen would open their shops, and the pubs would fling wide their shutters, and the sidewalks would come alive with the bustle and roar of busy Londoners. Tonight all was quiet. The street seemed unfamiliar, the houses and shops strangely alien, their signs and windows barely visible through the fog. If Vincent arrived soon, we should be able to load Bowser's body and be gone before the first souls stirred.

Then from the sooty darkness of the street opposite my window, a match flared briefly, a bright blue orange spark that drew my eye but was gone almost before it had registered in my mind. My feeling of ease evaporated.

The sensible thing to do, of course, was to ignore the flaring match, down another whisky and toddle off to dreamland to catch a few winks before Vincent appeared. And usually, I am sensible. But the fact that I had a dead body wrapped in a rug and stuffed under the four-poster made me nervy as hell.

The kitchen door creaked as I slipped outside. I waited on the back steps for a moment in the vain hope that my eyes would adjust to the darkness, but the clouds were so thick and the night air so charged with fog and mist that I couldn't see my hand when I waved it before my face. Hardly optimum conditions under which to search for a mysterious figure. Still, I started off down the alley that ran behind Lotus House, parallel to the street, aiming to flank the doorway where I'd seen the fleeting glow of the match and come upon the match-wielder from behind. A good plan, if only I'd been able to execute it, but that was deuced difficult with no moon, a blowing mist and a fog as thick and viscous as custard. I stumbled along, slipping over soft, rotting fruit (at least, I hoped it was rotting fruit and not worse), tripping over oyster shells and broken crates, and generally making enough racket that any minute I expected Bowser to lift the sash of Arabella's window and demand to know what the devil was going on.

At the end of the alley, I paused to reconnoiter the street before dashing across to the other side. The pavement was shrouded in darkness; there was no sound or movement. Several minutes ticked by as I waited for the telltale flame to appear again, but my patience was not rewarded. I scanned the street once more, then lifted my skirts and flitted across the road, finding sanctuary in the shelter of a doorway. Staying close to the buildings, I crept up the sidewalk, gingerly placing one foot in front of the other and praying that I wouldn't take a header over a decaying apple or an empty ale bottle. Lotus House came into view across the street, looking forlorn and deserted, a pale wisp of smoke eddying from the fireplace in my study.

I carried my revolver with me, and now I took a firm grip on it and leveled it waist high in front of me as I sidled along. I was thirty paces from where I'd seen the match spurt into flame, and I covered that distance at the speed of an arthritic snail, with my fingers locked around my weapon and my nerves screaming in anticipation. Likely, the match-wielder was a vagrant dossing down for the night, smoking the end of a gasper he'd picked up in the street. This part of London was full of beggars and transients, sleeping rough in doorways and begging the price of a drink from passersby. The scrape of shoe leather in another alley some hours

ago haunted me, though, and I wouldn't rest easy until I'd discovered who was enjoying a smoke across the street from the Lotus
House in the wee hours of the morning.

I didn't fancy playing cat and mouse much longer, so when I
got within spitting distance of the doorway where I'd seen the figure, I took a deep breath and leapt the rest of the way, brandishing my pistol and saying something infernally idiotic, like "Hands
up," or some such novelistic trash. At any rate, it was ineffective,
as there was no one there to hear such a trite command (much to
my relief). I was alone, though I made a rapid circuit up and down
the sidewalk just to be sure, and I was turning for home when a
harness jingled and the clop of horse's hooves echoed down the
empty street. I put on speed and caught Vincent as he was turning
into the alleyway behind Lotus House, scaring him half to death
as I hissed his name from the shadows. The horse, a dirty white
raw-boned nag, shied violently, and the cart rattled like thunder.

"I was hoping to do this without waking the neighborhood," I
said as I crawled up beside Vincent.

"'Twill be your own fault, then, for jumpin' up at me like a
bloody Pathan. What the blazes are you doin' roamin' around out
'ere?"

I told him about the figure across the street. "Whoever it was,
he's gone now," I said.

"P'raps I'll slip round and have a look meself," Vincent said.

"Suit yourself, but don't be long."

Vincent tied the horse to the post behind the back garden and
glided stealthily away into the darkness.

Mrs. Drinkwater's grey plaits had come undone and she was
burbling away contentedly with her head still on the kitchen
table. I touched her shoulder and she bolted upright, hair and

spittle flying, fingers clutching her chest, and gasping like a harpooned seal. "Sweet Mother of Jesus," she cried.

"Bloody hell," I whispered ferociously. "Get hold of yourself, woman."

Mrs. Drinkwater recognized my face, and her eyes rolled back into her head. She smoothed her hair and wiped the drool from her cheek, glaring balefully at me.

"You scared me half out of my wits, you did," she said. I refrained from commenting that such an event must have left her devoid of any. On occasion, I do the admirable thing.

Mrs. Drinkwater remained indignant. "It's bad enough I have to sit here all day and night with a corpse in the house, and then you come in creeping about like a murdering Fenian. I almost had a heart attack, I did, and it would have been your fault if I had. I wonder who'd make your tea and cook your meals and carry your dead bodies then?"

Well, she had a point. I made soothing noises and despite her brush with death, she eventually (although grudgingly) staggered upright and followed me upstairs to Arabella's room, where we dragged the carpet containing Bowser's body out from under the four-poster and into the hall, keeping one eye open for stray bints. Bowser's head bounced vigorously on the stairs as Mrs. Drinkwater and I hauled him down the steps by his feet. The carpet displayed a distressing tendency to unroll as we tugged on it, and I sent Mrs. Drinkwater to the kitchen for a rope. She returned bearing a length of twine and with Vincent in tow. He shook his head in response to my unasked question.

"Looks like fair sailin'," he said, "provided we get the cargo loaded soon."

We trussed Bowser like a birthday present, wrapped our arms

around the awkward package, lurched to our feet and wobbled through the hall into the kitchen and out the door, down the garden path and through the gate to the cart, where we deposited our bundle with oaths and groans. I'm not ashamed to say that we dumped Bowser into the cart with all the tender consideration we'd have given a side of beef, for I was heartily sick of the old goat by then.

I issued my last instructions to Vincent. "Bring back the carpet when you've finished. You can have whatever you find in his pockets. Mind you don't flog what you find where it'll be easy to trace."

He gave me a scornful look, as though such tutoring was strictly superfluous for a talented fingersmith like himself, and climbed into the cart.

He'd raised his hands to flick the reins over the horse's back, when someone coughed ominously.

"I say, isn't that a body in that rug?"

THREE

Now when you're caught red-handed, with your skirts up (or your trousers down, as the case may be) and all your cards showing, the best thing to do is run a bluff, for it's a known fact that the more you bluster and blather, the less likely someone is to ignore what's staring him in the face and accept the fact that you weren't lifting the old girl's purse, just helping her across the street. It's amazing what you can accomplish if you're brazen enough and can adopt the appropriate tone of outraged dignity, or dignified outrage, as the case may be. Yes, indeed, I probably could have bamboozled the gentleman that now stood facing us, if only my petticoats had been showing and not Bowser's shiny black boots.

The first thought that came to mind was to tell this cove that what he saw here was none of his business and to be on about his own; an argument that generally worked in this neighborhood as any knowledge was likely to be guilty knowledge, and the less one knew, the less likely one was to spend any time in gaol as an accomplice. But our visitor seemed inordinately interested in our little scene in the alley, regarding us with the intensity of a theatre critic on first night. I half expected to read about us in tomorrow's paper: "The scene in which the criminals dispose of the body is crippled by the amateurish acting of Miss India Black, and the inauthentic accent and costume of the young man who plays the urchin."

My next thought was to concoct a story about a brutal fight in my parlor last night, with blood spilled on my fine carpet, ruining it beyond repair and thus necessitating its removal, which would have been a fine story since there was a dead body to lend verisimilitude to the tale. However, that meant I could no longer deny the existence of the corpse swaddled in the rug.

I was hanged either way, it appeared, so I decided on the frontal attack. "Shove off, mate. This is no concern of yours."

"On the contrary, India. This affair is most definitely of concern to me."

The fact that the bloke knew my name brought me up short. I tried to make out his features in the swirling mist, but all I could see was a tall, slim gent in a top hat and overcoat, and the pale gleam of what might have been a smile, or perhaps the bared teeth of a predator moving in for the kill.

"I don't believe I've had the pleasure of your acquaintance," I said.

He gave a throaty laugh. "I can assure you, there will little pleasure involved."

I suppose he thought he'd intimidate with that line, but it only served to start my blood boiling. You don't survive long in my line of work if you're cowed by bullying and threats. I rapped on the cart with my knuckles. "Drive on, Vincent," I said.

The stranger took three quick steps, and his hand shot out with lightning speed and grasped the horse's harness. "Ever seen the inside of St. Bartholomew's Poor House, boy? Not a pretty sight."

A thin grey light was beginning to ebb through the fog, heralding the arrival of dawn. Time was running out; I needed to get Vincent on his way. The Bulldog was tucked into the waistband of my skirt. I pulled it out and pointed it at my uninvited guest. "This is your last chance to leave on your own two feet."

The stranger chuckled. "Two murders in one night? You'll surely hang, India."

"I didn't kill Bowser."

"Who?"

"The cove in the carpet."

"Oh. You mean Sir Archibald Latham."

Sir Archibald Latham? Oh, hell.

The nag tossed his head, and the man tightened his grip on the halter. "Expired naturally, did he?"

"If you could call a senior civil servant dying in a whorehouse while dressed in a black bombazine gown, brandishing a whip and covered in rouge, 'expiring naturally.'"

This chuckle sounded genuinely amused. "Is that what the old boy got up to? Well, well. I would have never believed that about him. He was always such a stick at the office."

"Do you think you could reminisce about the gay old times at a later date? I've a body to dispose of."

The stranger relinquished his hold on the harness and patted the horse's muzzle, as if to say there were no hard feelings. "You needn't worry about that."

"Oh?"

"I'm going to do it for you."

Vincent had been sitting silently, listening to the conversational exchange, and, I'd no doubt, calculating how best to remove himself from the scene without attracting too much attention. The man's offer stirred him to speech. "Oi, that'll cost you, India."

I'd already reached the same conclusion. Perhaps it was my natural cynicism, or a lifetime spent negotiating exchanges of goods and services, but I knew there was nothing altruistic about the stranger's offer. It was also damned odd.

"And whatever would induce you to offer such assistance?" I asked, waving the Webley Bulldog for emphasis.

"We've no more interest than you in having Sir Archibald's body found in a whorehouse."

I didn't ask who "we" might be; I didn't want to contemplate the idea that there were any more like this cool, arrogant fellow keeping an eye on India Black.

"Where is Latham's wallet?" he asked.

Vincent uttered a sharp cry. "Here, you said that 'twas mine, India."

There are times when you stand on principle, but I personally haven't experienced any such moments in my life. "Give the wallet to the gentleman, Vincent. I'll see that you're compensated." A rash offer on my part. For all I knew, Bowser might have been flush with cash, but daylight was upon us and I needed Bowser's corpse off my premises as quickly as possible.

With Vincent's help (delivered somewhat churlishly and with a great deal of grumbling), the man pulled the body from the cart, broke open the twine and unrolled the carpet in a twinkling. Then he conducted a thorough search through Bowser's pockets with such skill and rapidity that even Vincent, still sulking slightly, watched in silent admiration.

The stranger found Bowser's wallet, opened it, extracted the bank notes from it and passed them to Vincent, whose eyes widened at the largesse. "Blimey, that's a 'andful."

I felt it best to establish my own position after the stranger's generosity. "That's that, then, Vincent. Don't expect anything additional from me."

"Don't spend it all at the George and Dragon," said his benefactor. He unclipped Bowser's hunter and chain from his vest. "You might as well take the watch, too. Someone will help themselves down by the river, if you don't." He flipped the watch to Vincent, who caught it expertly and tucked it into a trouser pocket.

When he'd finished rifling through Bowser's pockets, he and Vincent (who'd suddenly switched allegiance and now scrambled eagerly to help) rolled the carpet round the body once more and secured it with the twine.

"There you are, boy. Do you know the old Hartley and Speke warehouse at the jute docks? The one that closed last year?"

"I do."

"There's a shed round the back. Leave him on the ground outside."

Vincent touched his cap (a sign of deference I thought might have been overdone), flicked the reins across the horse's back and jogged off, the cart rumbling and squeaking, with Bowser's body bouncing in the back. The sky had turned progressively lighter while we'd been having our confab in the alley, and I could begin to make out the features of the stranger. He was immaculately attired and twirled a malacca cane in his hand, with a fancy silver handle in the shape of a griffin. He was a handsome devil, if you cared for cold grey eyes, swarthy skin, blue black hair, and an aristocratic mien, though good looks and hereditary holdings never have impressed me much. All men look the same with their trousers down; there's no mystery at all to the lads then. This fellow, though, struck me as something altogether different than your run-of-the-mill public school Adonis.

There was something almost feral about the man, in his silent and undetected approach down the alley, his quick and efficient movements, and his cold and appraising eye. He scrutinized me thoroughly, and I stared boldly back at him, but I must confess that I averted my gaze first, feeling rather like a mouse in a python's cage. That deadly gaze was unnerving enough, without anticipating the squeeze to follow. And I was sure the stranger hadn't yet obtained everything he wanted from India Black.

We stood silently and watched the cart disappear around the corner into the street, then he dusted his hands together and said: "Quite a night's work, eh? Now I'll have the case and be off."

"The case?" I asked.

"The black leather portfolio."

I stared at him blankly.

He gestured impatiently. "Latham's case. He had it with him when he entered Lotus House. It's not on the cart. Where is it?"

In the mad rush of disposing of Bowser's body (it was still damned difficult to think of him as Latham), I'd forgotten the existence of his black bag.

"It's upstairs," I said.

"Fetch it, then, and I'll be on my way."

That was the first pleasing news I'd had in the last eighteen hours. We trundled up to Arabella's room, the stranger staying close by my elbow, presumably so I couldn't snatch away the case from under his nose. The room was undisturbed, Bowser's black gown and enormous unmentionables strewn about the floor. The man threaded his walking stick through the leg hole of the petticoat, lifted it from the floor and regarded it musingly. "Poor old Archie," he said. "Who'd have guessed?"

"We all have a secret," I said. "What's yours?"

He gave me an arrogant smirk. "I never share confidences, India. It's a sign of weakness. Now let's have the case and I'll be gone."

I'd have gladly done that, if only to get the smarmy bastard out of my establishment. Only one thing prevented me from doing so: the case was gone. I crawled under the bed, opened the closet, pawed through the bedclothes, searched behind the curtains and under the cushions in the chair, rummaged through the dresser drawers and the oak wardrobe, my heart sinking as I realized the magnitude of what was missing. My visitor declined to join the search, just stood aside and watched me flail around the room while his brows knitted and his face grew black as thunder. Finally, I could no longer avoid the obvious.

"It isn't here."

"Then where is it?"

"I don't know."

His walking stick beat an impatient tattoo on the floor. "Was there anyone with Latham when he died?"

"One of the bints. Arabella Cloud, she calls herself."

He seized my arm in a talon-like grasp. "It's imperative that I have that case. Find the girl and ask her where it is."

I gulped. In my swift search, I'd noticed that Bowser's case was not the only thing missing from Arabella's room; her portmanteau, a warped and spotted case of ancient vintage, had disappeared from her wardrobe, as had all of her gowns and stockings. Hope springing eternal (and to get out from under that basilisk glare my visitor was leveling at me), I dashed up to the third floor, to find the room I'd assigned to Arabella cold and quiet. The bed bore a faint impression of someone's body, but that was the only sign the girl had ever been in the room. My visitor was at the window when I returned to the bedroom, his lips drawn tight in anger, and his eyes the colour of a sabre blade, which did not augur well for me. He listened to my report with a skeptical air.

"Search the house," he said. "But quietly. The last thing either of us needs at the moment is an uproar."

So I crept in and out of bedrooms, tiptoeing cautiously around sleeping whores and freezing at every wheeze, sigh and snore. A quick reconnaissance of the rest of Lotus House confirmed my fears. Arabella had decamped. Likely, she was already down the street at Mother Fletcher's, testing the mattresses and spreading rumours. Eventually, I had to report that neither Arabella nor Bowser's case was anywhere inside Lotus House. This was not welcome news to the stranger with the silver-knobbed walking stick. He uttered an oath that made the curtains flutter, but his face was impassive.

"Does the girl have friends?"

"Not here. Arabella kept herself to herself."

"Family?"

"No doubt she has one, but I don't know anything about them."

"The girl worked for you and you know nothing about her?" The stranger's tone was faintly incredulous.

"We weren't at Christchurch together, no. She probably sold violets at Piccadilly Circus or ran a loom in the cotton mills or worked below stairs at a country house until the squire's son impregnated her and the housekeeper sent her away. That's all I know about any of the girls here." My brittle tone had no effect on the stranger; he just looked faintly bemused that I hadn't had Arabella fill out a ten-page application before buying her a couple of gowns and assigning her to a mattress.

"Describe her," he said.

"Dark brown hair," I recited. "Brown eyes, high cheekbones, pale skin."

The stranger raised an eyebrow, as if to say, "That's all?"

"A tiny waist. Big breasts and an arse the size of Lancashire." She was a whore. What else was there to notice about her?

"Is there nothing more you can tell me? No distinguishing marks? A mole, perhaps, or a scar? Did she have an accent?"

"We all have accents here," I said waspishly. "Depending on what the gentlemen want that day. Sometimes Arabella was Hungarian, sometimes from the East End, and sometimes she was the heir to the British throne."

My visitor frowned.

"Look, I just hired her to work here, not pose for a study of the 'Modern English Tart.' I didn't commit every freckle and beauty mark to memory. I've described her as well as I can to you."

There was nothing more I could tell him.

"Perhaps you could leave me your address. If the case turns up, I'll forward it to you." It seemed the only logical thing to say, under the circumstances, and I was hoping he'd take the hint and vacate the premises.

"You needn't trouble yourself, India. That case is miles away by now."

"Well," I said airily, "if you know where it is, you can collect it easily enough."

He gave me a mirthless smile. "Perhaps. In any case, I needn't trouble you any longer. I think it would be to our mutual advantage to keep what happened here tonight to ourselves."

His admonition was hardly necessary; I'd no intention of ever uttering the word "Bowser" again.

He took his leave of me then, gliding out the door and down the steps of Lotus House as coolly as if he were strolling through Hyde Park on a Sunday afternoon and hadn't spent the night in a brothel disposing of a dead body. The mist had stopped and the fog was burning off slowly as he disappeared down the sidewalk, and I have to say I was damned glad to see the back of him.

I spent the rest of the day in my room with the blinds drawn and a sleeping mask over my eyes. My midnight rambles through the city had been tiring, but the few hours spent in the company of that dark, calculating man had exhausted me thoroughly. I slept like the dead through the afternoon and into the early evening. Around six, Mrs. Drinkwater rapped abruptly on my door and careened into the room like a schooner blown off course. Through sheer luck she found the dressing table, and left me a pot of tea and a plate of beef sandwiches, which I fell on and devoured like a ravening wolf.

After a hot bath, I was feeling myself again, so I descended the stairs and mingled a moment in the dining room with the girls, who were just finishing their egg and chips and getting ready for a night's work. I adjudicated a dispute between Marigold and Lucinda over whose turn it was to wear the purple taffeta, listened to a complaint about the quality of wrist restraints I'd purchased for a discount from a brothel going out of business in the next street and gave my ear to a shockingly bold request that I supply the rouge for the house, as I could no doubt get it wholesale and save the girls a bundle. Next, they'll be unionizing. Soon I'd have to negotiate labour contracts with the Association of Risque Trade Suppliers. It was growing increasingly difficult for an employer to exploit the workers in this country. I'd have to write my MP soon.

Still ruminating over the difficulties of running a going concern in an era of labour unrest and rising costs, I retired to my office for a stiff whisky and a glance at the evening papers, which promptly made me forget the vicissitudes of business ownership. They were full of breathless headlines about the discovery of the body of Sir Archibald Latham, Member of the British Empire and Clerk to Lord Folkstone of the War Office. I read the stories with interest (naturally) and learned that Constable Thomas Peters (only three months on the force, poor lad) had been patrolling the streets of his district at eight o'clock when he was drawn to investigate the rear yard of an abandoned warehouse at the jute docks. "Something seemed amiss," he told the reporter (a mastery of understatement, if I've ever heard one). "And so I went round the back to see if anything was wrong."

To the young constable's dismay, he found the body of one middle-aged man, well dressed, the pockets of his black broadcloth suit turned out and empty, and bearing just the faintest impression of rouge on his veined cheeks. In a fever of excitement (his first dead body!), the bobby had blown his whistle, bringing his counterpart from the next district, and in a twinkling, the full force of the local constabulary had been brought to bear on the crime scene, Scotland Yard had been notified, and Inspector Miles Havelock of the Criminal Investigation Division was on the scene. In no time at all, the victim was identified, the widow notified (she was now in seclusion; requests for a few words were sternly declined by the family solicitor), and Inspector Havelock had assured the public that the killer would be found.

There were related articles extolling the virtue of Bowser—his first at Oxford, his prowess at rugby and cricket, his service to Queen and country—all the usual twaddle when respectable public Tories die. Just once, I'd like to read the real obituary: "Bloody fool, drunkard, poltroon and lout. Enjoyed buggering stable boys. Voted Liberal more than once." Now that would be worth reading.

The papers also contained the usual laments over the escalating crime rate and the inability of the Metropolitan Police Force to keep reputable citizens from being thumped on the head, all tinged with a wistful nostalgia for a kinder, more innocent era, when virtue reigned and the streets were safe. Wherever the writers of this kind of drivel had lived before now, it clearly wasn't London.

There was one question the eagle-eyed reporters seemed not to have asked, and that was what precisely had compelled Constable Peters to amble behind an abandoned warehouse. His intuition aside, it seemed an odd thing to do, or perhaps it was just a happy coincidence (at least for Mrs. Latham, who needn't worry any longer about when her husband would be home), but my money was on a dark stranger with a malacca walking stick, standing in the shadows and playing the role of deus ex machina.

I hadn't bothered to report the missing Arabella to the authorities. They'd have looked at me as though I should be occupying a bed in Bedlam. A prostitute who disappeared wasn't cause for alarm; she'd have run off with a suitor or found another house to work in or been lured away by another madam who promised her a bigger share of the takings (in that case, good riddance to her). To be truthful, I didn't want the police making any inquiries about Arabella, anyway. An investigation might turn up the interesting fact that she'd gone missing the very day that Sir Archibald Latham had been found dead by a clairvoyant peeler. I thought it likely that Arabella didn't want to take any chances of being connected to a customer's death, even if it had been an innocent one, and of course, it didn't look all that innocent since I'd seen fit to move the corpse somewhere else. Arabella probably had some secret in her past (don't we all?) and had reasons of her own for packing up and moving on. I wasn't going to lose any sleep over her, nor Bowser for that matter, but when I went to bed that night, I slept fitfully, dreaming of a haughty smile and grey eyes.

FOUR

Tuesday dawned, another chilly, cloud-shrouded day with a light drizzle that left a glaze on the pavement. The factories were working at full throttle, and the smoke from the tanneries and mills and rendering plants mingled with the vapors rising from the Thames and the soot from thousands of chimneys, creating a poisonous yellow haze that hung in the air like a veil. People scuttled past on the sidewalk, mufflers and scarves wrapped over their noses and mouths, blinking their eyes against the sulfurous murk.

The morning papers were still running hysterical columns on the dangerous London streets, and Mrs. Latham was still declining comment, but some of Bowser's co-workers had been interviewed, and all attested to their colleague's attention to detail, exemplary work habits and astute sense of judgment. One bloke weighed in with a sugary paean to Bowser's loyalty to the Royal Family and his "great regard" for the Prince of Wales, which brought a smile to my lips.

The day passed quietly enough. Lucinda's cousin Molly had arrived on the doorstep, fresh off the farm and ready for a life of glamour in the metropolis. I was grateful to have her, for Arabella's departure had caught me short, and there were clients to be serviced who were chomping at the bit for a fling with a real Slavic princess. Molly's eastern European accents were weak, but since her natural speech was a thick Yorkshire dialect that was nearly incomprehensible even to English speakers, I thought she might do. "Just keep the conversation to a minimum," I advised, "and if anyone questions whether you're really a Bulgarian countess, open your dress and show 'em your tits." In my business, that's sound advice in any number of circumstances. In any case, if she failed to convince the gents that she was genuine royalty from east of the Danube, she would still appeal to the tally-ho crowd, who would feel right at home saddling up a strapping maid who still had straw in her hair.

The hours passed quickly while Lucinda and I did our best to coax Molly into some semblance of alluring eroticism, not an easy task with a milk maid with chilblains and a distressing tendency to giggle at the thought of the male anatomy. By the end of the day, she was no longer spitting in the fireplace or erupting into laughter every time Lucinda (playing the role of client) whispered risqué suggestions into her ear.

Midway through the afternoon, Reverend Calthorp appeared, his pink cheeks aflame with virtuous dismay at the plight of the inhabitants of Lotus House, a handful of religious tracts in his hand. I was all for turning him out, but the girls wanted some sport, and I couldn't see the harm. He'd get an eyeful of quivering boobies and lewd winks, and be gone before you know it. He settled himself demurely on the horsehair sofa, an arm's distance from the nearest bint, and drank a cup of tea while he invited us all to attend next Sunday's morning service.

"What's the topic of your sermon, Reverend?" I asked. "The Immaculate Conception?"

Lucinda leaned over and slapped his knee. "If you need any help with some of the particulars, I'd be happy to offer my assistance."

The girls guffawed and Calthorp's blush ripened into full-fledged embarrassment. Well, what did he expect from a roomful of whores? Polite chitchat about the church fete and missions among the cannibals? Serves him right, the pious little prig. He at least had the grace to smile feebly at Lucinda's witticism, though you could tell he wasn't amused.

He sipped his tea perfunctorily and fixed his mild brown eyes on mine. "I'm surprised to find you all so jolly."

"Jolly?" I asked.

"Yes, considering that one of your fellow . . ." He paused. "Er, colleagues has gone missing."

Until that moment, I'd mostly forgotten the events of the previous day, focused as I was on whipping Molly into shape and dealing with the daily minutiae of running a first-class brothel in an unfriendly business climate. (The damned Contagious Diseases Act had been amended, for the third time, just a few years ago, and it was all I could do to keep my bints from being hauled in, examined for disease and registered as prostitutes. Up until 1859, soldiers and sailors were examined routinely, but in their infinite wisdom the parliamentarians deemed that exercise too humiliating for the poor fellows and decided whores were much less likely to have personal feelings about the subject.) At any rate, I hadn't given a thought for most of the day to Latham's missing case or the missing whore. Calthorp's question brought it all back in a flash.

"To whom are you referring?" I asked, though I knew damned well who he meant.

"Arabella Cloud, of course," said the padre, sipping his tea and wincing at Mrs. Drinkwater's version of this most innocent of beverages. "I understand that she is no longer with you."

"And how did you come by that information?"

Calthorp looked vaguely around the room. "Why, I believe Mary told me, on Sunday afternoon when I visited."

Mary looked mystified at this revelation; no doubt she'd been hitting the bottle again. Between her and Mrs. Drinkwater, it was beginning to feel like the local at closing time.

"It's a feature of this vocation, Reverend. Girls come and girls go. Isn't that right?" I looked around the room for confirmation, and several of my ladies nodded.

"'Tis indeed," said Lucinda. "The grass is always a shade greener on the other side of the street, so to speak."

"Still," said Calthorp, "I'd have thought you might have been concerned about Arabella. Something might have happened to her."

"And she might be sipping a gin and bitters at the White Hart right now," I said.

"Yes, but she could be lying injured somewhere or be in some kind of trouble."

"She's in trouble with me," said Mary. "She run off with my new tortoiseshell comb."

Calthorp looked at me beseechingly, his soft brown eyes glistening with moisture. "I have a premonition that Arabella is in danger and needs your help."

I laughed. "I think that's very unlikely, Reverend. Arabella Cloud can take care of herself."

"Still," he persisted. "Anything might have happened to her out there on the streets. Have you any idea where she might have gone?"

"None at all. She should never have left if she wanted to stay out of trouble." I rose briskly. For the life of me, I couldn't figure out why Calthorp was so obsessed with Arabella's whereabouts. Once she'd left Lotus House, she was as good as forgotten, from my point of view. Perhaps she was the proverbial hundredth sheep in Calthorp's eyes, the other ninety-nine being comfortably ensconced at Lotus House out of harm's way. In any case, I'd had just about enough of his interference.

"Girls, run along upstairs and make yourselves presentable. We'll have customers soon." I extended a hand to the clergyman. "I must take my leave of you, Reverend. I've some letters to write. Good day to you." I swept out of the room, not leaving him a moment to protest.

Mrs. Drinkwater caught me up in the hall, veering down on me like a high-altitude balloon navigated by a shortsighted chartsman. "Oh dear, miss. Something shocking."

This snared my attention, for after the death of Bowser and Arabella's flight and the appearance of the mysterious stranger, I shuddered to hear what Mrs. Drinkwater found shocking. But it was only the lack of Cuban cigars, the stock of which had mysteriously vanished from the humidor in the parlor sometime in the wee hours of Monday morning.

"'Twas that vicious little mongrel, Vincent," Mrs. Drinkwater growled. "He's no respect for the property of others." I daresay she was right.

"I'll walk to the tobacconist's shop and pick up a supply for the evening," I said. "It's not gone five yet. I've plenty of time." I pinned on a hat, selected a fetching little cape, took up my parasol and let myself out the front door.

The lamplighters were at work by then. Dusk had come early tonight, what with the thin drizzle and the nasty yellow brume that seeped into the streets. The gloomy atmosphere reminded me of my last stroll through these streets, when I'd gone in search of Vincent and returned to Lotus House to find someone loitering across the street. I'd no doubt now that the watcher had been the dark stranger who had arranged for Bowser's body to be found. As I passed the point at which I'd seen the spurt of flame on Sunday night, I peered into the shadows as a precaution and breathed a sigh of relief to find no one there.

An hour ago, the streets had been full of people hurrying home for their tea or on their way to down a pint at the local, but the crowd had dwindled. I passed a fellow traveler occasionally, tilting my chin politely in response to murmured greetings. The tobacconist's shop was only a few blocks from Lotus House, down a damp and narrow thoroughfare littered with horse droppings, wet straw and the bedraggled remains of the daily papers. I ducked in just as the proprietor was closing, haggled with him over the price of two dozen of his finest, and waited patiently while he wrapped and tied the parcel for me. The lock clicked shut behind me as he closed the door.

I threaded my way through the garbage choking the pavement, fending off the ragged brats who came out of nowhere to request a bit of the ready (polite term for it, really, actually more like being accosted by a group of Apache horse thieves). I used my parasol to rap one across the knuckles and hamstring another, and the whole troupe of little gangsters tore off in search of easier prey, leaving me alone on the deserted street.

A hansom cab turned the corner and rumbled to a halt twenty feet from me. The horse stamped and tossed its head, its harness jingling loudly, and the driver cursed and jerked the reins taut. Two burly men in billycocks and dusters alighted and huddled together on the sidewalk, reading the signs on the shops, scratching their heads and otherwise looking like two gents who'd been told to meet their friend at the Old Contemptibles only, look Bert, there ain't no such pub anywhere on the street. As I passed, the men lifted their hats in unison; the last time I had seen hands like that was on the lowland gorilla at the Regent's Park Zoo. I returned their pleasantries, but there was something about them that raised my hackles and made me half turn to look at them over my shoulder after I had passed. It might have been their eyes as they met mine, for theirs were as frigid as the Firth of Forth. Or it might have been those great hairy paws on the brims of their bowlers. Those weren't the hands of gentlemen of leisure. Whatever it was, I felt an icy arrow along my spine, and I quickened my pace.

But not fast enough. As I brushed past the two, a hand snaked out and caught my sleeve. "Pardon me, miss," a basso profundo voice muttered in my ear.

I swung away from the man and took a firm grip on my parasol. "Yes?"

"Someone wants to see you."

"I'm at home every afternoon between two and four," I said.

The man's smile could easily have been mistaken for a snarl. "Ain't you amusin'? Popular with your customers, I'll bet. Keep 'em laughin' while you skin 'em out of their pants and their money."

I glared at him. "Obviously you know who I am, but I'll be damned if I know where we've met. I wouldn't let the likes of you in my house."

The other fellow laughed. "Oooh, Billy. She's a fireball, ain't she?"

I yanked my arm from the man's grasp. "Unhand me," I said. I really must stop reading those trashy novels.

I raised my umbrella threateningly, but the action did not have the effect I'd intended, for the two men burst out laughing, squawking like a pair of lunatic parrots.

"You're a spirited filly," said the one on the left, and reached out for my arm. It's astonishing how far the point of a parasol will sink into a man's groin. It certainly surprised my assailant. He hit the ground like a felled ox, grasping his balls and squeaking urgently.

His companion's head swung menacingly in my direction. "Here, now. There's no call for that. You come along quietly now, and there won't be no trouble."

I lashed out with my parasol and clobbered him on the left ear, dislodging his billycock and sending it flying. He staggered a few steps, put his hand to his earlobe and stared incredulously at the smear of blood on his fingers. He shook his head like a horned Hereford bull and looked at me reproachfully. "I'm nearly vexed, I am. Now either you settle down and be quick about it, or you'll force me to take drastic action."

I pointed the tip of my parasol at him. "Do your best, you bloody baboon."

Then strong arms encircled me from behind, pinioning my own arms to my sides. I'd forgotten about the driver.

It was a sullen group that occupied the hansom cab. Billy sat with his hands in his lap, bemoaning the decrease in value of the family jewels and pausing only long enough to glare venomously at me. The other fellow's ear was beginning to resemble a cauliflower, and his collar was rusty with dried blood. We rode in silence. I strained to see out the window, trying to track our progress through the city, but the thug with the damaged ear leaned over and pulled down the shade.

"This is kidnapping," I said. "I most certainly intend to press charges against you."

The man fingered his ear gingerly and snorted. "Righto. And we'll tell the officer we picked you up in the Haymarket and already agreed to a price when you got stroppy."

There are disadvantages to being a whore, and one of them is that relations with the Metropolitan Police Force are, shall we say, delicate. After that, there was nothing to do but wait and wish that Billy and his friend hadn't had sausages and beans for lunch.

After half an hour, the cab stopped with a jerk, and the man raised the shade and peered out, nodding in satisfaction. "We're here, Billy." The only answer from Billy was an inarticulate groan. The driver jumped down and opened the door, and I was bundled roughly out of the cab and onto the street, before a great pile of grey stone that shimmered wetly in the light from the gas lamps. Before I had a moment to look around and orient myself to my surroundings, the two men each grabbed an elbow tightly (Billy displayed an enthusiasm that brought tears to my eyes) and hustled me inside the building.

Relief swept over me immediately once we were inside. I've more than a passing familiarity with most of the stations of the Metropolitan Police Force, and this wasn't one of them. It looked more like a bank or trading house or government offices. There were no signs of activity about. The place felt as empty as a tomb, an impression that was reinforced by the echo of our footsteps. The floors were a dingy black-and-white tile, worn and scuffed from the tread of many feet, and the narrow hall was dimly lit by electric bulbs. Heavy oak doors, each numbered with a brass plate, opened off the passage, revealing cramped offices. The desks inside were strewn with papers and neat stacks of documents tied with black ribbon.

"I swear I've paid my property tax," I said. "If you gentlemen hadn't been in such a hurry, I could've produced my receipt."

Billy grunted and dug his fingers into the soft skin just above my elbow. "That's a regular comedy routine you've got there. I wonder why you ain't on the stage."

Deep in the bowels of the building, we came upon a marble staircase with a banister of filigreed iron that wound upward into the gloom. We proceeded to climb, the two men lugging me between them like a sack of meal, my boots barely touching the steps. At the top of the stairs we turned down another long hallway, but at the end of this one, a wedge of light could be seen spilling out into the passage from an open doorway, and the distant murmur of voices reached our ears. The sound of our footsteps must have been equally audible to the persons in the room, for a shadow blotted out the light and a split second later a figure appeared in the hallway. With a sinking heart, I recognized my nemesis from Sunday evening.

He was just as aloof and unflappable as I remembered, giving me an appraising eye and the briefest of nods before he stood aside and my escorts ushered me into a long room with a fire blazing briskly in the hearth at the other end. It was a swell's office, all mahogany paneling, Persian rugs and leather-bound books lining the shelves on either side of the room. The fireplace sported a carved marble mantle and a painting of our Royal Highness, looking particularly lugubrious, as though she'd just learned that the Prince of Wales had been seen sporting with another actress. Two men stood before the fire, crystal glasses in hand, regarding me somberly.

My assailants deposited me before the fireplace with a flourish, but not before Billy took the opportunity to give my arm a savage squeeze with his ape-like hand and whisper, "Don't try that again, ducks, or you'll be sorry," in my ear. Then he and his friend (of the cauliflower ear) deferentially touched the brims of their bowlers and bowed their way out of the room, closing the great oaken door behind them.

The shorter of the two men stepped forward. With his dark curly hair, his bright, inquisitive eyes and his hooked nose, he wouldn't have looked out of place on a Saturday at Temple Emanuel or running a rag and bone shop in Whitechapel, only no self-respecting man of business would dare dye his locks such a sable hue or don the outfit the little man sported. I believe Beau Brummel would have hesitated a moment before choosing the striped trousers, canary yellow waistcoat, and the puce velvet jacket. It was Disraeli, of course, in the flesh, and if you think I was a bit disconcerted to find myself in the presence of Lord Beaconsfield, prime minister of Great Britain and its colonies, you'd be right. I'd had my hand kissed by minor aristocracy, but I'd never been this close to the seat of power before.

My first thought (isn't it always?) is that my fame had preceded me, and I'd been brought here to give Dizzy a gallop. But men who moved in his circle seemed to have no problem finding ready partners among their own class, and while I knew Dizzy's reputation as a connoisseur of women, his marriage was rumored to have been a happy one, and he'd been seriously cut up by his wife's death a few years before. Still, the strain of managing an empire and jollying along that gloomy old bag Victoria might have gotten to the man. I was pondering how to break the news that I'd retired on my laurels when the second man caught my attention, swirling the drink in his hand so that the crystal glass glittered in the firelight. He was a rum-looking cove, with reddish gold hair, a severe mustache and amber eyes that held not a spark of warmth. His skin was unnaturally white and glowed like alabaster in the light from the fireplace.

The prime minister waved a hand at a heavy sideboard lined with bottles and glasses. "May I offer you some refreshment, Miss Black?"

Stranger things have happened to me than being offered a glass of whisky by the prime minister, but for the life of me, I can't recall what they might have been. I muttered my thanks, accepted the proffered glass with what I hoped was a charming bow, and allowed myself to be shepherded into a soft leather chair.

"I trust your journey here was a pleasant one," Dizzy said, as though I'd received an engraved invitation and been escorted here by the Royal Blues, instead of kidnapped off the street by two Neanderthals. I wondered if there was a polite way to express this thought, but Dizzy was continuing on, oblivious to (or ignoring) the irony of his statement.

"Allow me to introduce William Endicott. Mr. Endicott is here on behalf of Lord Derby, the foreign secretary." Endicott was the rufus-haired gentleman. He turned a reptilian gaze upon me and blinked once, slowly.

"And of course, you have already met Mr. French of this office," said Dizzy.

The dark stranger who had disposed of Archibald Latham's body was at the sideboard, pouring a stiffish peg for himself. He didn't bother to look round, which was just as well as I was in no mood to smile and say hello. By this time, I'd regained my usual sangfroid, reasoning that I wasn't likely to be murdered in the office of the prime minister, and settled down to enjoy what promised to be an interesting evening. So I sipped my whisky demurely and waited for Dizzy to expound, which didn't take long, of course, as he could no more be silent than an Irishman can be sober.

"I hardly know where to begin," he said, and promptly launched into speech. "Two days ago, a representative of this government died rather precipitously, and somewhat unfortunately, at your, er, establishment. Also unfortunately, Sir Archibald Latham carried with him a case that held certain documents, containing rather sensitive information."

"Vital information," Endicott interposed. He'd screwed a cigarette into an ebony holder and was puffing away, the smoke dribbling out his nostrils. "Information of the greatest importance to this government."

"As you are aware, Miss Black, the case has gone missing." As if Dizzy weren't sure I'd gotten his point, he added: "From your, er, establishment."

The whisky was first-rate, but it was time to make known my position. "I didn't take the case," I said. "French was there when I searched Lotus House. He can tell you that I found nothing."

"We know the case is not in your possession," Endicott said. "We know where it is."

"Well, then. Why don't you just go and fetch it while I trundle back to Lotus House and attend to my business?"

"It's a complicated matter, Miss Black." Dizzy rose briskly and strode over to the fireplace, where he leaned against the mantle. "The case will soon be in the possession of Count Vladimir Maksimovich Yusopov, the head of military intelligence for Tsar Alexander II."

"If the case belongs to Her Majesty's government, why don't you tell Count Yusopov to hand it over? If he doesn't give it back, you can always boot him out of the country."

Dizzy sighed. "Dear me. I wish it were that simple. But for any number of reasons, we cannot make a public issue of the matter. It must be handled with the utmost discretion."

The faintest of lights had begun to dawn. "You mean, no one must know that the documents are missing."

Endicott frowned into his glass. "Precisely."

"Cause for embarrassment?" I asked. "Senior government official pops off in a whorehouse, losing state secrets to our bitter enemy along the way. Is that it?"

Dizzy looked unhappy. "You have summed up the situation quite succinctly. We cannot afford a public scandal; it would bring down the government." Endicott shot him a quick glance. In the shifting, uncertain light from the fireplace, I could have sworn it was laced with malice. But from the corner of his eye, he caught me studying him, and his expression smoothed immediately into the seamless mask he'd been wearing since I arrived.

"You said this count fellow would have the case soon. Where is it now?"

French spoke for the first time. "In the possession of one Major Vasily Kristoforovich Ivanov, Count Yusopov's most trusted agent. He is in London at the moment, awaiting Count Yusopov's return from Paris, where he has been for the past week."

"And how did this bloke Ivanov get his hands on the case?" I asked.

"Ivanov's men have been shadowing various officials from the War Office for several months."

"Including Bowser, I presume."

Endicott and Dizzy looked puzzled.

French's lip twitched slightly. "Sir Archibald Latham," he explained.

Dizzy had been silent for all of a minute, which must have been a terrible strain. "One of the destinations to which he was followed was your, er, establishment. We assume that the agent must have waited for Latham to emerge from what I understand was his usual appointment at your, er, estab—"

"Lotus House," I interjected, weary of this infernal dithering about my, er, establishment.

Endicott looked shocked that I'd interrupted the prime minister, but Dizzy didn't falter and ploughed on. "Er, quite. We further assume that when Latham did not reappear at his customary time, the agent was alerted that something unusual had occurred. He must have entered your premises, discovered Latham's body and purloined the case. We have sources within the Russian embassy who have notified us that the case has been delivered to Major Ivanov. Ivanov has deposited it into the embassy safe to await the return of Count Yusopov."

"How do you know that Ivanov hasn't already opened the case and inspected the contents?" I'd have wasted no time in doing so, and I assumed most of my fellow human beings would do the same, especially if they were Russian spies who'd just gotten their mitts on some secret papers.

"It would be more than his life is worth to look at those documents before Count Yusopov sees them. The count is the tsar's cousin and enjoys a rather close relationship with him. His subordinate, Ivanov, would not dare usurp Yusopov's right to deliver the information contained in those documents directly to the tsar."

"If you have sources in the embassy," I said, "why not have one of them recover the case for you?"

Dizzy sighed. "Alas, they are neither skilled enough nor in any position to do so without being compromised. We did, however, attempt to penetrate the security at the embassy last night. Unfortunately, our effort was detected and rebuffed, resulting in increased security measures that have made it impossible to make another attempt."

Tough luck, old boy, I thought to myself, but what I said was, "I don't quite see how this concerns me."

"We must try a new approach, Miss Black. We find ourselves in the unique position of having to ask for your assistance." Dizzy gave me a smile calculated to charm me out of my garters.

"How could I possibly be of service to you?" I asked.

Dizzy pursed his lips and looked at the ceiling. Endicott peered into his glass and scrupulously avoided my eyes. It didn't take any Gypsy blood to predict my fortunes were about to change. French, predictably, looked cool as dammit.

I cocked an eyebrow at him. "Go ahead, French. What can a whore do to extricate the British government from this embarrassing scandal? And won't there be an even bigger scandal when the story gets out that you had to ask a bint for help? Not very statesmanlike, that."

"It won't get out, India. Not from us, and certainly not from you," said French.

"You seem rather confident of that fact. What's to prevent me from selling my story to the papers?"

He smiled blandly. "You've a great deal invested in Lotus House. It would be a shame if you were to lose it."

A whore learns early how to run a bluff. It comes in useful when you're haggling over the price or the services, or when the bloke you're with has turned nasty and you have to talk your way out of the situation. Which, come to think of it, was exactly what had just happened with French.

"Put me out of business," I said, very coolly, "and I'll pay a visit to every journalist between London and St. Petersburg."

Dizzy had turned pale (no small feat, with that complexion) and was gnawing a fingernail. "Please don't be so hasty, Miss Black. You've no idea what is at stake here."

"Then why don't you tell me?"

Endicott raised an eyebrow and uttered a contemptuous cough. "Really, I hardly think the prime minister need bother to explain affairs of state to the likes of you."

"If the prime minister wants the assistance of the likes of me, he will." I sauntered over to the sideboard and freshened my drink, taking care not to let the decanter of whisky rattle against the glass and betray my apprehension. Dizzy was a politician and a man of the world; he looked ready for a confidential chat among friends. French's supercilious arrogance made my teeth ache, but I already knew he was a pragmatist and wouldn't scruple at doing whatever needed to be done. But this Endicott fellow was a pompous little tick and didn't bear crossing lightly.

French had taken little part in the discussion, and I'd been watching him out of the corner of my eye for the past few minutes. He seemed singularly disinterested in the conversation, his gaze roving the room but ignoring the occupants, turning his head this way and that, and finally (and most bizarrely), sniffing the air like a hound on the scent. He rose to his feet and began a rapid reconnaissance of the room, opening the door to the corridor, peering under desks and tables, and finally alighting in front of one of the large windows, draped in heavy curtains to keep out the winter chill.

Dizzy, Endicott and I had suspended our discourse and were watching him with curiosity, mixed with not a little concern on Dizzy's face that a trusted operative might suddenly have lost his mind.

French slowly extracted his handkerchief from his pocket, shook it out in his right hand, and grasping the curtains with his left, rapidly inserted his right behind the curtain and drew it out again. It contained Vincent's ear, which of course was still attached to his head, which still contained his mouth, from which a steady stream of curses now issued in that jackdaw voice of his.

"'Ere, let go o' me," he cried, writhing like an eel in French's grasp. "Oi, that hurts."

"As it should," said French coldly. "No one invited you to this meeting."

"Who is this guttersnipe?" Endicott demanded. "And how the devil did he get in here?"

Vincent took one look at French's frigid expression and the viper-like gaze of Endicott and quickly decided that outraged indignation wasn't going to cut much ice with those two. He gave me an appealing glance and said, "India, are ya alright? I saw them two brutes make orf wif ya and I followed 'em here." He looked suspiciously at the prime minister. "These fellers ain't 'urt ya, 'ave they?"

Dizzy looked shocked, at the lack of recognition or being suspected of such an outrage or because his accuser was a ragged tyke who smelled like an Arab slave ship. He recovered quickly, though (Dizzy's never at loss for words, it seems), and raised a placating hand toward Vincent, who was still glaring at him.

"Not to worry, my young friend. Miss Black is our guest and has been enjoying an evening discussing the latest developments in current affairs with us." He waved a hand at French. "Mr. French, you can release our visitor. I don't believe he means any harm."

French emancipated Vincent's ear, and Vincent shot him a look that clearly indicated he'd forgotten about French's largesse in the matter of Bowser's wallet. Vincent rubbed his ear vigorously. "Ya nearly pulled my ear orf, you did," he said accusingly.

"It would have served you right if I had," said French, depositing his handkerchief in the dustbin.

"Where in blazes are Smith and Jones?" thundered Endicott. "How in blazes did this child slip past them?"

Vincent bridled at this affront; the two thugs who'd brought me here were no match for him in skill or cunning, though they were certainly victorious in the muscles sector and were running neck and neck in the odor department.

"'Twas easy," he said scornfully. "Them two buggers was so busy draggin' India around they didn't even shut the door. I just slipped in be'ind 'em and followed 'em up the stairs and down the 'all. While you all were jabberin' and introducin' yourselves like proper gennelmun, I snuck in behind them dusty ole curtains and stayed still as a statue." Here he paused to glare at French. "'Til you winkled me out."

I cut in before Vincent lost his temper. "Thank you so much for coming, Vincent," I said. "And your concern for my honour is touching. I won't soon forget it. But as you can see, all is well."

"Run along," said French, not unkindly, for he certainly knew it was inquisitiveness that had brought Vincent here and not concern over my virtue.

Endicott was still sputtering, stalking around the room and uttering threats against Smith and Jones (you would think our senior ministers could show just a bit more imagination, wouldn't you, when it came to aliases?).

Vincent gave me a beseeching look. I could see he was desperate to stay and hear the rest of the story. I was about to add my own injunction to depart, but it occurred to me that had I *been* in any sort of trouble, the little toad might have been my only salvation.

"Oh, let him stay, French," I said. "He's been in a whorehouse before, so I don't suppose it will do him any harm to spend time in a politician's office. This might be the only civics lesson he ever gets."

"You can't be serious," Endicott fumed. "It's bad enough that we're talking to a harlot about government affairs. Now we're explaining the position of the British government to a filthy child off the streets."

"That will do, Endicott," French said sharply, before either Vincent or I could get out a word, which was fortunate for Endicott. "The boy is an associate of Miss Black's, and I might add, a very resourceful one. He might prove useful. In any case, it's growing late, and we have only a few hours to effect our plans."

I expect French's change of mind was due less to the lateness of the hour and Vincent's potential utility, and more to Endicott's insolence.

French nodded to Dizzy. "Prime Minister, you were about to explain what is at stake here and why we need Miss Black's collaboration."

He pushed Vincent into a chair next to mine and then stood upwind. No such luck for me; the stench rolled off Vincent in almost visible waves.

"Ah, yes," murmured Dizzy. "It would behoove us to explicate the matter to Miss Black. I've no doubt when she understands our plight and its fullest implications, we may count not only upon her sympathy, but her assistance as well." He tucked his chin and smiled bravely at me. "Our nation faces a grave peril tonight, Miss Black. You will grace us with your company for an hour, won't you, and let me explain to you this dire predicament we confront and how you might provide the succor we require in our time of need?"

He said it very prettily, with all the sincerity of a Romany horse trader, which indeed he resembled in his garish clothes and glittering rings, but I nodded gravely and sat down with an air of amiable attentiveness, while French lit a cheroot, Endicott settled back in his chair with a scowl on his face, and Dizzy put a boot on the fender, assumed a professorial air and began to talk.

FIVE

"It is ironic that your name is India, my dear, for that country shall be the subject of our conversation tonight." He looked down that formidable nose at me. "Of course, you are aware how vital the subcontinent is to the wealth and power of our tiny island nation?" Without waiting for me to confirm that I was in fact aware of the great amount of loot some of my fellow countrymen had pillaged from that unhappy country, he plunged on.

I'll summarize it for you, for if I repeated verbatim all that Dizzy told us that night, you'd be retired to Torquay and have forgotten your name by the time I finished the tale. Lord, that man loved to talk. The nub of the matter was this: in the summer of 1875, a handful of peasants (Orthodox Christian and Mussulman alike) in Hercegovina (part of the Ottoman Empire, and ruled at the time by Sultan Abdulaziz from Istanbul, or Constantinople, as the West persisted in calling the city) objected to paying their sheep tax after the harvest had failed. The Turkish ministers evidenced their sympathy to the peasants' position by dispatching their military to slaughter them. The butchering of Mussulman villagers went unremarked; the massacre of the Christians sent shock waves through the capitals of Europe. Andrassy, the Hungarian prime minister, issued an ultimatum to the Turks to stop the taxation of the luckless farmers and to guarantee the religious liberty of the Empire's subjects, an approach supported by Dizzy's Conservative government. The boys in Berlin went further, demanding that Christians be permitted to bear arms, a suggestion that nearly caused the sultan to suffer an apoplectic fit, as he had been under the impression that he was the caliph, heir to Mohammed and the undisputed ruler of the Sublime Porte (as the Turks liked to call their pleasant little realm). The sultan responded to Europe's meddling by brutally suppressing the spreading revolt.

Refugees poured out of Hercegovina into Austria, Serbia and Montenegro, with wild stories of Mussulman atrocities, which inflamed Christian sensibilities. Excitable as children, the leaders of Serbia and Montenegro wasted no time in declaring war on the sultan, at which act of audacious daring the rest of Europe drew a collective breath and wished, not for the first time (nor, I'd wager, for the last), that the bloody Serbs and Montenegrins would mind their own damned business. For their declaration of war meant that the great powers of Europe would be sucked into the vortex. The Russians, fellow Orthodox Christians, had long had a soft spot for their Serbian cousins and immediately declared their support in the war against the Turks.

The alarm bells went off in London, where Dizzy and his gang saw the Russian move as nothing more than a pretext for displacing the Turks and helping themselves to Constantinople and control of the Dardanelles. It was at this point in his lecture that Dizzy looked grave and motioned for us to follow him to the great oak table covered with maps, where he unrolled a chart and weighted the corners. He tapped Constantinople with his finger, then drew his hand along the coast of the Mediterranean, through Turkey into Syria, straight through Damascus and Jerusalem, until the moving finger reached Port Said, at the mouth of the Nile, where it stopped and tapped the map once more.

He fixed me with a stern look, and said: "Even a child can see the danger. If the Russians take Constantinople, there is nothing to stop them from marching all the way to Egypt."

Well, nothing but rocks and sand and a few thousand Mussulmans who'd like nothing more than to come swooping down out of the hills on the crusaders slogging through their territory, I thought, but there's no stopping Dizzy when he's in full flow.

"The Russian Bear could easily take the Suez Canal, cutting us off from India and bringing the British Empire to its knees."

I expected the music to swell patriotically at this point, but all I heard was Dizzy's fevered breathing and Endicott chewing the end of his mustache.

"Another Crimea," intoned Dizzy. "And we all know what that campaign did to the flower of English manhood."

"I think perhaps you're being a bit melodramatic, sir," Endicott murmured. "Lord Derby thinks the danger is greatly exaggerated."

The prime minister rounded on him, black eyes flashing and curls flying. "My foreign secretary spends entirely too much time enjoying the company of Count Shuvalov," he said acidly. "Lord Derby's friendship with the count renders him loath to act under the most auspicious of circumstances. If it were left to him, England would stand by while the tsar's army occupied Egypt."

"Who's Count Shove-a-lot?" whispered Vincent to me, leaning closer to do so. I nearly fainted.

"The Russian ambassador to the Court of St. James," French muttered under his breath.

Endicott's face was pale, except for two crimson stains across his cheekbones. He inclined his head stiffly at Dizzy. "My apologies, sir. I was merely trying to express the views of the secretary. After all, I am here as his representative."

"Quite so, Mr. Endicott." The prime minister smiled wanly. "I'm afraid the urgency of the situation prompts me to speak more warmly than I should."

"No doubt Mr. Gladstone's behavior contributes to your feelings on the matter," Endicott said, with a touch of spite.

If he expected his words to have an effect, they certainly did. Dizzy's face flushed unhealthily, and his eyes burned with contempt. "The old fool. Why can't he busy himself with church fetes and stay out of politics?"

"I don't understand," I said. "What's Gladstone got to do with this?"

Dizzy made a retching noise and stalked over to the sideboard for more whisky. "You tell her, French. When I think of that buffoon, my blood boils."

It was an open secret that Dizzy and the former prime minister hated each other as only a loquacious dandy and novelist with a whiff of the Levantine about him could hate a Bible-spouting, hymn-singing moralist. They'd been going at it tooth and nail since they were first introduced at a dinner given by Lord Lynd-hurst in 1835. For four decades they'd traded jabs, insults and of-fices, arguing over budgets, trade, the extension of the franchise, the disestablishment of the Church of Ireland, Anglo-Catholic church ritual, land reform, the British Empire, whether Vicky should be Empress of India (Dizzy won that battle, though the vast majority of the Indians seem unimpressed) and anything else they could think of to argue about, regardless of how petty it was. Possibly the nadir of the relationship between the two occurred when Gladstone succeeded Dizzy as chancellor of the exchequer. It was customary for the incoming chancellor to pay the outgo-ing chancellor the cost of his office furniture. It was also custom-ary for the outgoing chancellor to pass along the official robe of office to the incoming chancellor. When Gladstone refused to pay Dizzy for the furniture, Dizzy decided a fair trade would be the chancellor's robe, which he immediately spirited off to his country house in Buckinghamshire, where I suppose it remains to this day. It's hard to credit a story like this, when you're talking about two grown men, but it's true. You'll be able to look it up in the history books one day.

While the prime minister fortified himself with a tot, French picked up the story. "You may have heard of a place called Batak, Miss Black. It's a small village on the slope of Mount Rhodope, in Bulgaria. The peasants there are Orthodox Christians, or were."

"Were?" I asked.

"Four thousand of them were slaughtered last summer by the Bashi-Bazouks, Mussulman irregulars allied with the Turkish au-thorities. The incident was first reported in the *Daily News,* who referred to matter as the 'Bulgarian atrocities.'"

"Bah!" Dizzy exclaimed. "The stories were largely invention.

Coffeehouse babble. And no one seems to give a tinker's damn for the thousands of Mussulman villagers murdered by their Christian neighbors."

French shrugged. "Nevertheless, devout Christians, Mr. Gladstone among them, were outraged at the affair. There have been repeated calls for the British government to act."

"To act?" I asked.

"To attack the caliphate and liberate its Christian subjects."

"Gladstone wants you to invade the Ottoman Empire?"

"Ridiculous," Dizzy expostulated. "The man is a prize idiot. We hold millions of pounds in bonds issued by the Turks. If we invade, the bonds will be worthless. And then there's the matter of what to do with the Russians. We don't want to fight Ivan again, only twenty years after the horrors of Gallipoli. But we can't allow the Russians in Turkey, not at any cost. We're in a damned tight spot. We have tried to remain on the sidelines, urging the Turks to refrain from attacking their Christian subjects and warning the Russians to stay out."

Endicott stirred himself and fetched more whisky. "It's deuced difficult siding with the Turks against the Russians as long as the bloody Turks keep slaughtering Christians. Mr. Gladstone is outraged, and he's doing his best to incite the public to support a move against the Turks."

"He may be incensed," said Dizzy. "I've never doubted the old parson's faith, but it has no place in politics. Good God, just imagine if each man allowed himself to be swayed by moral compunctions; we'd never get a damned thing accomplished in Parliament." He shuddered at this unspeakable idea and fortified himself with a drink. "The man's a lunatic if he thinks Britain should mount another crusade to take on the Saracens and free their subjects from bondage. And don't think Gladstone doesn't have another motive behind all that proselytizing. He'd like nothing more than to see this Cabinet humiliated and this government fall. He's got an eye for the main chance, does Gladstone."

I've often wondered how a politician can keep a straight face when he talks, decrying as he does in his rivals the very same ethics he shares.

"Whatever his motives," said French, "Mr. Gladstone has struck a chord with the British public. In September he published a pamphlet on the situation in the Ottoman Empire. It sold two hundred thousand copies in less than a month. You may have seen it yourself, Miss Black. *The Bulgarian Horrors and the Question of the East?*"

I vaguely remembered the tract; Calthorp had brought in a stack on a fine autumn day, mustache trembling with suppressed fury at the horrors inflicted on the Bulgarian peasants. Since he'd waded through a swarm of unfed, unwashed and unwanted children to deliver them to Lotus House, I hadn't been able to muster much sympathy for nameless, faceless villagers half a world away.

"The British public be damned," Dizzy spat. "I've known sheep with more intelligence."

"Sheep they may be, but some of those sheep will be voting in the next election, and if it were held tomorrow, I've no doubt they'd be voting for Gladstone's party," said Endicott. He glanced obliquely at Dizzy and smiled spitefully. "People have taken to calling him the 'Grand Old Man.'"

"Pah," Dizzy spat contemptuously, venomous as a cobra. "God's Only Mistake, more like."

"Ten thousand people came to Blackheath to hear him speak

on the Bulgarian massacre." Endicott twisted the screw a little tighter. He was enjoying this, the devil.

"The 'alleged' massacre," Dizzy growled.

"I'm merely trying to illustrate that the people seem to back Gladstone on this issue," Endicott said.

"A point that Lord Derby no doubt finds persuasive in suggesting that we step aside and hand India to the Russians," said Dizzy.

"The secretary has suggested no such thing, Prime Minister, as you are well aware." Endicott and Dizzy glared at each other across the map.

I yawned; there's nothing so dull as watching men (even men the likes of the British prime minister and some muckety-muck from the Foreign Office) argue over politics, except watching men argue over religion or sport. "Pardon me for interrupting," I said, "but I'm still waiting for an explanation of why I was abducted off the street."

"Allow me to explain, my dear." Dizzy frowned. "That old fool Gladstone has been frothing at the mouth, whipping the press into a frenzy of Christian outrage. He's here in London now, at Claridge's, making the rounds of the papers, submitting hysterical letters to the editors and addressing every Women's Institute meeting in the city. And he's making no secret of his support for Russian intervention. He made a public display of himself at a performance of Tchaikovsky's "Marche Slav" at Covent Garden last month, weeping copiously into his handkerchief. He even went so far as to attend an anti-Turk rally at the Athenaeum a month ago in the company of Count Shuvalov."

"Shocking," I muttered, under my breath.

"Wonder if that Lord Derby was there with 'em," Vincent whispered. "Sounds like 'e ain't too particular 'bout the company he keeps."

"And while Gladstone dallies with the Russian ambassador, the tsar's army is preparing to descend on Constantinople," said French.

"The key to India," I added helpfully.

"Quite so," said Dizzy. "A few weeks ago, I dispatched Lord Salisbury to Paris and Berlin, attempting to enlist the aid of the French and German governments in issuing an ultimatum to the Russians to stay out of the Ottoman Empire. But delivering an ultimatum without threatening consequences is futile. And if the tsar and his ministers believe that Britain will act only in concert with France and Germany, and that those countries may not support us, then the Russians may still proceed with impunity to Constantinople. Consequently, a week ago I took the opportunity of speaking at the lord mayor's banquet, warning Russia that in the event we are forced to war, Britain will fight, alone if necessary, and that her resources are inexhaustible."

"You stated the matter quite emphatically." Endicott stroked his mustache. "You said that Britain was not a country that had to ask itself if it should enter into this campaign, but that it would enter the campaign and not terminate it until right was done. Stirring stuff," he added dryly. "If only you'd had the foresight to inquire whether the British army was capable of fulfilling that commitment before you made it."

I expected Dizzy to slap Endicott's mug with a glove and demand satisfaction at dawn, but the prime minister only sniffed and turned his back, ostentatiously positioning himself so he wouldn't have to look at the upstart minister from the Foreign Office. Endicott permitted himself a smirk and retired to his corner.

By this time, I was getting impatient. The whisky was first-rate, and the malicious bickering between Dizzy and Endicott entertaining, but I was tired of geopolitics and listening to Dizzy whinge about Gladstone. I had a business to run, and without me on the premises, I was liable to return to Lotus House to find it ransacked and the tarts drunk as lords and wearing my gowns. And they'd probably grant any number of discounts to their favorites, if I weren't there to enforce the retail rates.

French noticed my impatience. "We've nearly reached the end of the story, Miss Black."

"How nice. I was beginning to think I'd been transported into a novel by Mr. Trollope and might never see the light of day."

Dizzy smoothed his lapels. "Immediately after my speech at the lord mayor's banquet, I summoned a representative of the War Office and requested that he provide me with an estimate of the number of troops needed to hold Constantinople and Gallipoli. The estimate"—and here Dizzy passed a hand over his eyes and looked like the oysters he'd eaten for lunch had rebelled—"was shocking."

"The Intelligence Department at the War Office had previously advised that forty-six thousand troops were all that was necessary," said French. "The estimate they offered the prime minister after the speech had risen to seventy-five thousand men."

"I take it we do not have seventy-five thousand men," I ventured.

"We don't have *forty-five* thousand," said Endicott.

Dizzy shook his head. "I've suggested the department be renamed the Department of Ignorance. Those fools have placed me in an untenable position. I have declared that Britain is prepared to stand alone against Russia, when the truth is that we are simply not capable of doing so."

"We could bluff our way through," said Endicott. "Save for a rather unfortunate circumstance."

French relit his cheroot with a taper. "The prime minister prepared a memorandum to the secretary of war. The memorandum expressed the prime minister's concern and displeasure at the change in numbers. It also contained a detailed description of the potential loss of funds to the government and certain British investors if Britain were to attack the Porte and the Turks default on their debts. The memorandum was dispatched, along with the original documents containing the troop estimates, to the War Office by messenger on Sunday afternoon. The messenger took a detour. The documents never reached the War Office."

"Bowser," I said.

"Sir Archibald Latham," French confirmed.

"And the documents are now at the Russian embassy, waiting to be opened by Count Yusopov," I said.

French nodded. "So our sources tell us. Count Yusopov is returning tomorrow from Paris. We must recover the case before it reaches him and the weakness of the British forces is revealed. Once the Russians have that information, they'll be on the Bosporus before you know it."

"So you see, Miss Black," Dizzy went on, "the very future of England depends upon the retrieval of that missing case. Find the case, and we may prevent Russia from marching into Constantinople."

"I still don't see how I can be of help."

The three men exchanged a look, and I felt my heart sink. I

might not have had any idea what I could do, but those gents clearly had a scheme in mind, and since I hadn't had a hand in making it, it was a sure bet I wouldn't like it.

Dizzy bestowed another dazzling smile on me, the kind he no doubt gave his publisher when he persuaded him to publish that dreadful novel *Tancred*. "We want you to get the case back for us."

"Me?"

"You," said Endicott.

Vincent leaned toward me and muttered, "I got a bad feelin' 'bout this, India."

"How would you suggest I go about doing that?" I demanded. "Waltz up to the door of the Russian embassy and ask Yusopov to hand it over?"

"I don't think he'll give up the case quite that easily," said Endicott. "But we've no doubt you'll be able to find an opportunity to collect it for us." The same smirk he'd displayed earlier was now pasted across his face. "Count Yusopov is rather susceptible to feminine charms."

"Something you have in abundance, my dear," said Dizzy, in a blatant attempt to worm his way into my good graces.

"And where will I meet the man? Strolling through Hyde Park? Buying a beefsteak at the local butcher's shop?"

French looked impatient at this frivolity. "We've made arrangements, of course. Tomorrow evening you'll attend a gala ball at the embassy. Yusopov returns from Paris just in time to attend the function. His first opportunity to review the documents will be immediately after the ball, but we propose to delay his doing so by creating a diversion and stealing away with the case."

"What kind of diversion?" I asked.

"Not to put too fine a point on it," said French, "you."

"And who's going to steal the case?" I asked, with a sinking heart.

"You."

From his pocket, French produced a small envelope. "Here is your invitation. If you've nothing suitable to wear, please avail yourself of the services of Monsieur Gaspard. He's expecting you."

Reluctantly, I took the envelope from his outstretched hand. "Precisely what sort of diversion did you have in mind?" I was certain I wouldn't like the answer.

Dizzy had the grace to look abashed, something I thought him incapable of doing. "You see, that's how we can be assured that you will gain access to Yusopov. He has certain, er, proclivities."

In my line of work, that could mean anything from primates to pineapples.

Dizzy extended his hand and gave me another dazzling smile. "Mr. French will tell you more," he said, and thus ended my audience with the prime minister.

Mr. French did, as he escorted me back to Lotus House in a stylish barouche drawn by a pair of matching blacks, their breath smoking in the cold night air. French handed me in, then settled into the seat beside me. Vincent sat across from us. I'd have made him ride on top with the coachman, but French showed a surprising degree of compassion, unless of course he wanted you to steal government documents from the Russian embassy, and then he was prepared to blackmail you with impunity. French and I were uncomfortably close; I could feel the weight of his arm against mine. I shifted away from the contact, to the far side of the cab. I might be a whore, but I wasn't going to let the man take any liberties with me. Not unless he paid for the privilege.

"Mr. Endicott and I will be with you at the embassy tomorrow night, but we cannot do anything to assist you in finding the case. It's critical that the government isn't implicated in the matter."

"So if I'm discovered in the act of lifting the case, I needn't suggest the authorities contact you to clear up things."

"Precisely."

"Remind me again why I'm doing this."

"Lotus House."

"Ah, yes. For the privilege of keeping what I already own, I'm to lie back and think of England?"

"You could characterize it in that fashion."

"So what's Count Yusopov's pleasure?" I asked. "Whips and chains? Livestock? Jellied eels?"

"He's an admirer of Sappho." French turned to look at me, and I felt his breath on my cheek. "You'll have to bring someone along. I trust that won't be a problem."

"You could have asked first. Every whore has something she won't do."

"And what is it that you won't do, India?"

"I never share confidences, French. It's a sign of weakness."

Vincent cut in. "Yer payin' ain't ye, Mr. French? I can fix ye up with a woman quicker'n ye can say 'snap.' And she'll be cheaper than ye can find anywhere else."

"Hold on, Vincent," I said. "If I'm going to play slap and tickle with another woman, I'll choose the lucky lady." I shuddered at the thought of the disease-ridden hag Vincent would likely produce.

"I admire your entrepreneurial spirit," said French. "But under the circumstances, I think we must honour the lady's wishes. There is, however, one thing you can do for me, Vincent."

"Wot's that?"

French rummaged in his pocket and produced a handful of coins. "You can hand over the items you cadged from the prime minister's office. This should compensate you for the money you would have received if you had pawned them."

"Wot are ye on about, guv?" Vincent contrived to look innocent, without, I might add, any noticeable success.

French sighed. "Pray do not insult my intelligence, Vincent. Empty your pockets and take the money. I happen to know that Lord Beaconsfield is inordinately fond of that ivory-handled letter opener you have secreted on your person. It was a present from his wife."

Reluctantly, Vincent withdrew the aforementioned letter opener from his sleeve and placed it in French's hand, then held out his own for the coins.

French waggled his fingers impatiently.

Vincent wheezed mournfully and extracted a star-shaped crystal paperweight, a small silver inkwell and a gold-nibbed pen. French critically examined each item slowly, then pocketed them.

"Is that all, Vincent?"

Vincent nodded resentfully.

"You wouldn't lie to me, would you?"

Vincent shook his head vigorously. I was about to inform French that Vincent was constitutionally incapable of telling the truth, but why should I interfere? I hoped Vincent had kept some choice bauble for himself; it would serve French right.

After French had collected Vincent's loot, paying him what I considered an unseemly sum for returning stolen property, we spent the remainder of the drive to Lotus House hashing through the details of our plans for the next evening. It wasn't much of a plan. I (and my confederate) were to woo Yusopov upstairs with our maidenly charms, lull him to sleep with some vigorous sexual activity, and then I was to pop downstairs to Yusopov's office, open the safe (the combination of which French provided me, courtesy of some mole in the Russian embassy), secure Latham's case, and hotfoot it out the door and down the street, where I would find French waiting. The first part of the plan didn't present any problems: I was confident in my abilities to first charm, and then exhaust Yusopov. The latter section of the plan (hotfooting it out of the embassy) seemed rather vague, omitting as it did certain details such as the existence and location of armed guards.

"Not to worry, India," French said blithely (he wasn't going to be in the embassy, performing for Count Perverterov, was he?). "The guards will be exhausted after pulling duty at the ball. They'll be snoring in their beds by the time you have the case in hand."

The barouche dropped us at my front door, with instructions for me to be ready at nine o'clock the following evening and for Vincent not to be anywhere near the Russian embassy then. Vincent nodded obligingly, but I knew I'd likely see his face peeking out from behind the aspidistra.

As I've said, I didn't find it the least bit odd that the PM would enlist a whore to engage in some skullduggery on behalf of the government, and I made my plans accordingly.

If Yusopov wanted to enjoy the Sapphic arts, I had just the person in mind, and the following morning, I walked briskly around the corner to the Silver Thistle and inquired for the Jamaican Queen. Moments later, I was engulfed in a haze of perfume, my face buried in the ample bosom of Rowena Adderly.

"India," she squealed. "How delightful to see you." She held me at arm's length and assessed me with an expert eye. "You're looking particularly luscious, my dear."

I extracted myself from her grasp, no small feat as Rowena had the grip of an octopus in heat. "Hello, Rowena. You're look-ing well yourself." And she was a damnably fine-looking woman: statuesque and coffee-coloured, with a billowing cloud of dark curls, a lilting Caribbean accent, and plump lips that made men salivate. She plied her trade out of the Silver Thistle and did a rushing business in men newly returned from the colonies, where they'd acquired an affinity for Negresses, Indian nautch girls and Arab maidens, obtaining a small fortune along the way. Rowena's talents were legendary on the London docks, but her personal taste ran to her own sex. Hence my visit this morning: if you're going to do something, you may as well do it with style, and who better to give this affair some class (not to mention verisimili-tude) than a real live tom? I didn't have any doubt that Rowena would be willing to join me in my escapade. She'd been trying to get into my petticoats for years.

Of course I couldn't tell her the truth. I'd concocted a tale on the drive home, and now I spun it for Rowena, after we'd ex-changed the usual pleasantries and complaints about customers, peelers and the Contagious Diseases Act. I'd given considerable thought to how I might explain the case and what was in it and why I wanted it, bearing in mind that while Rowena might jump at the chance to strip off my knickers (not that I was planning on things getting to that point), she'd be even more likely to offer her assistance if I could enlist her sympathy, having, as I said, a soft spot for yours truly.

So I laid out a yarn that would have made Dickens's readers weep, how I'd promised my mother to take care of her dearest friend in her old age, how the friend had suffered grievously from a rare disease that could only be cured by taking the waters at Baden-Baden, how I'd borrowed the money from one of my customers, a Russian nobleman (Count Yusopov, by name, the rascal) and delivered to him as security the deed to Lotus House, how I'd repaid the debt but had been shocked and dismayed to learn that Yusopov had no intention of returning the deed to me, unless I agreed to provide him with services that no tart should ever have to provide.

I did my fiction credit, if I do say so myself, letting tears well up in my eyes at just the right moment and allowing my voice to choke when I mentioned dear Mother. Rowena lapped it up like a cat laps up cream (beautiful she may be, and possessed of a naïve cunning, but not what I'd call a scholar), her plump lips parted in amazement, her eyes growing luminous with unshed tears as my voice faltered and finally blazing with indignation at Yusopov's treachery. I knew the last bit would get her, you see, her being a fellow property owner.

At the end of my tale, she was ready to do battle, and willingly agreed to join me in attending the gala at the embassy (it never occurred to her to wonder how I'd managed to wrangle an invitation) and in recovering my stolen deed. I invited her along to Monsieur Gaspard's, for I intended to take full advantage of the offer to have a suitable gown run up for the soiree, as it was the only compensation I was going to receive for my services (I didn't count French's gracious offer to let me stay in business as remuneration), and I didn't see why Rowena shouldn't receive some recompense as well, since I'd lied to her to get her to join in my scheme. Thus we spent the next few hours being fussed over by a petite, cranky Frenchman, who talked through his nose and smelled of Camembert, but was a dab hand with silk and lace.

SIX

That evening, at the appointed hour, a hansom cab drew up to the Lotus House, and Rowena and I joined Endicott and French for the drive to the embassy. We looked, if I may admit so, ravishing. Monsieur Gaspard had done us proud. He'd decked me out in a watered-silk gown of ice blue, with a plunging neckline that showed the swell of my breasts to perfection, and the new cuirass bodice fitted my curvaceous figure like a glove. Rowena had fared as well, for she sported a moiré gown of pale yellow in the same style that glowed warmly against her coffee-coloured breasts and arms. Her Majesty's government (albeit unknowingly) had sprung for lace gloves and matching cashmere shawls for us both.

No woman of a certain class would attend a social affair unescorted, and it had been arranged that French and Endicott would act as our attendants, though I suspected their real role was to see that I carried out the retrieval of the case. Rowena and I had preened like peacocks in front of the mirror at Lotus House, but our sartorial splendor was wasted on the two men. French was reserved as always; Endicott even chillier, though he seemed momentarily taken aback when the dusky Rowena climbed into the cab, turning to glare at French before composing his face into a marble scowl and sulking all the way to the embassy. French, who'd known about Rowena since I'd vetted her with him on the ride from Dizzy's, assumed an air of innocence, which was about as convincing as a crocodile masquerading as a brindled gnu. Rowena was too experienced to do more than glance curiously at the men before turning away to gaze out at the streets of London as we traveled. We rode in silence, while the cab swayed and the driver cursed the carriages and pedestrians that impeded our progress.

The Russian embassy occupied a handsome mansion in the Regency style in Belgravia. The building was ablaze with lights when we drew up, the windows hung with scarlet and gold banners, the flag bearing the double-headed eagle of the tsar snapping in the breeze. Inside, an orchestra was playing a Strauss waltz, and the gay melody carried out into the street, where a throng of carriages and hansom cabs discharged a crowd of well-heeled revelers. The men were in white tie and tails, looking haughty and self-important, and the ladies decked out in gorgeous gowns, long white gloves and ermine wraps. There was a crush at the front door, as the parties jostled for entry and waited in line to be announced by a Slavic-looking cove in a tailcoat and crimson sash. French offered me his arm, Rowena tucked her hand into

Endicott's, and we passed through a double line of guards standing like a row of statues, spectacularly turned out in long grey coats with light blue stripes and gold cartridge loops, light blue *beshmets* or waistcoats, grey trousers and tall fleece caps of light blue. Each guard wore a wicked looking sword at his side.

"Terek Cossacks," whispered French, when we'd exited the corridor of guards. "One of the oldest of the Cossack hosts. That sword they carry is called a *shashka*. You never want to face one of those."

We entered a great hall with a marble staircase and illuminated by a chandelier of glittering crystal and gilt. Endicott handed the footman a card. The footman read the script, blinked, cast an anxious glance at Rowena's toffee-coloured skin and bit his lip. Endicott's growl recalled the man to his duty. "Mr. William R. Endicott and Miss Rowena Endicott," the footman stammered. In the light from the chandelier, Endicott's hair was the colour of burnished gold, his face as pale as the marble columns in the hallway.

"Siblings?" I hissed in French's ear. "Couldn't you have come up with something better than that?"

"I thought a wife might be stretching things a bit thin."

"You're not a nice man, French."

"I'm in politics. Being nice is a disadvantage."

We swept through the hallway and into the dining salon, where dozens of tables were scattered about, all covered with snowy white damask, gleaming crystal and individual silver candelabras. I'll say this for the Russians, they don't let the plight of the serfs stand in the way of a good party. The buffet tables in the dining salon groaned with food: caviar in silver bowls resting on a bed of crushed ice, oysters on the half shell, lobster and venison, borscht and dumplings, ices and puddings and chocolate gateau. There were iced buckets of Taittinger and Veuve Clicquot, and bottles of vodka, Madeira, brandy and claret. The rooms of the mansion were no less impressive, being decked out in that over-the-top style the Russkis favor, the one that makes most tarts envious, all velvet, gilt, marble, jewels and silk. In the ballroom, couples twirled dreamily around the parquet floor to the music of Tchaikovsky while diamonds and emeralds twinkled in the candlelight. A waiter scurried over with a tray of glasses, and French handed round the champagne.

Rowena swallowed appreciatively. "We'd nothing like this in Kingston."

French nudged my elbow. "There's your man," he whispered, and nodded discreetly at a paunchy, bearded fellow in white tie, with a chest full of medals and a luxuriant mustache, who was laughing uproariously at some anecdote being related by his companion, an overbred English woman with an aristocratic, horsy face. Yusopov had an air of languid dissipation, heightened by his flushed cheeks and the way his eyes drooped at the outer corner, as though he'd only just gotten out of bed.

He must have felt my eyes upon him, for he lifted his head and looked me squarely in the eye. His candid appraisal left me feeling as exposed as if he'd stripped me naked. He must have approved, for he bowed slightly and leered at me, raising his champagne glass in a wordless salute.

Beside me, I heard French's indrawn breath. "Quick work," he muttered.

"Can you blame the man?" I'm accustomed to the effect I produce in men (with the evident exception of French, of course, who looked at me with the same interest as a chess player would regard a pawn). "Just don't get cocky, boyo," I said. "I haven't gotten my hands on that case yet."

"I've no doubt you'll be successful tonight," said French, still marveling at the way Yusopov had honed in on me.

I returned Yusopov's gaze, simpering and pouting and otherwise announcing my availability. Then I shared a smile with Rowena, whispering to her behind my fan, and she tossed the count a look of frank interest, giving him an unobstructed view of two coffee-coloured breasts swelling out of her pale yellow gown. She smiled invitingly, put a proprietary arm around my waist and her lips to my ear, as though we were sharing a confidence and would likely share a bit more before the evening was over, and if Yusopov played his cards right, what we shared might be him. The count swallowed convulsively, muttered something into the ear of a uniformed lackey hovering nearby, and then turned his attention back to the equine-faced woman with difficulty. Rowena and I were subjected to a moment's scrutiny by the uniformed man, who was no doubt filing away our faces for future reference.

The game was afoot, but Yusopov played at a slow pace. No doubt he had certain social obligations to fulfill, for he circulated around the room, slapping backs and kissing hands and engaging in fervid discussions with various official-looking gents, but he made sure Rowena and I knew of his interest, casting a number of lusty glances in our direction and toasting us with the ever-present glass in his hand. As the evening wore on, his cheeks grew pinker, and beads of sweat appeared on his forehead.

We spent the better part of three hours guzzling champagne and dancing to the latest tunes. French proved surprisingly light on his feet, if not particularly attentive. He spent his time tracking Yusopov over my shoulder as we pirouetted around the ballroom floor, and quizzing me about the blueprints of the embassy he'd shown me the night before.

"And Yusopov's office is on the second floor, right below his bedroom."

"I know," I said. "You've told me ten bloody times." French's mouth was an inch from my ear and his hand was nestled in the small of my back. It was unsettling, this pleasant interlude with a man who'd done nothing but cause trouble since he came into my life. Fortunately, the moment was ruined when French spoke again. "There's little margin for error. You'll have to work quickly."

"You'd be surprised how many men prefer it that way," I said, swaying gently in time to the music.

"Rowena knows what's expected of her?"

"Yes. Stop fretting. It won't be the first time Rowena and I have rolled a customer and made off with his valuables."

"Should I check my pockets to confirm I still have my wallet?"

"I'd never steal your wallet, French. You'd be after me with all the hounds of hell. I plan to say auf Wiedersehen to you tonight and trust you'll never darken the doors of Lotus House again."

"You're an ungrateful wench, India."

"Ungrateful?" I yelped, sotto voce. "And for what should I be grateful?"

"Inspector Havelock of the Metropolitan Police hasn't stopped by to see you, has he?"

"That's low, French. You helped me dispose of the body."

"Indeed I did. But no one, least of all an unimaginative plod like Havelock, would believe it. Your word against mine, India. How do you like your odds?"

I stamped on his ankle with the heel of my slipper and had the satisfaction of hearing him grunt in pain.

"Not very nice of you, old girl."

"I'm a whore. Being nice is a disadvantage."

At one point in the evening, I thought I detected the familiar odor of *eau de Vincent,* but as we'd just swept past the caviar bowl on the buffet, I couldn't be sure. I kept a close eye on the table to see if the linen covering moved, but it remained still and I presumed Vincent, in a rare fit of obedience, had followed French's orders to remain away from the embassy.

Endicott and Rowena went galloping by, Rowena's teeth gleaming and Endicott looking grim and hanging on for dear life. She gave me a wink as they thundered past.

"Did I detect some animosity between the PM and Endicott last night?" I asked. "I thought you were all on the same side."

French executed a turn that left me breathless. "Endicott works for Lord Derby, the foreign secretary. He must advocate Lord Derby's position with respect to matters in the Ottoman Porte. Lord Derby is by nature quite conservative about the expansion of British hegemony. Indeed, some say he is an isolationist who will never find any cause or purpose compelling enough to warrant the use of military force, short of an outright invasion of a British dominion. The prime minister sees things a bit differently. He favors a more aggressive attitude, both in the extension of our empire and the protection of it. He doesn't intend to let the Russians gain so much as a toehold in any area he deems to be within Britain's sphere of control."

"If they differ so much on the issue, why is Lord Derby in the Cabinet?"

French shrugged. "Politics makes strange bedfellows. And he's much too prominent to be excluded from the Cabinet. That would have created difficulties within the Conservative Party."

"I thought a brothel was full of intrigue and drama, but there's more theatrics in politics," I said.

"The stakes are rather larger, though."

The music ended, and among polite applause we retired to one of the tables in the dining salon, with plates piled high with some of the delectables on offer. Rowena and Endicott joined us. Her face was flushed a dusky rose, and her dark eyes were lively.

She fanned herself vigorously and tucked into a mound of oysters. "Lord, what a spread! Did you see the meringues?"

Endicott screwed a cigarette into his holder and struck a match. "Perhaps you should exercise some restraint with respect to those oysters. Don't forget you've got work to do tonight."

Rowena ogled me across the table and patted Endicott on the knee. "Don't you worry, my lad. I've appetite enough for both oysters and India."

Over Endicott's shoulder, I saw a chap approaching, a tall, lithe figure elegant in the full dress uniform of a Russian major. French had seen the man, too; I felt him stiffen reflexively at the sight of the Russian.

"He looks a right villain," I whispered, and he did, with a face as lean and cruel as a wolf's and unnaturally green eyes. He looked as though he'd be more at home on the snow-swept steppes, cursing the peasants and applying the knout, than threading his way through the elegant tables of the dining salon. I knew his type: the kind who sent a frisson of fear through a bint when he walked in the room. You just knew he was going to ask for something you didn't want to supply and were damned glad you wouldn't. One glance at him and I had to hold back a whinny of fright.

He approached our table and bowed stiffly to French.

"Major Ivanov." So this was the military agent who'd acquired Latham's case. I was surprised that French accepted the outstretched hand.

"I didn't expect to see you tonight, Major. I thought you were with your regiment."

"No doubt I'll be rejoining my regiment soon." He smirked. "I have good reason to believe we'll be called into action shortly, to deal with those recalcitrant Turks."

"Bully for you," said French.

"It should be quite an interesting little war. The Turks haven't fielded a decent army since Kara Mustafa Pasha nearly took Vienna in 1683. I expect we'll be in Constantinople in a matter of weeks, once we cross the Danube. But enough talk of war. Who are your charming companions? Be a good fellow, French, and introduce me."

The Russian fawned over Rowena and I, clicking his heels and kissing our hands. Endicott looked nauseous, and never more so than when Ivanov clasped his hand and shook it heartily. "A representative from Lord Derby's office? Splendid! Count Yusopov will be so pleased. Have you spoken to him yet?" Ivanov plopped down in the seat next to me without waiting to be invited.

"We haven't yet had the opportunity," said Endicott stiffly. "He's been rather busy." Endicott looked meaningfully at a table near the window, where Yusopov could be seen single-handedly reducing the champagne stocks and fondling the knee of the rotund young woman seated next to him.

Ivanov chuckled indulgently. "How he enjoys these festivities.

All Russians do. We understand the brevity of life and take our pleasures where we find them. Unlike you English. So earnest. So staid." His eyes swung round to me. "Except here I think we have a young lady who is not so earnest."

"I am enjoying the party, Major. The refreshments are delicious and the music sublime."

"You rival the music, my dear," said Ivanov gallantly. "Perhaps you would do me the honour of dancing with me later?"

"Certainly," I replied.

"Wonderful. I shall look forward to it." The Russian cocked an eyebrow at French. "And now, Mr. French, what may I and my comrades in arms expect from the British lion? How soon will we be locked in mortal combat, eh? The prime minister's speech at the lord mayor's banquet has the generals in St. Petersburg all aflutter. I've been summoned back to the mother country myself, in preparation for posting to God knows where."

French blew a smoke ring and looked bored. "You'll be leaving England? What a pity."

"No doubt our paths will cross again. You English have a habit of turning up in the oddest places." Ivanov leaned across the table, and his brilliant green eyes twinkled merrily. "Or perhaps we may become allies in this war. Two Christian nations closing ranks to end the reign of terror of those despicable Turks."

French's smile was wintry. "How like Russia to cast this war as a holy crusade. I could have sworn her chief interest in the Ottoman Empire was not the religious persecution of its Christian subjects, but its deep-water port at Constantinople. The British government will not stand aside and let you violate the territorial integrity of the Porte."

Ivanov's smile was lupine. "This must be an event of the first instance. I was unaware the British government concerned itself with the territorial sovereignty of other nations, except in the event it determined that the interests of Great Britain required the invasion of that sovereignty."

"Naturally, a nation will put its own interests first," said French.

"Naturally," Ivanov said with mock solemnity. "But perhaps your Mr. Gladstone feels differently. He is a man who places his religious beliefs before his political ones. He has expressed to the ambassador his distress at this administration's failure to act. And from what I have read in your newspapers, many here in England support his view. Perhaps we will be allies, after all."

I was glad Dizzy wasn't around to hear this last, for we'd have no doubt been subjected to another one of his screeds against Gladstone.

"Do Mr. Gladstone and Count Yusopov share an interest in theology?" I asked. Yusopov's hand was out of sight beneath the tablecloth, but its location could be ascertained by the behavior of the rotund woman, who was jumping like a spurred colt and uttering muted squeals of pleasure.

Ivanov followed my gaze and let out a bark of laughter. "The count enjoys certain religious rites more than others." He rose gracefully, kissed my glove and Rowena's, and shook hands with Endicott and French. "I must ask your pardon; there are duties to which I must attend." He bowed and stalked gracefully away through the crowd.

"He's a scary chap," said Rowena. "Did you see those eyes?" She shuddered theatrically, which made her breasts quiver like Mrs. Drinkwater's blancmange and attracted the attention of every gentleman in a twenty foot radius.

Even Endicott sat up and took notice, until he was diverted

by the sight of a short, thickset fellow with a luxuriant mustache and bald head bearing down on our table like the daily express from Manchester. "Good God," he groaned. "Here's Penbras, come to make our lives a living hell."

The stout fellow dropped into a chair, raised a shout of "Ho, waiter, whisky," and thumped Endicott on the back. "Willie, my boy. How are you?"

"How the devil did you get in here?" Endicott hissed. "The press isn't usually allowed at these functions."

"I've got connections, Willie, as I've told you a hundred times. Not everyone views me with the loathing and suspicion that you do. I'm welcome in lots of places your regular journalistic type is verboten." He beamed round the table. "Allow me to introduce myself, ladies. Peter Penbras, of the *Morning Chronicle*. Correspondent, bon vivant and world traveler."

"Poltroon, fabricator and con artist," said French, almost affectionately, I thought. Observing the proprieties, he introduced us to the stout bloke.

Penbras took my outstretched hand and pronounced himself delighted, eyes roving unashamedly. With reluctance, he dragged his attention from me and turned to Rowena.

"Willie, you've outdone yourself, my lad. Who is this winsome creature?"

Endicott choked on his champagne, spewing a fair amount of the ambrosia over his shirt front.

"Dear me," said Rowena. "He does get excited at the smallest thing." She extended her hand. "A pleasure to meet you, Mr. Penbras. Please, call me Rowena. Everyone does."

"Then I shall do the same, my dear. I say, do you think I should fetch some water for Willie there? He's turning purple."

"He'll be fine," said Rowena. "These spells often last a few minutes."

Penbras winked and helped himself to a slice of cold tongue from French's plate. "Good grub here, ain't it? And the likker is first-rate. I do love these embassy flings."

"What brings you out tonight, Penbras?" Endicott asked. "A whiff of scandal? Carrion wheeling in the sky over the embassy tonight?"

"Whisky," said Penbras to the waiter. "And be quick about it, my good man. My throat's as dry as the road from Cardiff to Swansea." The waiter hurried off, clucking under his breath about British manners. Penbras watched him go with an air of benign amusement, searching absently through his pockets. "I say, Endicott, you wouldn't offer a friend a gasper, would you?"

"Certainly I'd give a friend a cigarette," Endicott said, resting his hands on the table and studying his manicure. A long minute ticked by.

Penbras grinned. "You're not subtle, Willie. Not the least bit crafty or sly, my man. That's why I like you. I just wish you'd play cards with me sometime."

"You're a mischievious bugger," said French. "I'm surprised the ambassador let you through the door."

Penbras waved a hand airily. "His Excellency and I have known each other for donkey's years. He's good copy, always has something to say, and he loves to see his name in print. Almost as much as Dizzy does."

"Most politicians are cut from the same cloth." French opened his case and offered Penbras a cigarette.

"Thanks, old man. You're a decent chap, despite what Endicott says about you."

French smiled but didn't rise to the bait. Endicott was staring round the dining salon, studiously avoiding the journalist.

Penbras extracted a small notebook and the stub of a pencil from his coat pocket. "Either of you gents got anything to say about the crisis in Turkey?"

"No," said Endicott. French shook his head.

Penbras sucked his teeth. "Rumor has it the PM is annoyed with the lads at the War Office. Got 'em shaking in their boots over there, calculating their pensions and drafting up their notices."

French smiled. "Isn't that how civil servants usually spend their time?"

Penbras looked thoughtful. "My source seemed confident something unusual has happened. Said it had something to do with Dizzy getting bad news about English troop strength."

French smoked languidly. "I can assure you there is nothing to this tattle."

Penbras tacked, sailing in a new direction. "What a shame about poor old Archie Latham," he said.

Endicott bridled. "*Sir* Archibald."

"Right," Penbras said. "Damned shame, that. We're none of us safe walking the streets. Especially the streets around the jute docks. Damned odd thing, for Archie to be trolling about down there in the dead of night. Something strange about that." Penbras assumed the expression of a newborn babe. "Wouldn't you say so, Willie?"

Endicott rose abruptly. "Listening to your gibberish is tiresome, Penbras. I'm here to enjoy myself. Shall we dance, Rowena?" He swept her away to the dance floor with her mouth still full of meringues.

"Stiff brute, ain't he?" Penbras said cheerfully. "About as much fun to play with as a starving mastiff. Now I enjoy going a few rounds with you, French. You're a fine sparring partner. You understand the give and take of the game, unlike your surly friend there."

"*Have* you something to give me?" French asked.

Penbras cocked his head to one side, like an appealing pup. "Maybe I do. Have *you* something to give *me*?"

"Perhaps later."

"Ah. Well, I was hoping you might confirm or deny the rumors about Dizzy and the War Office."

"I can't do that, Penbras. But I'll tell you that the prime minister's position on the Russian aggression in Turkey remains unchanged."

"You don't mind if I don't write that down, do you?" Penbras stroked his bald head. "What else would he say, if he wants to keep those Slavic bastards from the Bosporus? I was hoping for something a bit more definite."

"Stay in touch. Perhaps I can offer you something more specific in the days to come."

Penbras looked thoughtful. "Two questions come to mind when I hear you say that. One, why would a member of Dizzy's inner circle volunteer to toss me a juicy morsel? And, two, supposing that he does, what's it going to cost me?"

"Your source in the War Office."

Penbras chortled. "Oh, ho. Hoisted on my own petard. No doubt you think I'll lunge at the chance to acquire a source in the PM's office and gladly sacrifice my contact at the War Office to get it." He wiped his eyes, clucking gently. "I'll have to mull that over, but I must tell you, it's a privilege to enter the ring with a man who understands the role of strategy." He took a final drag of his cigarette and crushed it out in Endicott's plate. "I'm off to tackle Ambassador Shuvolov. He's promised me a few words on the Russian struggle to save the Christians of the Ottoman Empire. Mustn't tarry." He waggled his fingers at us, drained the last of his whisky and rumbled off to seek out the ambassador.

"How the devil did he get wind of the cock-up at the War Office?" French stabbed out his cigarette with considerable force.

"Who's his source, I wonder?"

French shrugged. "Impossible to tell. The senior officials are political appointees and generally loyal to the prime minister. But there are dozens of people who might lean toward the Liberal Party or Gladstone personally. And Penbras could be paying some lowly clerk for the information."

"Do you think he knows anything, really?" I asked.

"He's sniffed out something. He knows just enough to be dangerous." French took his watch from his pocket. "It's nearly midnight, and Yusopov's barely glanced at you in the last hour."

"I can change that," I said.

"Do," said French. But I was not to get my chance at Yusopov yet, for Ivanov materialized from among the partygoers and reminded me of my promise to dance with him. I left French brooding at the table, pondering the identity of Penbras's source and worrying whether Yusopov had gone in for a bout of celibacy, and let Ivanov sweep me onto the dance floor for a spirited caper. I couldn't help but feel some misgivings at the masterful way he whirled me around the floor, my feet barely brushing the parquet. Holding his lithe, strong body was a bit like embracing a leopard, and if he'd wanted to break my neck with one swipe of his paw and carry me up the nearest tree, he could have done so easily.

Watch this one, India, I said to myself. He's more dangerous than French.

"Is this your first visit to the embassy, Miss Black? I don't recall ever seeing you here before, and I could certainly never forget a young lady of such charm and beauty."

"Thank you, Major. Yes, this is my first time here. The embassy is lovely. I've never seen such exquisite décor."

He smiled mirthlessly at the lie. "And how did you come to be here on the arm of Mr. French? Are you old acquaintances?"

The last thing I needed was a grilling about French, since I knew nothing about the man and would be hard-pressed to invent any stories about a brother fagging for him at Eton or sharing digs with him at present.

"A recent acquaintance," I said cautiously, which at least had the virtue of truth, if not being particularly informative.

"An unusual fellow," mused Ivanov. "I quite like him, although I suspect he doesn't feel the same about me."

"Really? Why?"

Ivanov looked down at me, green eyes glowing in the lamplight. "Possibly we are too much alike, and we know each other too well. What is the expression? Familiarity breeds contempt?" The music ended with a flourish, and the band struck up a waltz.

"Another dance?" asked Ivanov.

"I think not," I said.

"I am not boring you? I should so hate to be tedious to such a lovely woman."

Ivanov's green eyes were mesmerizing, his gaze predatory.

"Certainly not, Major. You are . . . stimulating company. I'm just a bit fatigued."

"But you cannot leave yet. You have not met the count."

I yawned, feigning indifference. "Perhaps another time."

"It would be a shame to attend a party at the embassy and not be introduced to Count Yusopov."

As if on cue, the uniformed lackey who had received Yusopov's instructions when he first laid eyes on Rowena and me appeared at Ivanov's elbow. Ivanov smiled down at me. "You have come to the attention of the count. He would very much like to meet you and your friend with the delightful smile." He took me by the hand and gestured at the lackey. "If you would be so kind as to accompany this gentleman, the count will be along shortly."

I tried to catch French's eye, but he was embroiled in an intense discussion with a somber fellow in military dress. The underling escorted me off the dance floor and up the winding staircase to the third floor, where I was shown into a parlor swagged out in velvet and gilt. A fire burned brightly in the grate, and a table covered in snowy linen had been laid for three. The table held a cut-glass bowl of caviar and a bottle of vodka in a bucket of ice. Through a connecting door, I saw a massive four-poster in carved teak, turned down for the night. Apparently Yusopov was confident that Rowena and I would be receptive to his overtures. I suppose when you're a Russian aristocrat, related to the tsar, and the head of military intelligence for Russia, you don't have to deal with disappointment very often.

The door to the room swung open and Rowena waltzed in on the arm of the lackey, who bowed to her, then to me, then to both of us again, and he disappeared into the hallway, closing the door softly behind him.

Rowena collapsed into a chair. "Wherever did you find that pretentious little toad?"

"Endicott?"

"Yes, bloody Endicott. Stiff as a dildo and not half as entertaining."

"He's in government."

"That explains a multitude of things." Rowena sniffed the caviar and inspected the label on the vodka bottle. "Those Russians love fish eggs, don't they? Give me a cut of rare roast beef any day."

"Have a swig of vodka," I said. "It may be hard sledding tonight."

Rowena tilted an eyebrow and looked smug. "Not for me, darling. You know I've been dying to get you out of that corset for ever so long."

"Remember what we're here for, and don't get distracted."

"There's nothing says I can't enjoy my work while I'm doing it."

"Ladies," a voice boomed, and Count Yusopov glided into the room, if a portly, middle-aged cove may be said to glide. He was bubbling over with spirits and full of the devil. He bowed low over my hand and kissed it, letting his tongue wander idly over the knuckles while I swallowed the urge to knee him in the crotch and flee, but I couldn't, of course, as I'd yet to lay hands on Latham's case. Yusopov spent a good five minutes slavering into Rowena's palm and mewing like a kitten, while she yawned and rolled her eyes at me.

"Ladies"—he beamed—"please sit down and enjoy some refreshment." How he could be hungry after devouring our hands was beyond me, but sit we did, and watched as Yusopov spooned caviar onto the Meissen plates and poured us generous glasses of the ice-cold vodka. He raised his glass in a toast. "To English roses," he said, gazing salaciously at us over the rim.

"To English roses," we echoed.

He tossed off his vodka in one swallow and we followed suit. It burned like brimstone on the way down, but not as badly as some of the rotgut gin I've tasted. Yusopov smacked his lips and poured another, then shoveled a dollop of caviar onto a cracker and popped it into his mouth.

"The finest beluga," he said. "Harvested from the sturgeons of the Caspian Sea." He gave us a confidential wink. "I serve a slightly inferior brand in the dining salon. I hardly think the hoi polloi will know the difference. But for ladies of quality, only the best."

I won't bore you with a blow-by-blow account of our conversation. Despite the fact that Yusopov was a Russian toff with a diplomatic address and a chestful of medals, he wasn't any different than Dick from the insurance company when it came to making small talk with whores; they all want to brag and make more of themselves than they are, which is damned amusing since they're forking over cold cash for a bit of the rumpo and not trying to convince a maid of their prospects. No, when it comes to chatting up whores, men are all the same. For make no mistake about it, the count had pegged us both as ladies of experience, and being a man of experience, he intended to take full advantage of the situation.

He spouted on for a good while about his estates along the Volga, and his close personal relationship with the tsar, and how important and busy he was, while Rowena and I tutted and exclaimed and smiled coquettishly and displayed our décolletage. I was wondering how long it would take the count to get down to business, as it was getting on toward two o'clock in the morning, and Rowena and I still had to portray *Sappho and Anactoria on the Isle of Lesbos* before we could lull Yusopov to sleep and nip off with the case, when he finally inquired whether we ladies would enjoy looking at some pictures.

I didn't think he had in mind a visit to the National Gallery, and I wasn't surprised when he whisked us down the hall to a locked room containing a number of paintings that might have done duty as illustrations of female anatomy at the Royal Medical College, though, come to think of it, they might have been a bit risque for the young medicos. Yusopov was inordinately proud of his paintings, commenting on perspective, brush strokes and pigment, as though he was the art critic for the *Times*. Truthfully, I'd seen better pictures in the bawdy houses of London, but it doesn't do to ruin a man's illusions, so I pretended an awed admiration while I calculated just how long it would be before the bugger would be down for the count.

Yusopov ambled down the row of pictures, paused before a gaudy excrescence entitled *The Milkmaids Find Love* and gazed with veneration at the canvas, which depicted two Rubenesque dairy maids applying their milking skills to each other's udders. "My dears, tell me what you think of this particular work."

"Lovely," I said, with forced enthusiasm.

Rowena's ardor was genuine. She slipped a hand around my waist and pulled me close. I heard Yusopov suck in his breath. Rowena's lips traced the arc of my neck. "An accurate depiction of reality, wouldn't you say, India?"

Faster than you can say "Bob's your uncle," Yusopov herded us down the hall to the bedroom, locked the door behind us, pitched us onto the four-poster and pulled up a chair to watch the action. He was randy as a bull in springtime, and if I do say so myself, Rowena and I gave a marvelous performance. We thrashed around on the bed like two Grecian wrestlers, flinging gowns and stays and petticoats with abandon, and moaning like, well, whores. The headboard thumped the wall and the springs shrieked like a banshee, and any minute I expected the guards to come bursting through the doors in an effort to stop what was obviously an assassination attempt. They knew the count well, however, for we remained undisturbed.

There was nothing for it but to put our backs into it. It was, I think, the finest such performance of my life. 'Twas easier for Rowena, as she didn't have to act at all. Indeed, she was enjoying herself a bit too much, and once or twice I had to bite her ear and remind her in an urgent whisper that the point of this exercise was to recover my stolen deed and, for God's sake, try to remember that. She'd mumble agreement, then fasten her lips on mine, stifling further conversation.

I kept stealing surreptitious glances at Yusopov to see how close he was to satiation, and that was an exasperating business, for I've yet to see the man who can rival the count for sheer bloody stamina. But finally, I could see he was just about ready to cross the goal line, and I put the whip to Rowena in a bid to push him over. She had a mouthful of my knickers and Yusopov was pumping away like a piston when a key turned in the lock, and the three of us froze, still as statues. The door swung open slowly, and a woman in a silk dressing gown and carrying a candle stepped into the room. Yusopov struggled upright, fumbling with his trousers, and held out a hand to her. "Oksana," he cried.

The woman regarded him malevolently, then turned her hostile gaze on Rowena and me.

"Oh, dear," I said. "Hello, Arabella."

SEVEN

It had all the makings of a Gilbert and Sullivan operetta, with Yusopov echoing "Arabella?" in a puzzled tone, and me saying "Oksana?" in a disbelieving voice, and Oksana staring at me incredulously, and everyone flailing around in various stages of dishabille and trying to talk at once. When the dust had settled, Rowena and I were left trying to explain our presence in Yusopov's bed chamber, while Oksana (it's going to take some time for me to get used to calling her that) paced the rug, looking daggers at me and assuring Yusopov it couldn't possibly be a coincidence that I had appeared at the embassy within forty-eight hours of Latham's case disappearing from my brothel. Yusopov seemed inclined to agree. He was rather surly about the whole affair, having been denied the opportunity to spread his seed, so to speak,

and consequently looking angry, red-faced and somewhat con-
stipated. The upshot of the thing was that Yusopov arranged his
trousers and summoned the embassy guards (though not without a bitter smile and a shrug of the shoulders, as if to say he re-
gretted not seeing the end of our performance), and Rowena and
I were hustled away to a cold, barren room in the embassy attic.

"I never believed that silly story about your stolen deed,"
Rowena grumbled. We were sitting back to back, with our feet
bound and our wrists tied together. It was bloody cold, especially
since Yusopov and Oksana had been disinclined to let us dress before tossing us into the room. No doubt the temperature might
be that of St. Petersburg on a summer day, but for an English-
woman, it was icy.

"It's true in a sense," I said, shivering. "If I don't get those documents back, I *will* lose Lotus House."

"What makes you think Yusopov hasn't already read the documents? You're probably wasting your time worrying about getting it back."

"He arrived from Paris just before the ball started, and he was
within sight of French all evening. Then we were with him from
the end of the party until just a few minutes ago. He wouldn't
have had time to look over the papers yet, unless he's doing it as
we speak." A thought I didn't want to contemplate.

"How well do you know this French fellow?" Rowena asked.

"Not very," I admitted. "About the only thing I know is he's got
a heart of steel and he's a blackmailer to boot."

"I suppose that means he won't be shinnying up the drainpipe
to rescue us."

"Doubtful. He was emphatic that the government not be implicated in this."

Rowena squirmed, huddling closer for body warmth. "What do you reckon they plan to do with us?"

"I think they're figuring that out at this moment."

Our captors had deposited us in the empty room, locked the door behind them and disappeared down the stairs, hissing at each other like a pair of cats.

"Maybe Yusopov developed a fondness for us, in our brief time together," said Rowena. "I don't think we can bank on any sympathy from that woman; she looks a merciless bitch."

"I can't believe I was taken in by her," I moaned. "I knew that accent was too good for a girl from Weymouth. And to think how much money she took from me. Ungrateful strumpet."

A further thought struck me: Arabella's perfidy might extend further than occupying my premises under false pretenses. I'd assumed Bowser had died of a heart attack. It certainly wouldn't be the first time a corpulent gentleman had become too stimulated in the company of a tart and keeled over. But Arabella might have pried Bowser's secret out of him and, seizing her chance to make off with the case, helped transport Bowser from this veil of tears. If so, she was directly responsible for my current situation. I wouldn't soon forget that.

"Bit of a dish, though," said Rowena in a wistful tone. "You don't reckon there's any chance she's . . ."

"No," I said curtly. Though I had to agree that here on her home ground, Oksana had looked every inch a real Russian countess, dressed to kill in a gorgeous crimson silk gown, her luxuriant brown hair, high cheekbones and haughty attitude adding verisimilitude to the picture.

"I thought being a spy was glamorous work," Rowena said. "There ain't much glory in it, if you have to work in a brothel."

"There's not much glory in sitting half-naked in a cold room, either," I said. "Is there any play at all in that rope?"

Rowena wriggled experimentally. "Not a bit. Tight as a Tory's wallet."

I craned my neck to look out the dormer window. The sky was black, the stars hard points of light against the velvet background. Dawn was still several hours away, not that that signified anything, though it would be much more difficult for Yusopov and Oksana to do anything with us in the light of day, whether their plan was to spirit us away to another location for God knew what purpose or to dispose of our bodies.

"They'll have to do something before daybreak," I mused, giving voice to my thoughts.

"What happens at daybreak?" Rowena yawned.

"It becomes much more difficult to explain the presence of two Englishwomen being carted around by the embassy guards."

"And you think the average peeler will give a toss about the fate of two bints? He won't risk his job for the likes of us. These Russian bastards could cart us out of the country and no one will lift a hand to help us."

I didn't say anything, but I feared she was right.

I must have dozed off, for the next thing I knew I was coming to groggily and trying to place the sound that had disturbed my slumbers. Rowena was snoring gently, her chin tucked on her chest, but over her snuffling, I thought I detected a faint scratching at the door. Rats, I thought, and had composed myself for sleep once more when the sound came again, followed by the faintest of whispers.

"Miss Black?" The voice was familiar but seemed oddly out of place.

"Miss Black, are you in there?"

"I'm here," I whispered. "Who's there?"

"It's Charles Calthorp, Miss Black."

You could have knocked me over with the proverbial feather. "What the devil are you doing here?" I asked, forgetting my manners in my amazement.

"If you'll open the door, I'll tell you."

"I can't open the door. Rowena and I have been bound." At the mention of her name, Rowena awoke with a snort.

"What's going on?"

"Rescue has arrived," I said, though Charles Calthorp and his air of bumbling ineptitude did not inspire confidence. I thought it more likely that he might soon join Rowena and me in our dungeon, particularly if he continued to persist in holding a sotto voce conversation through a locked door.

"I say," whispered Calthorp. "Are you injured? They haven't hurt you, have they?"

"We're not injured," I whispered back. "Can you find a way to unlock the door?"

There ensued such a long pause, I was sure that Calthorp was having a prose with the Almighty about the morality of breaking and entering, or perhaps he had been stricken with fear and bolted, leaving Rowena and me to lament our best (and perhaps only) chance of escape, but eventually the diffident whisper sounded again through the keyhole: "I'll have a look round." Another longish pause. "I'll be just a tic."

"Just bloody well get on with it, would you?" Rowena had not awakened in a good mood.

"Right," said Calthorp. He sounded offended, but his footsteps crept stealthily away, and Rowena and I settled down to wait, which didn't entail much effort as with the cold, our shackles and our cramped positions over the last few hours, we'd didn't have the ability to move anyway.

"Who's this character?" asked Rowena.

"He's a clergyman from St. Margaret's. One of those celibate padres whose mission in life is to convert the heathen: in this case, the girls at Lotus House. He comes round so often, I'm thinking of charging him rent. You mean to say he's never called at the Silver Thistle?"

"I've yet to see the man," said Rowena, "so I couldn't say for sure, but I've had no visitors of the theological persuasion who wanted to save me from my wanton ways. Had more than a few who paid to watch me practice 'em, though."

A key grated in the lock, and our prison door swung open. Charles Calthorp peeked uncertainly into the room, a candle in one hand and a set of keys in the other.

"Oh, good work, Reverend," I said. "How the devil did you get your hand on those keys?"

"Never mind that, untie us," Rowena snapped. "Let's get the hell out of here."

Calthorp blinked, either at the barked command or our nearly natural state.

"Our clothes are in the corner," I said. "If you'll loosen these ropes, we can be dressed in an instant."

His stupor evaporated. He fumbled in his pocket and drew out a clasp knife, which he opened and applied to our bonds, sawing energetically. As the knife had probably seen no more strenuous duty than cutting his after-dinner cheese, it was dull as a retired schoolmaster, and it took a considerable amount of time for Calthorp to sever the ropes that bound our wrists and ankles. Rowena and I lurched to our feet and stumbled around the room cautiously, chafing our wrists and trying to restore circulation to our limbs. When we'd regained our strength, we found our discarded clothing and dressed rapidly, while Calthorp stood with his back turned, no doubt diverting himself by reciting the Nicene Creed or ticking off the Holy Days in the correct order.

"What *are* you doing here, Reverend?" I asked, when I'd stuffed myself back into Monsieur Gaspard's creation, which was a bit worse for the wear from my gymnastic routine with Rowena. "And where did you find those keys?"

"Why, I found them hanging in the kitchen, behind the door," he said, looking almost scandalized at the paucity of my knowledge of proper housekeeping procedures. He cocked his head, listening anxiously for footsteps. "It's most fortunate for you that I am here, Miss Black. My mind quakes at the heinous acts you might have been forced to perform for that beast Yusopov."

One person's heinous acts are another's bread and butter, but I thought the lesson would be wasted on Calthorp, who still hadn't satisfied my curiosity. "But why are you here? Surely you couldn't have known Rowena and I were at the embassy."

"Oh, no. That was a stroke of luck. You see, Yusopov has a reputation among the young ladies who work the street in Haymarket. He often selects the most unfortunate among them, the most needy, the most destitute, and entices them here to the embassy with promises of food and money. Once they are here, they suffer the most degrading forms of perversion and filth at the hands of that lecher." Calthorp's mustache bristled indignantly.

"'Twasn't so bad," Rowena opined, slipping on her stockings.

"Go on, Reverend," I said.

"Tonight I learned from one of the girls that Yusopov had chosen a very young girl, a mere child, with whom he planned to indulge his carnal desires." Well, well, I thought. Yusopov, you sly dog. How many women could the portly count handle in one night?

"I came here tonight and waited outside until the ball was over and the servants were distracted, eating and drinking the leftover items from the buffet. Then I slipped upstairs to see if I could find young Helen and take her home. I was going through the bedrooms on the third floor when I heard a terrible row coming from Yusopov's quarters, and a moment later, the two of you were marched up here and locked away. I've been waiting for everyone to retire before I attempted to free you."

"Very astute of you, Reverend." Rowena had finished her toilette and was peering out the window. "Now, how do we get out of here?"

"The same way I came in. We must creep down the stairs and out through the kitchen. All the servants are asleep."

"What about the guards?" I asked.

"There are two sentries posted at the front door and one patrolling the rear of the house, but if we are careful, we can slip past him when he's at the far end of the garden. Failing that, we can always distract him somehow."

It was a remarkably simple plan, briskly recited, and it sounded nothing at all like the sort of blundering enterprise I would have thought Calthorp would propose. Coupled with the fact that he'd penetrated the Russian embassy in the dead of night without alarming the guards and had rescued Rowena and me from an undetermined fate, I determined that I might, just might, reconsider my opinion of the little man.

"Very well," I said. "I shall meet you and Rowena in the kitchen in a few minutes. There's something I have to do before I leave here."

"Not that bloody case," Rowena groaned. "That's what got us into this predicament in the first place."

"What case?" Calthorp was reconnoitering the hallway. He glanced at me, puzzled.

I sighed. There was nothing for it but to deliver the monologue about my mother's poor friend and the debt to Yusopov and the count's refusal to return the deed to Lotus House. It was a difficult performance under the circumstances, with us freezing in that garret, with the sleeping embassy liable to awaken at any moment and with Rowena in the background rolling her eyes and emitting little gusts of suppressed laughter. But Calthorp (bless his naïve little heart) ate it up, frowning when I told him of the poor dear friend and her dreadful medical condition, and going pale and breathing fire at the count's treachery.

"The swine," he said, when I'd finished. "Please allow me to assist you in locating this case."

"Thank you ever so kindly," I said. "But I mustn't drag you into this affair. I know where the case is kept. If you'll hand over those keys, Reverend, I'll just run and collect it and meet you both downstairs."

But there was no staunching Calthorp's zeal to help me recover my stolen deed, and so in the end, the three of us crept cautiously downstairs to the second floor, with the clergyman in the lead holding the candle, me carrying the keys and Rowena in the rear (cursing me soundly under her breath). We paused now and again to listen as the building creaked and the sleeping embassy staff rattled and snored in their beds. At last we reached the door to Yusopov's study, and Calthorp held the candle flame close to the keyhole while I inserted various keys into the lock and prayed that one would fit. I had almost exhausted the keys and my patience when I felt the bolt turn beneath my fingers, and we were in.

Hastily, I pulled the door closed behind us. Yusopov's study was as garish and tawdry as the rest of the embassy, with a heavy carved desk of teak and a painting of the tsar mounted on a rearing stallion (quite accurately represented, I might add) of dappled grey. A few coals glowed in the fireplace, but the room had the desolate feel of any other office when the occupant has gone home for the night.

I went first to the safe, hidden behind a painting of some ancient bloke with a drooping mustache and a worried expression. French had shared its location and its combination, which I now entered as rapidly as I could with Calthorp breathing down my neck and wondering aloud (rather too loudly) how I'd come by the combination. It was the work of a moment, and I opened the safe with a flourish, only to find a set of tarnished fish knives and a stash of caviar where I'd hope to find Latham's case.

"It isn't here," I said. "Look for it."

"But how did you know the combination to the safe?" Calthorp asked. "Where . . . ?"

I grabbed his lapels and jerked him to me. "Later, Reverend. Now please shut up and help me look for the bloody thing."

Calthorp (dazed) and I (frantic) conducted a swift search, while Rowena kept watch at the door. It was Calthorp who won the prize, prying open a locked cabinet and giving a soft whoop of triumph as he triumphantly held up the late Archie Latham's black leather case. I took it from him and knelt to open it, careful to keep my back to him. I glanced at the contents only briefly, content to see the letterhead of the War Office repeated throughout the stack of documents.

"That's it," I whispered. "Now show us the way to the kitchen door, Reverend."

"It will be my pleasure," he said. "Permit me to carry the case for you."

I was loath to let it go, now that it was in my possession, but Calthorp seemed bent on being the gentlemen, and who was I to argue with the gallant knight who'd ridden to my rescue? I relinquished the case into his possession, took up the candle, and led our little procession through the darkened hallways and public rooms of the embassy, with Calthorp whispering directions to the kitchen. It was a great relief to crack open the kitchen door and breathe the dank, polluted air of London, and see the moonlight cascading over an expanse of manicured lawn that terminated in a row of plane trees that separated the embassy property from an alley.

Calthorp put his hand on my shoulder. "Allow me, Miss Black. I'll just slip out and ascertain the location of the sentry." He melted away into the darkness with all the expertise of a Zulu scout, which roused my admiration once more, falling over rubbish bins and tripping over paving stones being, I would have thought, more in his line. Rowena and I waited on the flagstone path, and I occupied my time imagining the casual way I'd fling the case onto Dizzy's desk and humbly accept his profuse and ecstatic expressions of gratitude. Even French couldn't fail to be impressed; and then perhaps I'd see the last of that arrogant cove with the malacca walking stick. I saw no reason to mention Calthorp's heroics. You may think me churlish and grudging; I don't give a tinker's damn if you do. I'd taken the risk, why shouldn't I have the credit?

But as so often happens in life, just as I was congratulating myself, imagining the look on French's face and gloating like the owner of the prize-winning pig, fate intervened. Pride goeth before a fall, per the Old Testament, and truer words have never been penned. There was a thumping sound out there in the darkness, followed by a muffled oath and then a shout of surprise from Calthorp, half-stifled, to be sure, but loud enough to rouse the Cossack guards. I heard the clatter of steel and the thunder of booted feet coming round the corner of the building, and suddenly lights were blazing from the windows and the beams from several bulls-eye lanterns were crisscrossing the lawn.

I clutched Rowena's arm and gave her a shove. "Run for it," I cried.

Our best hope was to bolt like rabbits, while the confusion and excitement raged. If we stayed any longer, those searching lantern beams would find us, and I wasn't keen on a return ticket to the room in the attic. We darted away into the cover of darkness, headed for the border of plane trees and the freedom beyond.

I gathered my skirts in my hands and raced across the lawn. The grass was slick with moisture, and my dainty heels were useless. I kicked them off, feeling the ground cold and wet beneath the soles of my feet. It would be a miracle if Monsieur Gaspard's creation survived the night.

A Russian sentry came looming up out of the darkness, his eyes still full of sleep, but he'd had the presence of mind to draw his sword. We collided at full pace, and I heard him grunt with pain and utter a strangled curse as I went down, flung like a rag doll to the ground. Rowena hared past, hurtling the fallen sentry and looking like a ghost as her pale yellow gown fluttered away into the night. Not cricket, you might say, but I'd have done the same if I'd been her. The Russian staggered around, holding his breadbasket and gulping for air. I lay on the ground, too winded to flee, counting the seconds until the guard regained his breath and remembered he had a sword in his hand and thought to use it. Well, India, you're in a pickle this time, I thought. Losing Lotus House will be the least of your worries.

The sentry drew a great shuddering gasp, straightened his spine and began looking round for the object that had felled him. His eyes fell on me, and with a guttural oath (I presume, for he spoke Russian, but the tone was unmistakable), he grasped the nape of my neck, hauled me upright and shook me like a terrier shaking a rat. He was angry as only a professional soldier can be when laid out by a slender woman in an evening gown, which, if you've never seen it, is very angry indeed.

The streets of London are a hard school; a girl learns early how to protect herself. I'd done my fair share of grappling with amorous drunks and fighting off loutish sailors, and if this Russian swine thought to carry me off as a prize, he'd pay a heavy price for his insolence. I was wheezing like a barrel organ myself, but I summoned the strength to lash out at my captor, raking my fingers across his face, aiming for his eyes. He inhaled sharply and struck me a blow across the mouth with the flat of his palm that made my teeth rattle and tears spring to my eyes.

If he wasn't going to play nicely, neither was I. I let myself go limp in his arms, flopping like a puppet, and signaling that I was through playing the hellcat. It works every time, especially with these muscular, oafish sorts who can't believe a woman would ever get the better of them. His grip on my neck relaxed. He sheathed his sword and patted his cheek, where my nails had left a calling card. He was railing softly at the perfidy of women (that sounds the same in any language, as well), when my toes drove into his crotch with all my weight behind them. He pitched over like a felled oak, clutching his gonads and barking like a seal. I felt absurdly pleased with myself: that was two assailants in two days I'd cut to size with a well-placed blow. But it wouldn't pay to linger to enjoy my triumph. A number of dark figures, more guards by their hoarse Russian voices, were quartering the lawn, searching for intruders. At the edge of the plane trees, fisticuffs had ensued; I could hear the thud of body blows and the ragged panting of two men engaged in hand-to-hand combat.

A shadow appeared at my shoulder, and I let out a squeal of surprise.

"Hush. This way, India."

"French?"

"There's no time to lose. Follow me."

Footsteps pounded toward us, and I heard the metallic swoosh of a sword being drawn from its scabbard.

French shoved me in the direction of the trees. "Run for the alley. Endicott should be there," he said. "I'll join you presently." He turned to face the oncoming swordsman, and I saw that he carried his malacca walking stick, from which he now drew a sword. The Cossack who was bearing down on us took one look at the slim blade and gave a dreadful smile. He of course carried a *shashka*, that great, single-edged weapon of the steppes that bore no guard to protect the swordsman's hands, so that he might cleave his opponent's body with the blade as near the hilt as possible, then draw it backward, slashing brutally downward as he did so. I waited for French to extract a revolver from his pocket and shoot the Cossack bastard, rather than going into battle with his rather effete swordstick, but French took up an en garde position, for all the world as if he were competing at some international fencing competition. I half expected him to touch swords with the guard before being slashed to ribbons by the fellow's *shashka*.

It did not seem the proper time to mention that French looked seriously outmanned in the sword department, that there were sounds of battle coming from the direction of the alley, and that Endicott might be preoccupied at the moment and unable to play nursemaid to a fleeing whore. In any case, being a spectator at a sword fight in the dim hours before dawn did not seem a sensible thing to do either, and I was just about to creep stealthily away and retreat to Lotus House to lick my wounds without troubling either French or Endicott any further, when a fleshy hand closed on my wrist and I felt a breath, redolent with fish eggs and vodka, on my cheek.

"Don't run away so soon, Miss Black. I have not yet finished with you." Yusopov chortled harshly, a great rumble that started in his belly and exploded in my face in a fishy gust.

French whirled at the sound of his voice, the point of his swordstick glittering in the light from Yusopov's lantern. He and Yusopov locked gazes, French looking as cool as though he'd just met the count strolling through the race-day crowd at Newmarket, and the count just as unflappable, with an amused smirk parting his whiskers.

"Put down your sword, Mr. French." Yusopov issued a sharp command to the Cossack sentry with the unsheathed *shashka* (a phrase that sounded vaguely erotic, but believe me, there was nothing sensual at all about it), and the fellow stopped short, eyeing French warily. Yusopov spoke again, and the fellow retreated a few steps, but he did not return his blade to the scabbard, turning it loosely in his hand and looking ready to attack at a command from Yusopov.

"I believe I've the whip hand here, as you English say," he said. "Intruders on the embassy grounds, a violation of Russian territorial sovereignty and all that. The laws of diplomacy are quite clear on the rights of foreign powers in cases such as these."

"The laws of Great Britain are equally clear," French drawled. "You've no right to detain British citizens."

Yusopov swept an arm in an encompassing gesture. "Your English law does not apply here, Mr. French. You might as well be in St. Petersburg."

"You may find yourself exiled to the northern reaches of Siberia, if you embarrass the tsar by holding an official of Her Majesty's government against his will."

"It's just as likely that I'll be rewarded for delivering to the tsar certain valuable information from the British War Office," Yusopov mused aloud. "Perhaps a posting to Paris. Paris would be lovely. The finest champagne and French fillies would make a pleasant change from overcooked mutton and rain."

"You'll free us immediately," said French, "or face the consequences."

Yusopov laughed his great belly laugh again, spreading a cloud of caviar-scented breath. Really, the man needed to learn some elementary hygiene practices. "What consequences? I hardly think Mr. Disraeli will want to publicize this affair. How will he explain one of his aides attempting to burglarize the Russian embassy?

He would find it so mortifying, so humiliating, to acknowledge the incident. Mr. Disraeli would have, what do you English say? Egg on his face? No, I think it more likely that the prime minister will want this embarrassing episode kept out of the public eye." Yusopov pursed his lips and looked shrewd. "And I've no doubt that the prime minister would prefer that Mr. Gladstone remain ignorant of this matter. Such irresponsible behavior might well call for the formation of a new government, under a steadier hand."

"You're wasting your breath, sir." French sheathed his swordstick and held out a hand to me. "Miss Black and I must be going."

"Not just yet, Mr. French. The young lady has something I want." Yusopov's hand contracted around my wrist. "Where is the case?"

"I don't know," I said.

The amused smirk disappeared. "Oh, come now. This is no time to be coy."

"I don't know where it is." I waved my hands. "As you can see, I don't have it."

"Plainly, the case is not in her possession," said French. He looked insufferably smug. The idiot probably thought I'd taken the papers from Latham's case and stuffed them down my petticoats.

Yusopov swung round and issued a brusque command to the sentries. The guards snapped salutes and rushed off, swords clanking and lanterns swinging.

"We shall soon see if the case is here." Yusopov looked at me speculatively. "I suppose you think I'm too much the gentleman to search you."

"I would never accuse you of that," I said.

"Here," French objected, "that won't be necessary." Sweet of him (and so English, too) to protest the injury to my honour, but since Yusopov had us cornered like rats and we weren't leaving the embassy grounds until he was satisfied I didn't have the documents on my person (not to mention that he'd already seen most of my wares earlier in the evening), it seemed much the wisest course of action to submit to a search.

"I usually charge for the privilege, but under the circumstances, I'll waive my customary fee," I said.

"You needn't submit to this appalling degradation." French's brow was furrowed in indignation. I suppose in the heat of the moment, he'd forgotten I was a whore. Or maybe he was just a poor loser and hated being forced to capitulate to Yusopov.

So while French fretted and fumed and threatened serious repercussions, I acquiesced to having my person searched by the count, who, by the way, was a dab hand at ferreting out a girl's secret hiding places, including some I hadn't known I had. Naturally, since I'd last seen the case in the possession of Calthorp, the ambassador's search was in vain, though he may have derived some secondary form of satisfaction from it, as evidenced by his heavy breathing and sweaty palms.

The guards returned from their treasure hunt with their tails tucked between their legs, having turned up nothing untoward in their search of the embassy and its grounds, except the hall porter's secret stash of brandy and the wheel of cheese gone missing from the embassy kitchen the week before (located, I believe, under the bed of one of the scullery wenches).

Yusopov looked pained at the news, twirling a mustache and belching softly. He paced a few steps in one direction and then back again, while the guards shifted nervously and glared at French with their hands on the hilts of their swords. Finally, the portly figure came to a halt, grasped his chin with one fleshy hand and subjected French and me to the minute scrutiny of a Harley Street practitioner.

"I must say, Mr. French, that I am very displeased with your extraordinary audacity in bringing this disreputable young woman here. I'm thinking of lodging a formal protest with the British government."

French yawned affectedly. "If that is the best you can do, Count, I would suggest you stand aside and let us leave now."

Yusopov's mustache twitched violently. "It appears we have reached what the Americans call a Mexican standoff."

"Indeed," said French. He put his hand under my elbow, nudging me in the direction of the alley. "Miss Black and I will be going."

"Give my regards to Mr. Disraeli, and tell him that if I ever catch one of his flunkies in my embassy again, he'll have to explain himself to the *Morning Chronicle.*"

I expected French to draw himself up in that lordly manner of his and demand that Yusopov retract his reference to "flunkies," but he merely nodded coldly at the count and hustled me away through the waning darkness. We didn't stop until we were a good quarter mile from the embassy, and then French came to an abrupt halt on the stoop of a pub, under the sickly yellow glow of a gas lamp. He was laughing as he looked down at me.

"That was cool work, India. How the devil did you get that case out of there? And where did you hide it?"

"Stop gloating, French. I don't have the case."

That shut his trap, as I knew it would. He stared at me, slack-jawed. "You don't mean to tell me it's still in the embassy."

"It's not at the embassy either."

"Then where the deuce is it?"

"The last I saw of it, Reverend Charles Calthorp was carrying it off under his arm."

For the first time since I'd met him, French looked discom-fited. "Who the bloody hell is Reverend Charles Calthorp?"

"An ecclesiastic type," I said, "who has a thing for trollops."

French groaned and passed a weary hand over his eyes. I must admit to feeling a bit tired myself, having snatched only a few minutes sleep stark naked in a cold room, which is the same as having no sleep at all, so I spared French the Dickensian version and briefly explained Calthorp's involvement. At the end of the story, French frowned and chewed his lip, staring off into the eastern sky where the sun had begun to peep over the horizon. In the grey light of dawn, his face looked haggard. Thoughtfully, he lit a cheroot and smoked meditatively.

At length, he asked, "What do you know about this Calthorp fellow?"

"Other than the fact that he's an infernal bore," I said, "abso-lutely nothing."

"What about the girls at Lotus House? Has he spoken to any of them at length?"

"There's Mary. She's spent a considerable amount of time with the man."

He crushed his cheroot beneath the heel of his boot. "I must speak to her now. There's not a moment to lose."

He strode off, and I trotted after, wincing as my bare feet located every pebble on the pavement. "How about a cab, French? I had to leave my shoes behind."

It was a great relief to set foot in Lotus House. I woke Mrs. Drinkwater from a sound sleep, ordered tea to be sent to my office, then sent her to summon Mary. I sank gratefully into a chair and examined the soles of my feet, which, during the night's activities, had acquired a layer of filth that rivaled anything I'd ever seen on Vincent. French paced the rug before the hearth, lost in thought.

"Am I correct in supposing that you do not think Calthorp's appearance at the embassy was entirely coincidental?" I asked, probing a tender spot on my heel.

"You are. I don't believe in serendipity."

"But what could he want with those documents from the War Office?"

"I am hoping your girl may be able to tell us something that will clarify the situation."

Mary and the tea arrived at the same time. Mrs. Drinkwater had thoughtfully provided a tray of biscuits, which were hard enough to have been minted by the exchequer.

Mary wasn't best pleased, having been roused from a sound sleep twice in the last four days to deal with a Calthorp exigency, but she perked up considerably when she spied French's handsome countenance and raven black hair. She sat down on the sofa, letting her dressing gown fall open casually to display a curvaceous leg and arranging her boobies to their best advantage, while she smiled winsomely and batted her eyelashes in French's direction. I was tempted to tell her not to waste her time with the man, he being about as warm-blooded as the average viper, but to my surprise (and not a little consternation), French gave her a roguish smile and planted himself on the sofa beside her. Mary leaned over so as to allow French an unobstructed view of her cleavage (free of charge, mind you—Mary and I needed to have a conversation) and fixed him with the look she usually reserves for dim-witted drunks with bulging wallets.

"I'm terribly sorry to have awakened you, my dear," French's tone was silken.

"Oh, la." Mary's lashes fluttered wildly. I stifled the urge to ask if she had a smut in her eye. "Think nothing of it, sir. I'm very happy to be of service to you. Indeed I am."

"I shan't keep you long. I'm endeavoring to locate an old friend of the family. Miss Black informs me that you are acquainted with Reverend Charles Calthorp."

The alleged association brought a flicker of disbelief to Mary's eyes, but being a whore, she was much too experienced at listening to men's lies to let it linger long.

"He's the curate of St. Margaret?"

"So he says. I ain't never darkened the door, so I couldn't say for certain."

"I believe you spoke with the reverend this past Sunday," said French.

"I did, sir. He come by to chat up the girls. He's dead keen on savin' our souls, is Reverend Calthorp. Not that he gets much joy in that line. Most of us ain't that interested in the hereafter, our concern bein' more the here and now. Not to mention that if Heaven is occupied by the likes of Reverend Calthorp, I'd ruther spend eternity with the sinners, drinkin' gin and eatin' cake."

Mary preened herself over her witticism and French smiled politely, but I could see he was anxious to get the information he needed and pick up Calthorp's trail. "It has been many years since I've seen Charles, but I remember him as an earnest young man," said French.

"Ever so sober," Mary agreed, "except when he's carryin' on about the Trinity or convertin' the heathen Chinee."

French wasn't interested in the salvation of Oriental souls. "Is that the extent of his conversation with you? Does he ever discuss his home or his family?"

"Oh, no. Reverend Calthorp don't talk about himself at all. He goes on about the things clergymen usually talk about, you know, like purity and wickedness and lust, and the sins of the flesh, and so forth. He gets awful frothed up about the sins of the flesh. And sometimes he talks about politics. He don't go in for entertainments of any sort, except politics. He's an eloquent son of a bitch, when he's ravin' about the Tories and Disraeli. You ought to hear him rattle on about old Gladstone. You'd think that old gent hung the moon, from the way the reverend gushes about him."

Had Dizzy been there, he'd have cursed Gladstone's name, denounced Calthorp as a traitor and bemoaned the fact that hanging had replaced drawing and quartering as the punishment for treason. French didn't rush to judgment as quickly, but the look he gave me was significant. "He's fond of the parson?"

"Fair worships the old bugger," Mary said brightly.

"Do you know the address of Reverend Calthorp's residence?" asked French.

Mary waggled a finger at him. "Not me, dearie. He's never said and I've never asked. No interest, you see. Penniless churchman ain't exactly my style. Nor barmy ones, neither. A handsome gen-tleman like yourself is more to my taste." To illustrate the point, she dropped a hand on French's thigh and let it meander lan-guidly in the direction of his crotch.

But French had no time for dalliance. He seized Mary's wan-dering fingers, shook her hand briskly, then jumped to his feet, clapped his hat on his head and charged out the door, ignoring Mary's pout.

"Wait," I cried, springing after him. "Where are you going?" But there was no answer, only the slamming of the front door of Lotus House.

EIGHT

A few hours later, after a bath and some breakfast, I was circling Claridge's Hotel, watching a good percentage of the London ton swagger in and out, while the doorman bowed deferentially and surreptitiously counted his tips as the door closed behind the august clientele. Gladstone might be a Low Church booby and a friend of the common man, but he came from the gentry and hadn't spared any expense in his lodging arrangements here in London.

I'd fairly flown to St. Margaret's where I had accosted the addled crone dusting the altar rail and demanded to know the whereabouts of Calthorp. The clergyman hadn't been seen yet that morning, and the old woman, who was employed as a charwoman and charged with cleaning both the church proper and

Calthorp's rooms in an adjoining house (and whose tongue I loosened with ten bob), said his bed had not been slept in the previous night. As I was leaving, the crone sunk a tooth into the coin and idly wondered at the coincidence of being asked the same question not 'alf an hour ago by a distinguished cove with a malacca walking stick.

With Calthorp having disappeared from view, the only lead worth following seemed to be his adoration of Gladstone, and since Dizzy had mentioned at our meeting that Gladstone was now residing at Claridge's, whipping public attention to a fever pitch over the Mussulman atrocities, then I should have to visit the hotel as well. Remembering also Dizzy's complaint that Gladstone (and quite likely, his devout followers) would like to see Dizzy's government implode in disgrace, it seemed plausible that Calthorp might have looked at the documents we'd recovered from the Russian embassy, realized their importance to Gladstone and hied off to Claridge's to deliver them to the old man on a platter. In fact, now that I had been exposed to the level of skull-duggery that seemed to go on in the political arena, Calthorp's visits to Lotus House might not have been as innocent as I had believed them to be. In actuality, the little God wallah might have been keeping an eye on old Archie Latham, just as the Russians had been. Calthorp's expertise at penetrating the embassy and escaping with the case seemed less and less like a stroke of luck and more like the doings of an experienced operative.

French was nowhere in view when I arrived at Claridge's. I'd arrived without a plan in mind, and so I sauntered back and forth for a few minutes, watching the doorman and a procession of elegantly attired ladies and gentlemen strut through the door and making mental notes about the alterations I'd need to make to my wardrobe to bring it up to snuff with the latest Parisian fashions. The doorman was ex-military; his ramrod bearing, shining buttons and stoic expression gave him away. He looked like the stern but kindly sergeant who raked young privates over the coals for coming in drunk, then tucked them into their bunks with tender affection. He'd have rallied the square at Inkerman, and volunteered to blacken his face and sneak out of camp through enemy lines to summon help. He'd know a great deal about carbines, native liquor and venereal disease, bayonet drills and whores, and I wouldn't stand a chance of getting through the front door while he stood guard. His type takes his duty seriously. Thank God, there's only a few like that in the military, or we tarts wouldn't have any custom at all.

I briefly debated brazening it out and affecting an entrance, figuring that if the old soldier gave me any guff I'd inform him that I was an acquaintance of Dizzy's, had dined last night at the Russian embassy, and what did he mean, denying entrance to a lady? After mature consideration, I concluded that my cozy evening with Count Yusopov would not impress the doorman. I'd likely be tossed into the street like yesterday's newspapers.

Nevertheless, there was one role I could play to the hilt, which the old codger might find sympathetic and which might provide me with some valuable intelligence at the same time. So I bowed my head and bashfully approached the doorman, doing my best to appear timorous and deferential, which is damned near impossible for me to do. My dress and coat were smart and clean, my boots polished and my hat wouldn't have disgraced any fashionable lady, but the keen eyes of the ex-military duffer spotted me before I'd made the second step.

"Here, you, miss," he cried, darting forward with an astonishingly rapid step to separate the goat (me) from the sheep (the cream of London society, which I was dangerously close to infecting with my unworthiness). I knew the fellow could spot a wrong 'un.

The last thing he expected, I'm sure, was that some wanton hussy would throw her arms around him and cling to him like a limpet, but that's what I did, crying tremulously, "Oh, sir, sir. Tell me it's true, sir. Tell me it's true."

There's not much a man of his experience can't handle. After shooting Indian mutineers out of cannons, hustling a swooning whore out of the sight of the London elite was mere child's play. The doorman tucked me under one arm and carried me away from the hotel steps. When he judged the distance far enough from innocent bystanders, he dropped me like a sack of flour and said roughly, "Now then, what are you up to?"

I looked beseechingly up at him. "Please, sir. I heard that Mr. Gladstone is staying at the hotel. Is it true?"

"What if it is? What business is it of yours?"

I staggered to my feet and clutched at his arm. "I've come to thank him. He . . ." Here I choked back a little sob. "He saved my life."

The doorman's brows crinkled. "What kind of daft talk is that? Did he fish you out of the Thames after you'd thrown your wretched self in, trying to escape your sins?"

"Please, sir. Don't be scornful of a poor wretch like me. Mr. Gladstone came to my house . . . that is . . . the house where I . . . work." I paused to emit another tiny sob. I must say, I'd have broken my own heart. Unfortunately, the doorman was a more severe critic. He seemed unmoved by my theatrics. I was going to have to put my back into it.

"He told us all about Jesus and God and salvation and how to save our souls, and I believed him." I gazed at the doorman with tear-stained eyes. "Oh, sir. What a relief it's been to know that I'm a saved woman. I shall never go back to my life of sin."

His craggy face softened. "Well, now. I'm very glad to hear that you've found the Lord and turned your back on Satan. I'd heard Mr. Gladstone spread the word of God among you, er, your kind." Must be chapel, I thought. How lucky can a girl get?

I pulled out my handkerchief and daintily dabbed my eyes. "That's why I'm here. I heard Mr. Gladstone was staying at Claridge's, and I wanted to thank him for leading me to Jesus. You couldn't let me in for just a minute, could you? To offer that great man my heartfelt thanks for saving my life."

He shook his head regretfully. "Sorry, miss. I've strict instructions, you know. And even if I didn't, you couldn't see him anyway. He went out this morning early, and he'll be gone all day. I heard him tell the desk clerk that he'd be back just in time for dinner."

Hallelujah. With any luck at all, Gladstone hadn't seen the documents.

"I so wanted to see him," I said wistfully. "You don't think, when he gets back, that you could let me in for just a moment?"

"I'm afraid I can't do that. The manager would have my hide." The doorman looked thoughtful. "Tell you what. You want to write a note to him? I could deliver it for you."

"That's very kind of you." I sniffed lugubriously. "But I can't write."

Having extracted some useful information, I strolled around to the rear of the building for a reconnaissance. I didn't expect to see French lurking among the dustbins in the alleyway; he'd have swaggered in the front while the doormen snapped a salute and the ladies in the lobby cooed in admiration.

The alleyway was busy with tradesmen delivering crates of vegetables and sacks of flour. A fishmonger's delivery wagon blocked the alley, exuding a briny odor and attracting a legion of cats. The felines paced cautiously underfoot, sniffing the breeze. The tradesman's entrance to the hotel was through a set of double doors, open wide to the chill wind. A portly fellow in a striped weskit and shirtsleeves stood at the door, a sheaf of papers in his hand that he consulted with regularity, meticulously ticking off items while he barked commands to the hotel staff and the deliverymen. He looked even less likely than the doorman to succumb to my charms.

The only other possibility of entrance into the rear of the hotel was a second, smaller door twenty feet from the portly fellow in the weskit and the gang of deliverymen. In case I harbored any doubts about the propriety of my entering through said door, it bore an elegantly painted sign advising No Entrance. Now, I've often wondered why establishments go to the expense of such absurd prohibitions on ingress; the only people who comply with such directions are law-abiding citizens and Christians. I hadn't the least concern about trying my luck at the door, but I'd have to wait until the deliveries were finished and the bloke in the weskit had finished his task. I turned and sauntered away down the alley, until I found a niche in the wall half hidden behind a brewer's dray which provided both an excellent hiding place and an unobstructed view of both the portly fellow and the second door.

Lord, but that fellow was diligent. I wish I had whores half as committed to their work as that man, but alas, it's difficult to find many strumpets these days who take pride in their occupation. Anyway, he scribbled on his list and bellowed at the hapless youths staggering under their loads of linen and cases of wine, their crates of pigeons and sides of beef, for what seemed hours, while I gnawed a thumbnail and anxiously eyed the darkening sky. I'd wasted too much time jawing with the doorman and watching brawny lads at work. The noon hour had come and gone, and the afternoon was waning. If I didn't gain access to the hotel soon, I'd miss my chance to toss Gladstone's room while the old bugger was away.

No doubt you're wondering why I was loitering in the alley behind Claridge's in what was probably a vain attempt at snatching back the case of documents from Charles Calthorp. I certainly had time to cogitate over that question while I waited for weskit man to finish with his damned list and go in for his tea. I didn't think that Dizzy or French would really make good on their threat to ruin my business or harass me personally. Surely they had better things to do than rearrange the life of one insignificant madam, like worry about the Russkis making nice with the Tibetans or Egyptian nationalists taking potshots at British tourists dining on the terrace at Sheppard's. Not to mention the bloody Irish. No, I was probably well out of things right now, and if I were an intelligent woman, I'd leave things as they were, slip out of the alley and return to supervise the evening's business at Lotus House.

The flaw in my character is not lack of intelligence, however, but an abundance of obstinacy. The only reason I'd gotten involved in this escapade in the first place was because Bowser had had the effrontery to die in my whorehouse. I was merely an innocent (at least in this instance) bystander. Since then my livelihood had been threatened, I had been blackmailed into performing like a lesbian trick pony for that lascivious bastard Yusopov, Rowena and I had been held captive in the attic of the Russian embassy (ruining a perfectly lovely, not to mention free, dress in the process), and I had narrowly escaped being skewered by a Cossack guard. And then there was that devil French. I'd be damned if I'd let that smug fellow get to those documents before me. I'm not just so much baggage to be picked up when useful, pilfered and plundered and then jettisoned by the wayside when no longer needed. I wanted the pleasure of sashaying up to Dizzy's office with a black leather portfolio under my arm and presenting him the documents that ensured he'd stay prime minister for at least a little longer. The poor soul needed all the help he could get; any man who'd wear bottle green velvet trousers in public needed a handler, in my opinion. Still, it would be pleasant to receive the heartfelt thanks of the most powerful man in England, not to mention the pleasure of watching French snarl as I performed my patriotic duty. I might even curtsy.

The slamming of a door and the rattle of cart wheels abruptly awakened me from my reverie. The tradesmen were climbing onto their wagons, the chap in the weskit had disappeared, and the double doors were now closed. I clambered out of my hiding place and walked quickly to the second door, glancing around to be sure I was unobserved. The brass knob was cold and sleek to the touch, and I turned it gingerly, willing the door to open. As I'm generally used to getting my way, it was a bit of a disappointment when the door refused to budge.

"Bloody hell," I muttered. Now what? There were streaks of orange and red in the smut-stained sky. Gladstone might have already entered the hotel and Calthorp turned over the case to him.

If Gladstone had the documents in his hands, then there was nothing more that I could do. Dizzy would have to face the press and produce some explanation for spouting anti-Russian rhetoric and threatening war with a British army just large enough to field a few football teams. I'd no doubt he was up to the task; the man did not lack imagination. But I still couldn't give up without one last attempt to creep into the hotel and find the case, if for no other reason than my own pride.

And then the brass knob turned in my hand, the door opened, and salvation appeared in the form of a short, ruddy-faced fellow with a cherub's cheeks, neat blond mustache and the handsome uniform of the Claridge's concierge. He drew back when he saw me, eyes widening in astonishment, but they narrowed quickly and he gave me a frank appraisal from head to toe. It was when he made his occulatory tour of my person that I knew the little angel was going to be my salvation. I recognized, you see, a kindred soul. Apparently, he felt the same degree of kinship. A slow smirk swirled across his face, like cream trickling into coffee. He held an unlit cigar in his pudgy fingers; now he put it between his lips and searched his pocket for a box of matches, all the while conducting his silent inventory of my natural charms.

"Good evening, sir."

"And a pleasant evening to you, my dear." He gave me a sardonic little bow, found a match, and scraped it into flame on the door frame. He took his time lighting his cigar, and when it was drawing nicely, he tossed the match in the gutter and gave me a frank stare.

There was a lilt in his voice that might have been the faintest brogue, an accent no doubt intended to charm the lady guests while he smiled obsequiously and catered to their every whim. I'd no doubt that the brogue would disappear and the voice deepen into hearty bluffness when the guest was a gentleman. I'd also no doubt that my new friend was of a most amiable disposition, eager to comply with the wishes and demands of the Claridge's guests, no matter how outré they might prove. Indeed, if I were a wagering woman, I'd bet my last farthing that the cherubic concierge leering at me over his cigar was exceedingly practiced in the art of procuring all manner of goods and services for his clientele.

"A Montecristo, sir? A stone's throw away, sir, at the tobacconist's shop on the corner. But don't trouble yourself, sir. I'll send a boy to fetch them for you." Delivered, no doubt, with an amiable smile.

"Baccarat? There's quite a nice club a few blocks from here. Very discreet, they are. And the champagne is a superior vintage." This in a confidential, man-of-the-world tone, while pocketing a sovereign.

"A young lady, sir? I think I can arrange something to your satisfaction in that department. Quality, sir? Oh, of the very highest, I can assure you. I'll escort her to your room myself, sir. We wouldn't want any embarrassment, would we?" A circumspect, but nevertheless sly, wink and a furtive exchange of the ready.

That was the kindred spirit I'd identified in the cove when I first laid eyes on him: we were both fixers. Live on the streets of London long enough and you learn to size up a man or woman in a split second. If you guess wrong, well, you might not live to regret your error. Having earned first-class honours in that department long ago, I felt reasonably confident that I'd calculated aright about the concierge. No doubt he had an arrangement with some local abbess nearby. This would require some skillful handling, but all that remained now was figuring how best to play the match.

He opened the batting. "I haven't seen you around here before, have I? I'd surely remember a ravishing creature such as yourself."

"You haven't seen me before. I've wandered off my patch."

He exhaled smoke and nodded thoughtfully. "Thought as much. Mother Nellie handles the business around here, and she hasn't said a word about a new girl."

"Nellie Rowe? Didn't know the old girl was still around. Getting a little long in the tooth, surely." I cut my eyes at him and smiled, so he could size up my own perfectly formed pearly whites.

He laughed harshly and blew a cloud of cigar smoke in my face. "She may be too sprung to ride, but she keeps a fine stable of fillies. Smart gal, that Nellie. We go back a long way."

"Always good to have associates you can trust." I paused, then added, "And it never hurts to make a new friend now and then."

He looked amused. "Are you my new friend, then? What a fortunate day for me. What's your name?"

"Rowena Adderly." Well, the bitch still owed me for running out on me just as I was about to become a kebab on the lawn of the Russian embassy.

He offered me a plump hand, cold as a dead squab, and introduced himself as Frank Netherly. "Rowena, dear, I'd love to stand outside and yarn with you all night, but I'm back on duty in a few minutes. What say we dispense with the preliminaries and go straight to the main bout?"

I do like a man who gets to the point; so many of them don't, blathering on about wives who don't understand them and mooning about mothers who neglected them (which is why they need to roger a sixteen-year-old wench in a bustiere, but I digress). At least Netherly was a man of business and through with polite conversation, which was fine by me as I needed to get inside that hotel and locate Calthorp.

I'd decided already that it wouldn't do to try and play on Netherly's sympathies. He had as much empathy for his fellow man (or woman) as a puff adder. The best approach was a straightforward appeal to the fellow's vanity and greed.

"It's lucky for me that I bumped into you, Frank. You're just the man who can see me right."

"Is that so?" He delicately picked a tobacco leaf from his tongue with his thumb and forefinger and examined it idly before flicking it away.

"I've an old customer coming into town tonight, with a fondness for make believe. You know, Frank, how some men like tavern wenches and some like governesses? Well, this bloke likes maids. Hotel maids. And not the kind of maids you'd find at your cut-rate establishments, either. He likes to take a room at the most expensive and proper hotels in town and open the door an hour later to find me standing there in an authentic maid's uniform. Bit of a game with him, you see, rogering his favorite bint in some of London's finest addresses."

Netherly was already shaking his head. I put my hand on his arm and opened my mouth before he could open his.

"Frank, I know you're a loyal friend to Nellie, and I admire you for it. I'm not here to move in on her territory. This is a one-off, so to speak. Help me out tonight and I'll never darken the door of the Claridge again. In and out in an hour. Nellie need never know." I squeezed his arm suggestively, and added, "And of course, I'll make it worth your while."

"You'll have to cough up a pretty penny, if you want me to undercut my business partner." Netherly contrived to sound righteous, but the greedy glint in his eye gave him away.

"What's your usual arrangement with Nellie?"

I could almost see the wheels turning while Netherly calculated how exorbitant a claim he could make and still be believed. I could have saved him the trouble; I had no intention of paying him a ha'penny for his trouble.

After a lengthy pause, he ventured a sum, studying me covertly to see if I'd faint.

"Pish!" I cried. "Is that all the old bag pays you?" Well, it was a decent enough sum, but while I was about my own business, there wasn't any reason I shouldn't queer the deal for my competition. "I'll pay you twice that amount."

Netherly's pink cheeks had deepened to a dusky red, whether from anger at Nellie's churlishness or cupidity at my own generosity, but before he could attempt to negotiate, I seized his hand and wrung it, exclaiming, "We've a deal, then. Excellent. Now if you'd be so good as to show me where the maids' uniforms are kept, I'll kit out, roger the old geezer and bring you your money before dinner."

"Wait a minute, Rowena, dear. I'd like my money now. Who's to say you won't just disappear the minute you've serviced the old boy?"

I looked shocked. "Goodness, Frank. I don't carry that kind of sum around with me. I'd be knocked on the head and left in the gutter. The old man will see me right in just a tic, and then I'll be down to pay you what we've agreed."

He didn't like it, but he didn't argue. I suppose my sincerity convinced him. Fool.

* * *

And that is how I came to be outfitted in a tidy black merino dress, starched white apron and a hideous mobcap that did nothing for my appearance. The dress was a bit too tight for comfort's sake, but apparently all the housemaids at Claridge's were woefully underpaid and underfed, for the largest dress Netherly could find fit my buxom frame like a sausage casing. For the sake of authenticity, Netherly had armed me with an ostrich duster, a dustpan and a broom. The only item I lacked was information: which room was Gladstone's and had he tired of bending the ears of prominent swells about the Bulgarian atrocities and returned to it already? In which event, I was too late.

But faint heart never stole a case full of War Office documents, and so I gathered my skirts and my wits and set off to ferret out the location of the old turnip-head's chamber. Getting into the hotel had been a challenge, but it hadn't half prepared me for the trial of prowling the halls of the place, trying to avoid the other maids and the porters carrying luggage to and fro, any one of which would have recognized me as an imposter and blown the whistle on my escapade. Not to mention trying to simultaneously keep a sharp eye out for Calthorp (to be avoided at all costs), French (likewise) and Gladstone (what to say to that bugger?), and to look modestly down at the carpet whenever I met a guest in the hall. Normally, that wouldn't be a concern, as most of London's upper class wouldn't acknowledge a servant if she was thrashing about on the floor and turning blue under their feet, but you never know when you might encounter a former (or current) customer, and that could prove embarrassing.

So I spent the better part of an aimless hour wandering the

halls, flicking my duster over the odd table and growing increasingly desperate at the time I was wasting, calculating my chances of sneaking a look at the register in order to find Gladstone's room, and hoping that Netherly wouldn't grow impatient waiting for his money and come searching for me. I could have given up and gone home at any time, slipping out the back door and leaving the field open to French, but by now this little game was exerting a strong attraction for me, something I hadn't felt since the last time I'd matched wits with Abbess Dorothy Claridge (an interesting story, that; remind me to tell you about it later). Perhaps life at Lotus House had become a matter of routine—riding herd over a bevy of hard-drinking, opium-smoking judies, listening with half an ear to the nattering of bewhiskered civil servants and army officers, fretting over bills. It was good to be on the game again, playing the crooked cross on the likes of Frank Netherly, matching wits with Russian spies, English clerics (if indeed Calthorp was the genuine article, but his pious moping had seemed honest enough) and crafty bastards with malacca swordsticks.

I took the servants' stairs to the ground floor, creeping along and peering around the turns of the stairwell to avoid any contact with the other employees. Once a door opened and a strapping porter appeared with a suitcase under each arm and started struggling up the steps in my direction. I might play the demure miss with the guests, but I reckoned I could brazen my way past this fellow, for he had the lumbering gait and vacant stare of any beast of burden. I sailed past him, my dress straining across my hips and bosom, looked him right in the eye and grinned saucily, and left him standing in open-mouthed admiration on the stairs.

I reached the ground floor, where all the public rooms were

located, and made a cautious exit from the protection of the stairwell. I'd come out into a gaslit corridor, with flocked velvet wallpaper and gold-framed pictures of London landmarks. To my right, the passageway terminated in a closed door with Manager's Office lettered in gilt, but to the left the hall led into the lobby, with its marble floor and carved mahogany columns. I could hear a low hum from the room and catch glimpses of fine ladies saun-tering along in the latest fashions, accompanied by well-heeled gents in evening dress, for it was getting on to the dinner hour.

Among that fashionable crowd, a housemaid in a too-tight dress would stand out like an aborigine at a polo match, so I was limited to scouting the lobby from the hall. I stationed myself against the wall, in the shadow and out of the glare of the flaring gaslights, and assumed an expression of moronic wistfulness. If I was caught out by the management, perhaps I could sell myself as a naïve youngster fresh out of the Lancashire mills and yearn-ing for the bright lights and beautiful dresses on display in the Claridge's reception area.

For the next few minutes I scanned the room, shifting my posi-tion occasionally to get a better view of the crowd in the lobby. I spotted Netherly ensconced behind a wooden desk, smirking and chatting amiably with a brainless young buck just in from the country; Netherly was scribbling on a notepad, a map, no doubt, to the nearest den of iniquity. I scuttled out of Netherly's range of vision and peered around the lobby.

I noticed Calthorp right away, seated prominently in the mid-dle of the room near the registration desk, with an unobstructed view of the front door of the hotel. He looked hellishly tired, his sleek brown hair rumpled and his glasses askew, as though he'd been up all night duping credulous whores and prowling through the Russian embassy in search of British military secrets. He sat stiffly in a straight-backed chair, his gaze locked on the hotel entrance, and his hands clasping the black leather portfolio on his knees. At least one of my concerns was lifted. Clearly, Calthorp was waiting for Gladstone to return to hand over the documents.

If Calthorp was here, French must be around somewhere. I risked a step forward and craned my neck for a better look. I spied a pair of elegant legs, one cocked over the other, protruding from a comfortable leather chair and a malacca swordstick balanced against the arm. The legs and the walking stick belonged to a fellow who appeared to take no discernible interest in the proceedings around him, for his face was buried behind a copy of the day's *Times,* with a languid hand appearing now and then to lift a glass of whisky and soda behind the curtain of the newspaper. Though he appeared to be absorbed in the paper, I had no doubt that French could provide an accurate account of every nervous twitch and fevered sigh of Calthorp's.

"Hello, dearie." A hand snaked round my waist and a moist mustache planted itself against my ear.

I flapped a hand irritably. "Go away, Netherly. I'm waiting for the old gent now."

"Now don't tell me you've thrown me over for this bloke Netherly. You'll break my heart, India."

I whirled around to find myself staring down at the bald crown and twinkling eyes of Peter Penbras.

Bloody hell.

Penbras cast an admiring glance at my attire. "Costume party at Claridge's? I can't believe I wasn't invited." He peered around me into the lobby. "Or could you be visiting this august establishment for some other purpose?"

I figured Penbras had deduced my occupation upon sight at the embassy, and so I decided on the frontal attack. "Bugger off, Penbras. I'm trying to make a living here."

He raised one of his bushy eyebrows. "Are you, my dear? Is it French you're waiting for, dressed in such a seductive fashion? I see him over there, pretending to read the paper, but I would hardly have thought dressing up games were his cup of tea."

"French is here?" Even to my ears, my question sounded remarkably lame.

Penbras gave me a dubious look. "Come now, India. Don't try to pretend you don't know your sidekick is sitting in the lobby, nursing the same drink for what must be all of an hour now. Clearly he's waiting on someone, and I assume you're waiting with him. Who could it be, I wonder?"

"You've got hold of the wrong end of the horse, Penbras. I'm to meet a customer here, and whatever French is doing here is a mystery to me. He doesn't advise me of his social calendar."

Penbras ignored my statement. "Myself, I'm waiting for Gladstone to appear. He's always good for a frenzied attack on the Turks, not to mention some choice quotes about our prime minister's ineptitude. But what the devil would French want with Gladstone, unless he's here to personally deliver an insult from Dizzy? That really isn't French's style. Perhaps French is here for another reason?"

Penbras glanced in my direction, waiting for some reaction to his speculation, no doubt. I didn't oblige him.

"If my customer gets cold feet and disappears because you're hovering around me, you're going to owe me ten quid."

Penbras looked shocked. "Ten quid! As much as that? You're a handsome woman, India, but Lord, that's high. Must be a hell of an outing for that price." Then his eyes narrowed. He was nobody's fool, was Penbras, and he'd quickly conned that I was doing my best to distract him. He turned back to the lobby and surveyed the crowd with a practiced eye.

"If not Gladstone, then whom?" he muttered. A moment later I felt him stiffen like a dog on point. "I say, India, isn't that clergyman with the glasses holding a government portfolio? Now that's mighty odd. I wonder how he came by it?"

This Penbras fellow was turning into an almighty pest. Things couldn't get much worse.

Well, yes, they could. Penbras looked at me thoughtfully. "You don't suppose that portfolio came from the War Office, do you?"

I was considering a reply to this question when salvation appeared in the form of a filthy tornado, barreling down the hall of Claridge's and into the rotund figure of Peter Penbras. I got a whiff of the human whirlwind as it went by, which was all I needed to confirm that Vincent was in the building. He disappeared down the corridor and out through the servant's entrance before I'd barely caught a glimpse of him.

Penbras was on his back, waving his arms and legs like an overturned beetle and making strangled noises of rage. I felt inclined to leave him there, for he was beginning to attract attention from the nearest inhabitants of the Claridge's lobby. His face had turned an alarming shade of red and was screwed up like a baby's. Any minute now, he'd be shouting the rooftops down. Time for me to exit, stage right. I scurried down the hall, just as Penbras recovered his breath and roared: "That boy stole my wallet."

Well, there was quite an uproar in the lobby of Claridge's after that, as you can well imagine. I saw it all from my new vantage

point, just around the corner from the saloon bar, behind a por-
ted fern. At Penbras's cry, Frank Netherly rushed to his side and
assisted him to his feet while trying to stifle the reporter's increasingly vociferous allegations of theft. The croakers who'd been
dozing over their papers woke up with a start, and several ladies
uttered muted screams at the disturbance. I could see Calthorp
(goggling at Penbras and Netherly, the case clutched tightly to his
chest) and French (well, just his legs, actually, as he'd taken one
look in the direction of the commotion and then retreated behind his paper once again). It took some time for the hurly-burly
to die down, but it did eventually, with the old gentlemen settled
in their chairs, new whiskies at hand, and the ladies petted and
reassured, and Netherly groveling to Penbras so he wouldn't write
a story about the crime wave at Claridge's, and Penbras no doubt
blackmailing Netherly for some juicy tips in the future.

There seemed nothing else to do now but settle down and wait,
following French's example. I was prepared for a long suspension
of activity, for it seemed like I had done nothing but cool my heels
for hours, but the wait proved short-lived. Suddenly there was
a bustle of activity at the hotel entrance, and Gladstone strode
into the lobby, followed by a retinue of earnest young men and
middle-aged matrons, clutching Bibles and babbling away. Every
head in the place turned in unison, and there were muted gasps
and muffled applause from some of the guests, while the rest
glowered and muttered and mentally calculated the days until
their next opportunity to vote Tory. Gladstone ignored them
all, advancing on the registration desk to collect his key with the
stately and measured stride of a former, and (if Calthorp had his
way) the next, prime minister. He was an impressive old bird, with
a slab of a face roughly hewn into a hawk-like visage, enormous

tufts of white side-whiskers, and a mouth like an Old Testament prophet who'd just gotten wind of the goings-on in Sodom and Gomorrah.

Calthorp sprang to his feet and, clutching the case to his breast, shoved his way through the ranks of Gladstone's retinue until he was close enough to grasp the great man's sleeve. Gladstone greeted his acolyte with 'a hearty handshake and a whispered confidence. I noticed that French had dropped the pretense of reading his newspaper and was now peering over the top of it, staring coolly at the greetings and bustle in the lobby. One of Gladstone's minions collected the key while Gladstone extricated himself from the crowd of well-wishers and hangers-on, conducting himself as a good Christian should, earnestly wringing the hands of the men and bowing gravely over the plump mitts of the ladies. Then the gaggle stumped out of the lobby in a determined fashion, on their way to sing hymns or to proselytize among the non-believers, no doubt, while Gladstone and four of his followers, including Calthorp, made for the stairs. French drained his whisky, folded his newspaper, and strolled after them. I turned and made for the back stairs.

I flew down the corridor and wrenched open the stairwell, and my feet fairly skimmed up the risers as I made for the first floor. I reached the door to the corridor on the first floor and cracked it open, wheezing a little, and waited to see if the Gladstone party was resident. At the far end of the hall, I heard the low rumble of male voices and caught a brief glance of five sober black suits as they passed the entranceway to the first floor and continued upward. On to the second floor, then, and I launched myself with vigor at the stairs, straining to breathe in my tight dress. Sitting around Lotus House, counting sovereigns and drinking gin, hadn't improved my general health any, and I was blowing like a nonagenarian whale when I made the second floor landing. I loosened the door latch and put an eye to the opening, just in time to see Gladstone's party emerge into the hallway and amble slowly toward me, talking animatedly among themselves, with Calthorp and the old man engaged in a whispered discussion. Snatches of their conversation floated toward me: "Wonderful crowd this afternoon . . . Christian brothers . . . teach those Turk-ish heathens a lesson," and more of the same ilk.

Halfway down the hall, one of the entourage halted the group's progress, produced a key, and opened the door to one of the rooms. The gentlemen filed inside, and I watched with a sinking feeling. Now Calthorp would produce the case and pro-vide Gladstone with the ammunition he'd need to attack Dizzy in the press, revealing not only the prime minister's bluff about the British Army kicking the Russians back to the Volga if they dared step foot into Turkey, but more damning still, Dizzy's desire to protect British investors at the expense of the Porte's Christian subjects. You'd think that a man of Gladstone's principles, being a member of the flock as he was prone to tell anyone who wan-dered into his path, would observe the Good Book's injunction against theft. Even a former prime minister has no right to see government documents without permission. But I suspected that the Grand Old Man thought the safety of a few thousand Serbian brothers and sisters in Christ justified the act of stealing War Of-fice documents and bringing down the government. It's amazing the means these self-righteous bastards will employ to achieve their ends.

In this case, however, it appeared that the Serbian brothers and sisters could wait until after dinner, for Gladstone and his follow-

ers (including Calthorp, *sans* case) appeared in the hallway again
and discussed dining at the hotel or wandering down to the club
for a beefsteak, while the same gent who'd unlocked the door
now secured it and dropped the room key in his pocket. For a moment, I considered catching them up before they got out of the
vicinity, claiming the need to enter the room to do a bit of clear-
ing up or to turn down beds, but Calthorp was too bloody close.
If I drew attention to myself, he'd surely recognize me, despite the
purloined uniform and the mobcap. India Black's charms, if I do
say so myself, are impossible to disguise. Just look at that narrow
escape from Penbras.

So I watched them stroll out of sight while I turned over various schemes in my mind. I was tantalizingly close to the object of
my exertions, but getting into the room would be no easy task.
My chances of obtaining the passkey from the registration desk
were nil; the clerk wouldn't hand over a key to a blowsy housemaid he'd never laid eyes on before, and I didn't have time to try
to charm it out of him. Netherly? It had been over two hours since
I had entered the hotel under false pretenses, and I doubted he'd
sit still for another tale. No, he'd be asking for his money, and if I
didn't produce it, I'd be out on my ear. The closest I had to an ally
in this game was French, and there'd been no sign of him since
I'd seen him in the lobby. At this point in the day's play, I'd have
welcomed the sight of that imperious cove.

I was standing in the hallway, contemplating the alternatives,
when one suddenly presented itself on a platter. The door next to
Gladstone's room opened and a willowy swell in an opera cloak,
top hat and pince-nez emerged, stopping short at the sight of me
loitering in the passageway. I could see right away there was no
chance of bewitching this one; he was a right mandrake. I could

see the faintest outline of kohl around his pale blue eyes, and his manicure was an improvement over mine. I chose the sniveling servant routine and in a trice was in the toff's room, turning down the bed (inexpertly) and arranging his toiletries (and my, there were a lot of them) on the dressing table, while the occupant of the room swanned off happily to enjoy the delights of the theatre (and no doubt, later in the evening, those of the first available sailor).

When he was safely out of sight and the door fastened securely behind him, I hurried to the window and flung it open, only to be met by a blast of sleet, snow and cold arctic wind. While I'd been romping around Claridge's, playing the role of servile maid, a bloody storm had blown in from the North Sea. That made my plan even less appealing. It was too much to hope for a balcony, but there was a narrow ledge of stone, no more than ten inches wide and rapidly accumulating a layer of ice, about three feet below the window and running the length of the building, which meant that it ran right under the window to Gladstone's room as well. The drop was a good twenty feet, though, and that checked me for a moment while I weighed up the available options for retrieving the case, which didn't take long as there didn't appear to be any others. I cast a quick look round and was relieved to see that Gladstone and the Mary Anne had rated quiet rooms that overlooked an interior garden, and at least I would not be exposed to view from the busy streets surrounding the hotel, though on a night like this the pedestrians would be striding along with their heads ducked down anyway, taking no notice of anything happening two stories above the ground.

I sighed. There was nothing for it but to give it a go, so I gingerly lifted a leg over the windowsill and groped for the ledge with the toe of my boot. I wasn't reassured when I found it; the footing was treacherous, and the sole of my boot skittered wildly along the ledge until I could steady myself using the window frame. I got the second foot over the sill and onto the ledge and cautiously canted my upper body out of the safety of the window until I was standing upright in the blowing sleet and snow, facing the building. I was damned reluctant to leave the safety of that open window, for with one step to my left, I'd have no secure handhold until I reached Gladstone's window. The brick façade of the building was as cold as ice and nearly as slippery, speckled as it was with frozen precipitation.

If a rozzer had wandered by that night, he might have been tempted to pull me in for lewd and lascivious conduct in a public place, for I've never hugged a man the way I hugged that wall of stone. I plastered myself to the cold façade, hardly daring to breathe and sliding along at a snail's pace. Blasts of wind shook me, and pellets of sleet stung my face. I put my head down and inched sideways, fast as I dared. Midway from one window to the other, it occurred to me that even as I was risking life and limb, French had probably observed Gladstone's departure, sauntered down to the registration desk and suborned the clerk to hand over the key to Gladstone's room. French might be in there now, collecting the case and congratulating himself on nicking it from under Calthorp's nose. The thought galvanized me, and I redoubled my efforts.

By the time I reached the window of Gladstone's room, I'd scraped my cheek badly, barked my knuckles a half dozen times, and the maid's costume had become a stiff cloak of ice. My teeth were chattering loud enough to rouse the dead, and I could no longer feel my feet. This was, of course, the worst possible time to think about the possibility that Gladstone's window would be locked. But that is what I did, cursing myself for a fool and wishing myself back in my warm study, with Mrs. Drinkwater lurching around the room, crashing into the furniture, bringing me whisky and building up the fire. Halfheartedly, I reached out and groped blindly for the handle. A gloved hand closed over my wrist.

NINE

The results were predictable: I shrieked and attempted to wrench free from the vise-like grip of the gentleman who was sharing my ledge. My boots shot out from under me, and my stomach lurched, and then the two of us went flying, arse over tea kettle, arms and legs flailing. The flight was brief, for the ground came up to meet us with shocking quickness. I felt an excruciating blow to my head, and then another to my ribs and the next thing I remember I was lying stunned on the icy grass, gasping for air and trying to curse at the same time, while the wind howled and the sleet and snow collected in my eyebrows.

"Bloody hell," I finally managed to expostulate, rolling over on my side and trying to collect myself. A dark figure lay huddled next to me. I leaned over and prodded it with my finger.

"French?"

It had to be him; no one else was so fond of sneaking up on innocent people and scaring the wits out of them. The figure stirred and groaned piteously (though I must confess the effect was wasted on me), then managed to sit upright, wobbling dangerously and cursing heartily, which seemed to indicate a rapid rate of recovery. At any minute I expected the French windows to the garden to open and the rescue squad to come blundering out into the wintry night, but apparently the sounds of the wind and the blowing sleet and snow had muffled the noise of our fall. No one ventured out of the warmth and light of the hotel.

"'Ill met by moonlight, proud Titania,'" French groaned between clenched teeth, clutching his side and straining to breathe.

"Indeed," I said icily. "I was hoping to encounter Oberon. Instead I've hit Bottom." Well, if the idiot wanted to quote Shakespeare just after taking a fall from a hotel ledge in the middle of a blizzard, I'd accommodate him.

"You infernal idiot," French said.

I considered that an unfair criticism. "Oh, I'm an idiot, am I? Whatever possessed you to creep up on me while I was balancing on an icy ledge two stories above the ground and clamp a hand on my wrist? I'd have expected you to comprehend the consequences of such a precipitate action." (Anger tends to make me verbose.)

French's hair had collected a considerable amount of snow and stood up in icy peaks. I couldn't see his face well, there being only a dim glow from the hotel windows illuminating the garden, but I could imagine him glowering at me from under those bristling black brows.

"I certainly didn't anticipate that you, of all people, would be disconcerted by my actions and behave like the silliest of your sex," he said, and began thrashing about in the snow, trying to find his footing. He must have suffered a grievous blow to the head when we'd tumbled off the ledge, for one might almost interpret his statement as a compliment, in a backhanded sort of way, of course. I had no time to consider the implications of the matter further, for French loomed over me, reached down and grasped my arm, and hauled me unceremoniously to my feet.

"We must gain access to that room, India. How did you get onto the ledge?"

I briefly explained (for the garden of Claridge's on a night cold enough to freeze the balls off a statue was no place for lengthy confabs) that I'd come out the window of the room next to Gladstone's.

French's grip tightened. "Have you a passkey?"

I tried to shrug off his hand and told him about my services for the Uranian opera lover. He seemed to notice then for the first time that I was not attired in my usual stylish fashion, but was wearing a servant's apron and a bedraggled mobcap.

I felt his critical gaze on my person. "Worth another try, I suppose, if you didn't look like a refugee from a shipwreck," he said. "But I fear that no guest will let you past the door of his room looking like that."

I was tempted to point out that he was not up to his usual sartorial splendor either, but I bit back the words. There would be time to hurl abuse at each other later.

"And how did you find your way onto the ledge?" I asked.

"I climbed up the drainpipe. And I fear that's our only hope now." He renewed his grip on my arm and commenced dragging me toward a dark corner of the building.

"Why the bloody hell didn't you just bribe the desk clerk for the room key?"

"This is probably a deuced difficult concept for you to fathom, but I didn't want to draw attention to myself."

Well, that was French's way: first a backhanded compliment, followed immediately by an outright insult. I couldn't resist another dig myself.

"And for that matter, why didn't you just waltz up to Calthorp in the lobby and demand the return of Her Majesty's documents? He couldn't very well refuse a representative of the government."

"I can see that discretion is another concept in which you require tutelage. The lobby was full of newspapermen, including that swine Penbras, all waiting for Gladstone and bored silly while they waited. If I'd confronted Calthorp and he'd made a scene, the news would have been all over the city by morning, with every opposition leader sniffing the wind and reaching conclusions I'd rather they didn't." By now we'd reached a secluded corner of the garden where two wings of the building met and a network of drains and pipes ran from the roof to the ground.

French let loose of my arm and glanced skyward. "Right. Up you go," he said peremptorily.

"What?" I'd barely mustered the nerve to leave the mandrake's window in the first place. I wasn't about to go ice skating on that narrow ledge again, at least not for the dubious pleasure of saving Dizzy's hide.

"It's better if we both go. I'll force the window, and you can collect the case. If anyone returns to the room, your presence will be easier to explain than mine."

"I think *you* need some tutelage in elementary logic," I sniffed. "You just said I looked like I'd had a dip in the ocean, remember?"

"Oh, you do. But you're wearing a maid's clothing, and you can always explain that you were caught out in the storm running an errand for one of the female guests. I, on the other hand, have no plausible reason for being in that room."

"If it's Calthorp that returns, he'll recognize me immediately. What then?"

"Then you throw the case out the window for me to retrieve, and employ some of your famous charm."

"I see. Deniability for you and Dizzy. Gaol for India."

"You won't be there long," said French, as if this were some consolation. "We're wasting time. Give me your foot, and I'll give you a boost."

It was a perilous climb up the frigid iron drainpipe, the sleet peppering our faces and hands, and the wind howling like a banshee. I went first, with French behind me. I floundered and groped and would have made little headway, but he was agile as a monkey and strong as a gorilla, wedging his shoulder under my bum (a liberty I wouldn't have permitted in ordinary circumstances, even though he was a handsome devil) and shoving me skyward. Maneuvering onto the ledge from the downspout was a damned-dicey business, but we finally succeeded, me with my heart in my throat and French spouting a torrent of invective, most of it aimed at me and my lack of gymnastic ability. Then we slithered along the ledge with all the grace of newborn colts, the soles of our leather boots glissading on the slick surface, French gripping my arm to steady me, until we reached Gladstone's window. There he extracted a folding knife with a wicked blade, inserted it deftly, and sprang the window latch with the practiced ease of a screwsman. I clambered in through the open window, scanning the room for the black leather portfolio. The room looked less like a bedchamber and more like the headquarters of some political or military campaign, for there were documents stacked on every surface, maps lying unfurled on the floor, and a number of gentleman's cases scattered around the room. After a rapid reconnaissance (for French had stuck his head through the window and was barking instructions to hurry, for God's sake), I found Calthorp's prize tucked away behind an armchair and gathered it up. I felt a thrill of triumph when I claimed it, for outwitting that pious pack of fools and laying hands on it before French. I had little time to bask in the warm glow of success, however, for French snatched the case from my hands at the window, and disappeared along the ledge on the slow journey back to the drainpipe without so much as a backward glance at me, leaving me to crawl out of the window and find my own way down.

A few steps into my excursion, it occurred to me that I had failed to close the window behind me, ensuring that when Calthorp and Gladstone and the rest returned to the room, they'd be greeted by a screeching gale, a drift of snow and ice on the Turkey carpet, and the sure evidence of an unwanted visitor to the chamber. For a moment, I wondered whether my oversight might lead to a general alarm being raised and our escape being circumvented, but then logic reasserted itself, and I concluded there was little Gladstone could do in the circumstances. He could hardly raise a hue and cry about the disappearance of a leather case belonging to Her Majesty's government, particularly one that had been purloined by one of his supporters.

It was laborious business, navigating that frozen ledge, like mountaineering on a glacier without the aid of crampon or piton, and by the time I'd reached the drainpipe I was weak as a lamb, shaking with cold and wet to the bone. French was nowhere to be seen; I assume he'd already begun to descend the drainpipe, so I hooked a leg around the pipe and attempted to grasp it with hands that were numb with fatigue and chill. That probably explains why, as soon as I'd relinquished my foothold on the ledge, I slid down the drainpipe at speed, plummeting to earth like a meteor. It was a lucky thing for me, but a bit unfortunate for French, who had decided to play the gentleman. For he was waiting for me at the bottom of the downspout, about to offer a chivalrous arm I suppose, when I barreled into him like a Swiss avalanche, sending him sprawling into the darkness of the snowy garden with a muffled oath.

I found him a few feet away, laid out like an effigy on a tomb, too stunned, I presume, to move.

"French?" I inquired, for the second time that night.

There was no response. Tentatively, I reached out my hand and shook him gently. I didn't want to be too close in the event he regained consciousness.

"French, are you hurt?" The only sound was the keening wind and the clatter of sleet against the windows of the hotel.

I groped until my hand found his face, cold as marble and damp with melting snow. I leaned over and put my ear to his nose, listening for the breath of life and debating whether to leave him as he lay or summon assistance.

There was a deep shuddering sigh, then a series of ragged breaths, and then French found his voice. "Imbecile," he croaked, and I knew it would be no time at all until he was back to normal.

"Where's the case?" I asked.

French waved a vague hand, indicating the world at large, and concentrated on breathing. I pawed around in the snow for a few minutes, praying that the impact hadn't sprung the lock on the case and scattered War Office documents and the PM's memo to the four corners of the Claridge's garden, until my hands encountered cold wet leather and I hauled out the portfolio, none the worse for the ordeal but for a touch of damp. I brushed off the snow and tucked it under my arm.

"I've got the case, French. Let's get out of here before Calthorp comes back and finds out someone's buggered off with it." The open window still nagged at me, and I wanted to put some distance between us and the hotel. Any minute, the disappearance of the case might be discovered, and a crew of clean-living, muscular Christians might come spilling out of the hotel, baying like hounds on a scent. When they did, I wanted them to find only snow churned into a bewildering pattern of sitzmarks, as though a gang of schnapps-drinking sportsmen had been schussing through the Claridge's garden on a lark.

"Can you walk?"

French snarled something inarticulate that I took to be an affirmative answer, and he staggered to his feet. I took his arm, but he shook off my hand with another of his patented growls and stalked off through the falling snow. I couldn't help thinking his behavior a tiny bit ungrateful. After all, I'd retrieved the case for him and Dizzy, probably saving Dizzy's career (at least for the moment—there's no telling about Dizzy; he'll be in the soup again soon of his own accord, no doubt), and ensuring that Gladstone and his party of gospel grinders didn't know how deeply British investors had backed the Sublime Porte. What Gladstone would have made of the War Office memo detailing the deplorable state of Britain's armed forces I don't know, but at a guess I figure he'd conclude that while they might be no match for the Russians, they could easily take on the hired thugs and indolent janissaries that comprised the Ottoman military. Gladstone was spoiling for a fight with the Turks, and there's nothing as militant as a Christian when he's convinced he's doing the Lord's work. On the whole, I preferred Dizzy's sabre-rattling theatrics for the Russians to Gladstone's barmy ideas about attacking Constantinople and freeing the Porte's Christian subjects from their Turkish masters. I didn't doubt that most of the lads in the army would prefer the comfort of their billets in England to dueling it out again on the Crimean peninsula, given the dismal performance there the last time round. Oh, no doubt some fire-breathers were chomping at the bit, anxious to test their skills and luck on the field of battle, whether against Cossacks or Afridis made no difference to them. But the average soldier probably preferred the comforts of barmaids and beer.

While I was conducting this political analysis and congratulating myself on my charitable work on behalf of Tommy Atkins, I'd been trotting along behind French, who was marching along at a ground-eating pace. It was bitterly cold; the sleet had changed into a heavy, wet snow, and the wind was still blowing with a vengeance. I stopped ruminating about Turks and Christians and began contemplating the medicinal benefits of a stiff peg of brandy, followed by tea and toast. We'd left the garden of the hotel behind and were trekking through an alley, making for Downing Street, when French uttered a muffled oath, stopped short and held out a restraining hand.

"What is it?" I said, having to shout to make myself heard above the shriek of the wind. "What's the matter?"

He didn't reply, only directed my attention to the end of the alley where a gas lamp burned feebly. A dark figure, cloaked and motionless, stood in the muted halo of yellow light. My heart sank as I contemplated the figure, for there was something diabolical about that silent, waiting apparition that made me shudder with fear. The man's unnatural stillness was more sinister than a flashing blade or a brandished pistol. I took a half step back and slid in behind French's stalwart form.

"Not one of your men?" I enquired hopefully.

He grunted. Good-bye tea and toast, I thought regretfully. The evening looked far from over.

When you're in a pickle, there are three things you can do: brazen it out, fight it out or run like the devil. Being a whore, I'm practiced at the first, avoid the second unless there's no alternative and prefer the third as it offers the best opportunity to preserve purse and person. Instinctively I looked over my shoulder, back down the alleyway, to suss out an escape route. What I saw made me clutch French's arm.

"Three more of them, behind us," I hissed in his ear, and he nodded grimly, never taking his eyes from the dark figure under the lamp.

He clasped my hand and drew me close, putting his mouth to my ear. "Follow me," he said. "If I give you the word, I want you to run. Don't stop for anything. Go straight to the PM's office. There will be someone there to help you." His grip tightened. "And whatever you do, hold on to that case."

"That's the plan?" I asked, in some exasperation. "I try to outpace four ruffians through a blizzard?"

"You're right. That's a bloody awful plan," French said. His tone matched mine. "I'm sure I can think of something else if you give me a minute." He pretended to think. "Ah, yes. Here it is." He paused for effect. "I could always take the case and leave you to your own devices."

I glanced over my shoulder again. The three shapeless forms I'd seen in the alley were closer now and had materialized into three bulky brutes bearing down determinedly upon us.

"Right," I said. "Plan one it is. Let's move, or those three hooligans back there will be inviting us to make up a table at the nearest pub."

We set off with French in the lead and me trailing along in his wake, checking now and then to see if the gap between us and the three men had narrowed. The few paces we covered seemed to take forever, with the dark figure waiting silently for us under the gas lamp, oozing menace, and the three men skulking along behind us like a pack of wolves stalking their prey across the steppe. We reached the street, and the motionless figure stirred and advanced slowly toward us, until we met just at the edge of the light.

"That will be far enough, Mr. French." The voice was cold, cultured, and unmistakably Russian.

"Ivanov," French said gloomily.

The Russian gave us a lupine smile. "This is an interesting game we play, is it not? A move here, a countermove there? But I believe my queen is about to take your rook, Mr. French, leaving King Dizzy exposed. Or so I would imagine, given the lengths to which you have gone to retrieve that case. I am trembling with anticipation, old boy. I simply can't wait to discover what you've been at such pains to keep secret. Why, you've even enlisted a whore to help you protect national secrets. I'd gauge that a sure sign of desperation." He gave me a mock bow, which sent snow cascading from his hat and the shoulders of his cloak. "Though I must congratulate Her Majesty's servants for their taste in ladies of the evening. A prime specimen, without a doubt."

There's something about being discussed like a prize-winning

Berkshire sow at the county fair that sets my teeth on edge, but for the moment the Russian had the upper hand. The three hoodlums had formed a semicircle around us, blocking any escape routes. They were a vicious-looking bunch, mustachioed and swarthy. A cudgel dangled from the hands of one; the other two had their paws buried in their pockets, ready to produce weapons if necessary. Now would have been a good time for French to produce a weapon of some sort to cover our retreat, but it was Ivanov who whipped out the barkers, matching Webleys that gleamed dully in the flickering lamplight.

"And now, I'll have the case," he said, "for it is much too cold to pass time in idle chitchat. We must get Miss Black back to her fireside, and you, Mr. French, must deliver some disappointing news to the prime minister."

I tensed, waiting for the signal to flee from French, but it didn't come. Ivanov jerked his head at one of his goons, who promptly obeyed the imperious command by wrenching the case from my grasp.

"Thank you for cooperating, Mr. French. It makes our interactions so much more pleasant when you are disinclined to play the hero, although I must say, I expected more from you."

"And you'll get it, Ivanov," French said. "I'll be after you."

"I believe you, sir. And that is why I must arrange for you to be briefly detained by these fine fellows." He gave us a wintry smile and a piercing glance from those glittering green eyes. "Do not struggle, and you will not be harmed. You will be released when I have gone."

I hoped he was telling the truth; one look at those three burly accomplices made me also hope that at least one of them was smart enough to understand that we were to be freed after the

Russian wolf had fled. Ivanov shoved one of the Webleys into his jacket and collected the case.

"Au revoir, French, and good-bye to you, Miss Black. Perhaps I'll have the pleasure of consulting you professionally someday."

"I don't do flunkies myself, but I'll set you up with a nice girl who knows how to satisfy the common soldier," I said.

"A woman of spirit. I admire that," said Ivanov, but I could see that my comment would not be forgotten, and I hoped I would never have the ill fortune to meet that sinister figure alone and unarmed. With his last remark, he turned on his heel and stalked away without a glance, pocketing the Webley as he went and carrying the case securely under his arm. My gaze followed him as he plunged into the blowing snow, and then, just as he was about to vanish, I thought I saw a small, black shadow detach itself from the doorway of a shop and disappear into the darkness after the Russian.

My image of spies, confidential agents and such took a grievous blow that evening, for I expected French to fly into action against our three guards once Ivanov had disappeared from sight, delivering a flurry of quick blows that stunned our thick-headed captors, and then charging headlong after Ivanov and the case. Instead, French stood brooding under the lamp, hardly glancing at the three wrong-uns that surrounded us. The minutes crawled by, the snow pile higher, and I lost all feeling in my hands and feet.

After what seemed an age but was probably only a matter of minutes, the fellow with the cudgel tucked it under his arm, extracted a hunter from his pocket and held it close to his nose, nodded to the other two, and then the three of them melted away into the night, leaving French and me alone in the middle of the blizzard.

"Why didn't you do something?" I demanded. "You just let Ivanov have the case without a fight."

"One against four aren't odds worth taking, India. Would you rather I'd have tried something heroic, getting my skull bashed in and leaving you to Ivanov's mercy?"

Put that way, I supposed I preferred the scenario that had occurred.

"What now? Should we go back to the embassy?" I asked.

French shook his head. "This is out of your hands, India. Go back to Lotus House."

"And what will you do? Have the British army mount a full-scale assault on the Russian embassy?"

"Nothing quite so dramatic, India," snapped French. "You heard what Ivanov said about playing a game? Well, he's upped the ante, but the contest is still on. We'll run him to ground." Then his voice softened, and I had to strain to hear what he said. "You've played your part, and you've played it well. Now go home."

His declaration took me by surprise, and I hesitated in replying, torn as I was between the suspicion that French was patronizing me and the thought (outrageous as it might seem) that he'd actually paid me a compliment. Consequently, and uncharacteristically, I couldn't think of anything to say. Presumably, French took my silence for acquiescence to his instructions to return to Lotus House, for before I could get a word out, he'd disappeared, leaving behind only a set of blurred footprints in the snow.

It was damned hard work catching a cab back to Lotus House.

There were very few of the wretched contrivances about, most of the drivers apparently having decided that there'd be no fares worth having tonight, and retreating to hearth and home. To make matters worse, the few drivers that were out seemed reluctant to pick up a maidservant who looked as though she'd taken a tumble in the Thames. I was finally able to flag down an intrepid soul who was so swathed in coats and scarves and addled by brandy that I doubted he could even see his potential customers. In any case, he didn't seem the least bit startled at my appearance, only received my instructions to relay me home as quickly as possible on such a night with a deferential nod and whipped his nag to the task. When we arrived at Lotus House, I ushered him into the sitting room with the promise of whisky and double the fare if he'd wait until I'd changed my clothes and then deliver me on to my destination.

Per usual, Mrs. Drinkwater had fallen asleep with her head on the kitchen table, less the effect of a hard day spent cleaning up after the whores than the result of the empty bottle of gin and the sticky tumbler on the floor beside her. I roused her up, and to her credit she didn't even blink at my countenance, but staggered around the kitchen, putting on the kettle for tea, cutting bread and making toast, and filling a flask with brandy. I rushed upstairs to the privacy of my room, where I discarded the form-fitting maid's costume without regret, toweled myself dry and selected an ensemble more fitting for roving about in the middle of a snowstorm. In a twinkling, I was back downstairs, bolting toast and scalding my mouth on a cup of tea, gulping a medicinal draught of brandy and rousing up the driver, who was dozing on the sofa in the sitting room.

No doubt you have deduced and are likely thinking that the

intelligent thing for me to do would be to don my dressing gown and dry my hair in front of the fire, a snifter of brandy in hand, while the forces of good (it was difficult to see French in this role, but at least in this pantomime, he seemed to fit the part) and evil (Ivanov: no question about his suitability as stage villain) battled it out without the assistance of India Black. This was, in effect, what French had ordered me to do, and no doubt most women would have followed his instructions to the letter, swooning all the while. I was made of sterner stuff, however. I did not take orders from anyone, let alone a dashing aristocrat prancing around London, playing at spies. Indeed, the surest way to ensure that I did something was to order me to do the opposite. I can't help it; a lifetime of fending for myself in the streets of London, scraping for crusts and customers, dodging blows from the peelers and attempts to reform me by assorted God wallahs, has left me with a rather jaundiced view of authority in all its guises. India Black answers to no man, no matter how attractive he might be. Of course, that was only part of the reason I'd laced on a pair of sturdy boots and commandeered a cab for a drive through one of the worst snowstorms I could remember. I'm a sporting woman by nature; even my line of work requires a calculating heart and a bold spirit. I'm not ashamed to confess that I'd become caught up in the game, thrilling at the chase, and I wanted to be in on the kill. And if in the case of Ivanov, that was a literal and not figurative event, so much the better.

TEN

The entrance to the prime minister's office was shrouded in darkness and appeared deserted, but as I ascended the steps, a stout fellow appeared from behind a pillar and held out a restraining hand.

"Hold on there, miss," he warned. I recognized him as one of the men who'd accosted me and delivered me to Dizzy (was it really just two nights ago?). He must have recognized me at the same time, for I heard his quick inhalation of breath and his hand moved inadvertently to cover his groin.

"How are your tallywags?" I inquired cheerfully. "I do hope I haven't caused any permanent damage," and swept past him into the building.

I had thought I would find a council of war underway, and

indeed Dizzy, French and Endicott were all gathered in Dizzy's office. Endicott was ensconced in a leather chair by the fire, brooding over a balloon glass of cognac and darting contemptuous glances in Dizzy's direction. French was standing at the window, watching the snow pelt down and smoking meditatively. Dizzy was fuming and sputtering like a wet Catherine wheel, his brow twitching and his fingers beating a tattoo on his knees. My entrance was received as expected. Dizzy put on a brave smile and advanced toward me with an outstretched hand. French nodded briefly at me, then turned back to his contemplation of the inky darkness outside the window, but not before I saw a slight smile tugging at the corners of his mouth.

Endicott flicked a disdainful glance in my direction and remained anchored in his chair. "What the devil are you doing here?" he asked, in that pompous drawl I found so annoying.

"I thought you might need my assistance again."

"You haven't been a great deal of help, Miss Black," Endicott said. "The case is in Russian hands, and Britain is about to be exposed."

"I got the bloody case for you, Endicott. It's not my fault that Ivanov and his crew seem to have outwitted you at every turn."

That spiked his gun, as I knew it would. He erupted out of his chair, cognac sloshing wildly, his cheeks burning brightly in his pale face. "Now see here," he began, in a voice that could have cut glass, but he didn't get any further.

"Mr. Endicott, you may wish to exchange insults with Miss Black for the duration of the evening, though I'd advise against it," said French. "Perhaps we should concentrate our efforts on determining a course of action and leave the trading of accusations for another time." He fixed me with a level gaze. "That goes for you as well, Miss Black."

I returned his gaze, without acknowledging the directive. As I said, I don't take kindly to authority.

"Quite right," Dizzy chimed in. They were the first words he'd spoken, except for a brief hello when I'd arrived, and so I knew the strain must be an awful one, to have rendered him mute for nearly five minutes. "We were just discussing the advisability of delivering a formal protest to Count Yusopov at the embassy."

Endicott had slumped back into his chair. That man had a future as an instructor in the art of sulking. Now he spoke sullenly. "What bloody good will that do? By now Ivanov and Yusopov know our troop strength and are toasting Russia's forthcoming conquest of Constantinople."

French selected a burning ember from the fire and held it to his cheroot. "They'll have to send the documents out of England by diplomatic courier or take it themselves. They don't dare telegraph the news from London as they'll be implicated in the theft of the case and create a diplomatic furor. Even Gladstone can't countenance a Russian theft of state secrets, no matter how chummy he is with the tsar's ambassador. As long as Ivanov and Yusopov are the only ones who know, the issue can still be resolved in our favor."

Dizzy looked sideways at him, brow furrowed.

Endicott sat up in his chair with a start. "Good Lord, French. Surely you aren't advocating the assassination of those two? Yusopov is the tsar's cousin. There'd be absolute hell to pay."

"I wasn't planning to advertise the fact that the British government was involved, Endicott. Nor was I necessarily contemplat-

ing their deaths. Merely removing them from the field of play for
a period of time might achieve our objectives. Killing them would
only be a last resort."

My admiration for French rose. I had pegged him as a typical
British aristocrat: clean living, rugby playing and foolishly ad-
dicted to that bizarre code of honour they instilled at places like
Eton and Harrow. I was pleased to see his scruples were more elas-
tic than Endicott's, who sneered at being in a whore's company
but wasn't prepared to consider violence even though the Empire
was teetering on the edge.

Dizzy was looking uncharacteristically uncomfortable, no
doubt considering that one ramification of eliminating Ivanov
and Yusopov was the possible tit-for-tat assassination of key per-
sonnel in the British government, including, just conceivably, the
British prime minister.

"That's a drastic course of action, Mr. French," he said. "Do
you think it necessary?"

French shrugged. "Perhaps. We should not eliminate it from
the list of options available to us."

"And what are those options?" I asked.

"We must locate Ivanov and the case. If he has delivered it to
Yusopov and the contents are now known, then we may have no
choice but to prevent those two from communicating the information to the tsar or his generals. If the contents are still unread,
then we must recover the case. We shall find a way," said French
decisively. "We've recovered it twice already; we can do so again."

"I hate to quibble, but Calthorp actually carried it away from
the embassy."

"That sniveling little toady," Dizzy spat. "How on earth did he
manage to pull off a feat like that?"

"There's more to Calthorp than meets the eye. I think it very likely that he was doing much the same as the Russian agents in the days leading up to Latham's death," I said. "He'd been making frequent visits to Lotus House, ostensibly inquiring after the girls, but perhaps he was keeping an eye on Latham from the beginning. On the day Latham died, Calthorp appeared almost immediately, and I found him hovering in the hall outside Oksana's room where Latham's body was hidden. He also knew that Oksana had disappeared from Lotus House, though he could only have learned that from one of the girls, and no one knew she'd done a runner except me. And in retrospect, Calthorp's explanation of why he was at the embassy just doesn't ring true. I think he followed us there. For a meek little clergyman, he struck me as quite skilled at sneaking into guarded embassies. To cap it all, I believe he's the one who raised the alarm outside the embassy. I heard him shout, and I think he did that when he was in the clear with the case, just to set the guards on us and give himself time to escape."

Endicott harrumphed, but French nodded sagely, as if he'd already worked this all out for himself and I was a prize pupil for having followed his logic. Insufferable man.

Dizzy was pacing the floor. "That Bible-thumping, hymn-singing hypocrite Gladstone," he sputtered. "Setting Calthorp onto Latham to try and steal that memo. He has no sense of honour, nor of shame."

I yawned. It had been a long couple of days, I hadn't had much rest (sleeping nearly naked in a freezing garret not counting as real repose), and I was not looking forward to one of Dizzy's lengthy screeds against Gladstone.

Apparently French wasn't either. "I agree that Mr. Gladstone has acted disgracefully in this affair, but we must turn our efforts to finding Ivanov and the case. We must know where we stand, and then we will know what we have to do. We cannot let Ivanov and Yusopov defeat us."

I thought that French might plump for knifing Ivanov on some dark street regardless of what happened to the case, such was the intensity of dislike for the man his voice betrayed. Or maybe it was patriotism; not being personally acquainted with that particular virtue, I might have mistaken the tone of voice.

"Dandy idea," I said. "How do we find Ivanov?"

The three men gazed vaguely around the room, as if the Russian might suddenly materialize in a puff of smoke.

"You've no idea where he is?" I asked. "Haven't you been keeping an eye on him, knowing that he'd be after the documents?"

"Of course we have," said French. "We've had operatives following him since Calthorp disappeared with the case, on the chance that Ivanov would get to Calthorp before we did."

"So, theoretically, British agents were somewhere in the vicinity of Claridge's when Ivanov relieved you of the case," I said to French. "Where were these stalwart fellows when Ivanov left us alone with his thugs and made off with the goods?"

For the first time since I'd met him, French looked slightly discomfited. "Unavoidably detained elsewhere," he muttered. Well, if it had been Smith and Jones who had been tailing Ivanov, I could easily understand how the fellow had evaded them. Even Vincent had outwitted those two.

"We assume Ivanov returned to the Russian embassy with the case, and we've watchers posted at all the entrances. If he leaves the embassy, we'll know it within minutes," said French. "As a precaution, we've also stationed men at all the Channel ports nearest London, and in the train stations near the embassy."

"So we wait?" I asked.

"*We* wait," said Endicott firmly. "There is no need for you to remain here. Your services, such as they were, are no longer required."

"Yes, my dear, Mr. Endicott is right," said Dizzy, not unkindly. "You should return to your, er, establishment. You've done your duty by us, and I shall be eternally grateful for the assistance you've rendered."

I glanced at French, but he studiously ignored me, puffing his cheroot at the window, his hands in his pockets.

I was about to hang up my gloves and skulk back to Lotus House, finally beaten by French's indifference, when a hoarse shout was heard down the hallway. The sounds of light footsteps could be heard running rapidly toward the prime minister's office, followed distantly by what appeared to be two galloping dray horses. I recognized the first set of footsteps, having heard them innumerable times in the vicinity of Lotus House, usually in full flight from some outraged shopkeeper or irate peeler. The others hadn't had my experience. French sprang for his walking stick and drew out that ridiculously slender blade, while Endicott jumped to his feet, brandishing a poker from the fireplace. Like any wise politician in the face of public disfavor, Dizzy had gone to ground beneath the desk.

The door burst open and Vincent (as I expected) careered into the room, with Smith and Jones (naturally, no one else could create such a commotion without effecting any results) lumbering after him. Vincent scanned the room quickly, then darted toward

French and ducked in behind him. The two guards (if that's not being unduly generous about their capabilities) skidded to a halt and glowered at Vincent, whose ugly mug could be seen smirking from behind French. The boy certainly knew how to make an entrance.

"Come here, you," growled one of the brutes.

Endicott sighed in exasperation. "How does this filthy guttersnipe manage to get past you two?"

French had his arm around Vincent's shoulder (something he'd regret later, when he found the lice) and was fending off Smith and Jones with his free hand. "Settle down, lads. The boy poses no harm to anyone."

"I'll pose some harm to him," Smith said. "He'll get a beating he won't soon forget."

"That's hardly necessary," said French, who suddenly noticed that he had made contact with Vincent. He rapidly removed his arm from the boy's shoulder and surreptitiously brushed his sleeve.

Smith and Jones subsided, glowering. Dizzy scrambled out from under the desk, contriving to appear as though he'd been searching for a lost pen, and settled into his seat, smoothing his thin curls.

"What are you doing here, Vincent?" asked French. He took a couple of steps upwind, as Vincent's clothes had begun to steam in the heat from the fire, and the odor of the London streets had begun to permeate the room.

"I was at that 'otel and saw that Russian bloke take the case away from you and India."

So Vincent had been the shadow in the doorway that had slipped away in pursuit of Ivanov.

"I followed 'im for ever so long. Lord, it was cold out there. My feet feel like blocks o' ice."

"Yes, yes," said French. "The weather's dreadfully inclement tonight. Now tell me, where did Ivanov go?"

"To Covent Garden," said Vincent. "To the op'ra."

I'd thought French a relaxed individual in the execution of his duties, but a visit to hear Rossini while carrying a portfolio full of British military secrets seemed cool indeed.

Vincent drew a breath and looked longingly at the bottles on the sideboard. "I've been runnin' a long way. I'm fair parched, I am. Any chance I could get a glass o' beer to wet me whistle?"

I thought French might balk at this corruption of Vincent's youth, but he went silently to the sideboard, opened a bottle of ale and brought it to Vincent. Vincent tilted up the bottle and drained it in one go, belched violently, nodded his thanks to French and continued.

"The Russian went into the lobby and talked to one of them ushers there. 'E wrote out a note and give the usher some money and away went the usher while the Russian bloke cooled his 'eels for a few minutes. Then that there Use-a-Paw feller come down the stairs and the two of them jabbered together for a long time. Then Use-a-Paw went back to listen to the screechin' and caterwalin' and that Ivanov bloke went out and caught a cab back to the embassy. 'E was inside about 'alf an hour or so, and then 'e come out with a woman and they got in a coach driven by one of them fierce lookin' fellers they got guardin' the place, and off they went."

"Did Ivanov open the case for Yusopov?" asked French. "Did he show him any papers from the case?"

"No," said Vincent. "They had a mighty palaver, and then Use-

a-Paw musta told the other fellow to get on with it 'cause that's
when 'e lit out o' there and 'eaded for the embassy."

"And Ivanov and the woman had the case with them when they
left the embassy?" Endicott demanded.

"S'right," said Vincent.

"Do you have any idea which direction they're headed?" asked
French. He was as eager as a hound on the scent, eyes gleaming
with anticipation. I could tell he was anxious to get stuck into
that bastard Ivanov.

"I followed 'em as far as Greenwich. I'd say they're 'eadin' for
Dover."

"Greenwich!" Dizzy exclaimed. "However did you manage to
keep up with them for such a distance? And in this weather?"

Vincent's thin chest puffed like a bantam rooster's. "'Opped
on the back of the coach. They never knew I was there. I jumped
off when they got near Greenwich. I figured they was on their way
to the coast. I didn't fancy spendin' the night out in the open.
'Course," he added hastily (never missing the chance to put himself in the good graces of those who could do favors for him), "I
'ad to 'urry back here to tell you wot 'ad 'appened. You see, none
of those coves you left at the embassy to watch for that Russian
fellow 'ad seen a thing. They was 'uddled in the nearest doorway,
keepin' out of the snow."

"Damn and blast," said Endicott. "Heads will roll over this."

"You ran all the way here from Greenwich?" French asked. He
went to the sideboard, poured a jot of whisky into a glass and
handed it to Vincent. "Well done."

"Thank'ee, guv." The whisky disappeared in a trice.

"Any idea what time you left Ivanov and the woman in
Greenwich?"

"Must 'ave been 'leven or so. I thought I 'eard church bells."

French extracted his watch from his pocket. "Nearly one o'clock. Smith, telegraph our man in Dover to be on the lookout, and summon my carriage. I'll be on my way as soon as it arrives. Endicott?"

Endicott quaffed the last of his brandy. "Not this time, French. I'll let this be your show tonight. I need to alert Lord Derby to these latest developments. You'll let me know when you have the case?"

That was optimistic thinking. So far, the score stood at Russia-two, Britain-nil.

French was already flying out the door, with Dizzy shouting best wishes and good hunting to him and Vincent and I scrambling after him.

"I'm going with you, French," I panted as we clattered down the stairs.

"You're not," he huffed back. "And neither are you, Vincent."

"Oi, I found 'em for you. Why can't I be there when you cut that Russian's 'ead off?"

"Yes, why not?" I gasped as we skidded down the hallway.

French came to an abrupt halt, and since Vincent and I had been hot on his heels, this action of course resulted in the two of us piling into French like a Prussian express. Not for the first time that night, I found myself patting French's cheek and searching for signs of consciousness.

"Bloody hell."

Ah, he was alive.

"I don't know who's the bigger threat: you or Ivanov," he said, sitting up and clutching his walking stick.

"Look, I've no time to waste arguing with you two. India, you can go, if only because you might be of some use in dealing with the woman, who I presume must be Oksana or Arabella or whatever she's calling herself. Vincent, you must go to Lotus House and wait for us there. You've done a damned-fine job tonight, better than any of those so-called agents I have working for me, but this could be potentially dangerous. I can't ask you to place your life in jeopardy."

I guess he didn't have any qualms in asking me.

"Now, guv, that ain't fair," wailed Vincent. "I can 'andle meself. I've duked it out with cutthroats before. I ain't scared."

"I don't doubt your courage, Vincent. But India is a grown woman, and you, however experienced you think you may be, have not yet reached the age of majority. Now be a good lad, and do what I ask you. I'll be back to tell you how it ends."

His face softened as he saw Vincent's downcast expression. He reached out a hand to ruffle the boy's hair, thought better of it, and quickly thrust it into his pocket instead, pulling out a handful of coins.

"I want you to do something for me, Vincent. Tomorrow morning, I want you to go to the nearest bath house and give yourself a good wash. Then buy some new clothes and a proper coat and cap for this weather. Have a good meal—the biggest beefsteak you can eat—and a pudding." French rummaged through his pocket and produced a card. "Then come and see me at this address at ten o'clock in the morning on Friday. I'll have some work for you to do. All right?"

Reluctantly, Vincent took the card, and (with a great deal less reluctance) the money. I'd have laid odds that French would never see him again, but who am I to educate the world on the ways of man?

"You sure you don't need me tonight, guv?"

Vincent as supplicant was something I never thought I'd see.

"No, lad. Off you go now. Remember, be there on Friday."

I felt a pang of sympathy for the boy as he trudged off, which lasted only a moment, as I knew that if the tables had been turned and Vincent selected to go with French, the cheeky sod wouldn't have given me a second thought.

French watched him go. "Right," he said, as Vincent disappeared through the great double doors into the night. "My carriage should be here any moment."

He looked at me intently, his cool grey eyes searching mine.

"Are you sure you want to do this? It will be a long, cold night, and there may be no joy at the end of it. In fact, there might be a great deal of ugliness."

I smiled. "I'm a whore, French. I've seen ugliness."

"Men killed? Run through with a sword, or shot in the belly, with their entrails spreading over the floor?"

If he thought to scare me into abandoning our quest, he thought wrong.

"Speaking of shooting someone, it seems a sensible man would equip himself with a pistol, rather than that willow branch you call a sword."

He gave a great shout of laughter. "Can't frighten you off, India? So be it. Let's see if we can run that Russian wolf to ground."

French's carriage arrived, a smart brougham with tufted seats of butter-soft leather and velvet curtains at the windows. An elegantly attired coachman in a woolen greatcoat and mittens touched his whip to his hat, and French handed me aboard. Inside was a brazier of warm coals for us to rest our feet on and a plethora of warm rugs and furs to keep out the cold. I swaddled myself in them, propped my boots on the brazier and settled in for the long ride. Ivanov and Oksana had a two hour start on us, but the weather would surely have delayed them, for it was blowing hard and had been snowing for hours, and visibility was limited. Of course the weather wouldn't help our cause either, but at least French had had time to alert his agent at Dover, and perhaps he could arrange a delay in the Russian party's departure. For surely the object was to get the case out of England and into France as swiftly as possible, where a summary of its contents might be telegraphed to St. Petersburg without arousing the suspicion of an English telegrapher. Given the effort expended by the British government to recover the case, the Russians knew it contained political dynamite, and the most important thing now was to send the information on to the tsar and his generals at the first opportunity.

"We've a long night ahead of us, India. It's nearly eighty miles to Dover. We'll have to stop frequently to change horses. No animal could be expected to last long under these conditions. We'll push them as hard as we dare, but I shouldn't think we can get more than four or five miles from them. Evans, my driver, will need a rest now and then, as well. That's going to slow us down considerably."

"Ivanov and Oksana will face the same issue, though. And if they believe they escaped from the embassy unnoticed, they may not be travelling with the urgency that we are."

"True," said French.

"Have we any chance of catching them in this weather?"

"We'll catch them," he said tersely. "Even if I have to follow Ivanov to Russia, I'll catch that bloody bastard."

I didn't doubt that French meant it; the only question was whether we would get to Ivanov before he'd had a chance to telegraph the dismal facts about Britain's military readiness to his superiors in Russia.

We crossed the Thames by the Westminster Bridge, the swirling black water dimly visible in the lights from shore. Chunks of ice bobbed along in the rapids, obscured almost immediately by the wind-whipped snow and the darkness. I looked at the dismal scene and my heart sank; I feared we were on a fool's errand. Thereafter, there wasn't much to do but to draw the velvet curtains against the cold and huddle beneath the traveling rugs in a vain attempt to keep warm.

The horses fought the elements with all the strength they possessed, straining in the traces, their hooves fighting for purchase on the icy road. Occasionally, over the shrieking wind, I could hear the faint jingling of their harnesses and the hoarse shouts of the coachman urging them on. The coach laboured and strained too, lurching from side to side as the wheels slipped in the snow and the horses pressed on through the drifts.

There were no other conveyances on the road that night, and certainly no pedestrians struggling through the blizzard-like conditions, all sensible people being safely indoors, tucked up in bed with a heated brick or a hot water bottle at their feet. I envied them that simple existence, for here was I, setting out in a freezing brougham, in what could yet prove to be a futile attempt to recover Latham's case, with a companion who made the Sphinx seem loquacious. I sighed. Not much hope of stimulating conversation to relieve the boredom, not with French staring moodily into space and gnawing his lower lip. I settled down in the rugs and furs and dozed uneasily, dreaming of feather beds and hot toddies.

After what seemed like hours, we juddered to a halt, the coach rattling over frozen cobblestones. I pulled back the curtains to find that we had reached the shelter of an inn, with the coach drawn up before the door where a lantern burned weakly, illuminating the sign of the Black Bull.

"We'll change horses here," said French. "And let Evans warm himself for a bit. We'll have a bite to eat and something to drink, as well."

I was too cold to be hungry or thirsty, but I threw off the rugs and furs and followed French into the warm snug. A low fire burned in the grate, and French strode to it and piled on a half dozen logs, stirring the embers and creating a roaring blaze in a matter of minutes. The sleepy-eyed publican stumbled down the stairs, still fastening his braces, and soon placed ale, bread and cheese on the table in front of us. I suddenly realized I was famished and tackled the food and drink with all the grace and delicacy of a pig at a trough. Well, it had been many hours since I'd had something other than tea or toast, and it's deuced difficult to chase Russian spies through a blizzard on an empty stomach.

After our cold repast, French dickered with the landlord over the cost of food, drink and horseflesh, looking shocked at the landlord's exorbitant demands and parsimoniously rubbing a few coins between his fingers so our host could hear the chime of Her Majesty's gold. After protracted negotiations, the coins changed hands, with French sighing in exasperation at the preposterous rental for two broken down nags and the publican looking melancholy at letting go of his two best pacers for such a paltry sum.

With a clap of his hands and a shout, French summoned Evans, and the Black Bull's ostler was soon backing a brace of

swaybacked geldings into the traces of the brougham. There were
no gambados or caprioles from these dobbins. They would look
more at home pulling a plough than prancing proudly in front
of French's elegant equipage. Well, needs must, and all that. We
trundled off, Evans struggling with the reins as the newcomers
jumped and shied.

The stop at the Black Bull was the first of many that night.
French would spring from the brougham and hurry into the
King's Bollocks or the Blind Wanker or wherever we happened to
be, bellowing for the landlord and demanding food, drink, horses
and information about any Russians who happened to be in the
vicinity. French and the landlord would haggle over the price of
brandy and coach horses, with French spending money with a lav-
ish hand (I'd love to have seen Dizzy's face when he saw French's
expenses for this trip). At two of the inns where we stopped, we
struck lucky: Ivanov and Oksana had been there before us, doing
much the same as us, bartering for the rental of horses and forti-
fying themselves against the cold with liquor and victuals.

Upon hearing this news, French would roar for Evans to finish
his whisky and go charging out into the night. The fresh horses
were harnessed to the coach, only to flounder courageously for
three or four miles until, exhausted and covered with snow and
ice, Evans steered them into another inn for food and water and
a well-deserved rest. Between inns I'd drift into a dreamless sleep,
only to be awakened every minute or so when the coach hesitated
at a drift, then broke through with a lurch. The coals in the brazier would die and my feet would begin to freeze, making further
attempts at sleep futile. By then it would be time to change horses
again, and I'd alight into the frigid wind and scurry out behind
the inn to relieve myself, returning to the chilly rooms to bolt

down some cold beef or fowl, and to drink a tankard of mulled wine or cider.

The landlord would refill the brazier with a shovelful of coals from the fire, and we'd be off again, only to repeat the same exercise a short time later. After several hours of this, I was beginning to think the horses were having an easier night than I was.

Though I dozed intermittently, I don't think French slept the entire night. I'd wake to find him with the velvet curtains parted, staring out into the darkness, though there was nothing to see. I didn't dare say anything, as his face was hard as stone and his eyes flared with an inner fire that brooked no conversation. I'd thought him a thorough-going professional, and so he was, but I was sure his pursuit of Ivanov had now taken on a personal aspect. I just hoped that when we came face-to-face with Ivanov and Oksana, French wouldn't let his feelings run away with him and do something stupid, such as challenging Ivanov to a fencing match when Ivanov's only weapon was a pistol. At least one of us was prepared; I felt the weight of the British Bulldog in my purse and calculated how to avoid shooting French if he persisted in attacking Ivanov with his swordstick.

Near dawn I roused myself from sleep to find French silently contemplating me, his arms crossed over his chest.

"What is it?" I yawned and stretched, noting that I'd lost all feeling in my feet and wondering when we would make our next stop. A warm fire and a cup of tea would be just the ticket.

"Who are you, India?" asked French. He was staring at me with the intense scrutiny Mrs. Drinkwater would give a mess of kidneys for the evening's pie.

"Who am I?"

"Don't repeat my question, India. You're stalling for time. Tell me, who are you?"

His question caught me off guard. To date, in our brief acquaintance, he'd shown no personal interest in me at all, something I attributed to the fact that he already knew everything about me that he needed to know: I was a whore, susceptible to blackmail and unexpectedly drawn to the excitement of the game.

"You know who I am. I'm the abbess of Lotus House."

"Yes, I'm aware of that fact. But that hardly defines who you really are. There are a number of anomalies about you that require some explanation."

"Do they? I wasn't aware that I had to explain myself to you, or to anyone else for that matter."

French ignored the rebuff. He's very good at that sort of thing.

"For example, there's your voice."

"My voice?"

"Your elocution, to be precise. You speak like an educated woman."

"I wasn't aware of any laws prohibiting prostitutes from speaking the English language correctly."

"And you have at least a passing acquaintance with Trollope and Shakespeare."

"A girl picks up quite a bit of knowledge around a brothel, if she keeps her ears open. Useless bits of information, really. But sometimes you can impress a customer with them. You'd be surprised what some fellows want from their bints. I knew one cove who couldn't get it up unless his judy recited 'The Charge of the Light Brigade.' Must have had a thing about young men and horses."

"So you're a magpie, collecting the sparkly bits of information that you hear and storing them away, dropping them into the conversation for the benefit of your clients. No education beyond that?"

"Not what you'd call a proper one, but I can add and subtract and, if it's not too difficult, do some elementary long division. Oh, and I can sign my name."

He gave me a skeptical look. "There's more to you than meets the eye. I wonder why you try to hide it."

I was growing irritated at this conversation. My private life was my own, and there was a limit to how much intrusion I'd tolerate. "You're the bloody spy, French. If you want to know more about me, presumably you have the resources to find out."

He smiled. "I wouldn't presume, India. I must admit that I am curious about you, but I respect your privacy."

I resisted the urge to feel his forehead, fearing that he'd contracted a fever in these appalling weather conditions, for nothing else could surely explain this very un-French behavior. It was time to turn the tables.

"As long as we're becoming better acquainted with each other, I've a few questions of my own," I said.

"You didn't answer any of my questions, India. But go ahead and ask me if you like. I reserve the right not to answer any of yours."

"Fair enough. For starters, do you have a Christian name?"

"I do. My parents insisted on it."

"Oh, so you have parents."

"Most people do. It seems a prerequisite for existence."

"I thought you might have been conjured into being by some force of nature."

"Hardly. Next question."

"You haven't answered the first."

"I expect you could find out my Christian name. I'm not the only person in England with a network of agents."

"If you're referring to Vincent, his limitations include illiteracy and a lack of access to Debrett's."

"Well then, you're an intelligent woman. You'll have to sleuth it out on your own."

"I hardly think you'd put me through the exercise for something mundane, like James or Henry. Your parents must have been unkind. I'm beginning to think you're ashamed of your name. It must be something hideous."

"Hideous?"

"Yes. Like Endeavour, perhaps."

"Not Endeavour, no. Nothing quite so Bunyanesque. And nothing run-of-the-mill like John or William, either." He peered at me in the gloom. "By the way, did any of your clients provide you with a précis of *Pilgrim's Progress* at some time in your career?"

"I'll admit to perusing a chapter or two, but some of the concepts are hard going for a whore, especially all that claptrap about virtue." I settled back in my seat, wrapping the traveling rug around me. It was damned cold in the brougham, but at least the game was amusing and passed the time.

"Ranelagh?"

"No."

"Gervase?"

"No."

"Peveley?"

"No."

"Theobald?"

"Good Lord, no. And while I don't mind you entertaining yourself on this journey, since it's turning out to be rather longer than expected, I find this exercise rather tedious."

"Oh, very well. You won't tell me your name. What is it exactly that you do for the government?"

"I work for the prime minister."

"Doing what?"

"Whatever he wants me to do."

"So you're Dizzy's man. Tory to the core?"

"I'm attached to the office of the prime minister, not the man. If the present government fell and Gladstone moved into Downing Street, I'd be at his beck and call."

"I thought you didn't like Gladstone."

"Whether I like him or not is irrelevant. I serve the prime minister."

"Have you an official title? Should I be addressing you as Special Agent or something?"

For the first time since we left London, a smile creased French's face. "I do have a title, but plain French will do."

"I'll bet you're admired for your discretion."

"It's one of the things that makes me useful."

The brougham gave a sudden lurch and made a sharp turn, which signaled our arrival at yet another inn. This one was the Green Man, which made me yearn momentarily for a hot London summer and strolls through Hyde Park. But when I stepped outside, the air was still frigid, the wind wailing, and the snow hurtling down. I hadn't thought the weather could worsen, but it surely had. I staggered through a knee-high drift into the warmth of the building and headed directly to the fire where I collapsed on a bench and propped my feet on the fender to warm them. I seldom drank spirits before noon, but whisky was indicated.

I was about to summon the landlord, but he and French were engaged in deep conversation (well, French was; the landlord was rubbing sleep from his eyes and fumbling with his buttons). The landlord listened drowsily to French, perking up now and then, probably at the mention of French's going rate for the best horses available. Then French asked a question, and the landlord came to life, nodding vigorously and waving his hands emphatically. French turned to me, face shining with triumph.

"Ivanov and Oksana were here not more than forty minutes ago," he said. "We've nearly caught them."

"Good news, indeed. But have you noticed the weather has taken a turn for the worse? We seem to be stopping more frequently to change horses. Can we manage to get closer to them in these conditions, or will they make Dover before us?"

French was frowning, chewing his lip in concentration. "You're right, we need to move faster. The brougham is deuced awkward on these roads. No purchase in the wheels, and too difficult to maneuver. Can you ride, India?"

"A horse?"

"Of course, I mean a horse. Can you ride?"

"Badly."

"Damn and blast," said French.

Well, it's not my fault my mother couldn't afford riding lessons. She'd been more concerned with seeing that I had a crust of bread at least once a day.

The landlord had decried my parched condition and had brought a bottle of whisky, glasses, and bread and meat to the table. He deposited the items on the table before me and coughed deferentially. "Pardon me, sir, but if it's a faster form of transpor-tation you're in need of, I may have just the ticket. If you'll follow me out to the stable, sir, I'll show you what I have in mind."

I left them to it; there was no point in my going along as French would do just exactly as he chose and ignore my opinion as to matters of transportation. So I introduced myself to the bottle of whisky (and shockingly bad, it was, but after it took the roof off your mouth it settled in your stomach with a lovely glow that nearly made up for the appalling taste). Another bottle of this turpentine would be the perfect accompaniment for our travels, and I helped myself to a bottle from behind the bar. The landlord returned then, stamping snow from his feet and brushing snow from his hat, and cursing the weather with enthusiasm. I told him to add the bottle to French's bill and was looking around to see if there might be any other items of interest I could charge to the taxpayer, when French came striding in, smiling broadly and clapping his hands with glee.

"On your feet, India! We're off!"

French never spoke in exclamation marks, so I knew he must have made trumps this time in a big way.

"Come and look," he said, gesturing toward the frozen waste outside. "Ivanov doesn't stand a chance now. We'll be on him like hounds on a stag before the morning is over."

I went to the door and spotted Evans holding the heads of two of the typical inn horses we'd been able to hire. Even the best of them were little better than half-starved, hammer-headed nags, and these were no different. This time, however, they were not harnessed to French's brougham, but to the object which had ex-cited such confidence in French that he'd run Ivanov to ground in short order: a bright red sleigh, with curved runners and a rak-

ish silhouette. And no roof at all. As I watched, the snow was piling up on the seats. Oh, dear. How dedicated was I to the chase?
It had been one thing, traveling in the relative comfort of the
brougham, with a brazier of coals and rugs for warmth. An open
sleigh in the midst of a raging snow squall was quite another.
French had flung open the door to the sleigh, brushing the snow
aside vigorously to clear the seat for me.

"Come along, India. There's no time to waste."

When I didn't vault in at his command, he turned to me and
gave me a piercing glance. Perhaps I looked a little bedraggled out
there in the wind, the feathers on my hat drooping and my skirts
wet from the snow. In any case, he came to stand before me, and
as he did, his face softened a bit. It was such a shocking sight that
I found it hard to pay attention to what he had to say.

"Do you want to stay here? I can send a man back for you when
I reach Dover. You needn't worry about coming on with me. The
journey's been difficult till now, and God knows, it will get worse
before it's over. This isn't a job for a woman. I shan't blame you
for staying."

That smug devil. There was no way I'd back down from a challenge like that, and he knew it.

"Oh, stop that insipid drivel, and let's get on with it," I snarled.

ELEVEN

The sleigh had room only for two, so we left Evans standing in the road before the inn in the first light of dawn, waving mournfully after us. I rather envied him, for the eggs and bacon, tots of whisky and warm feather bed he'd soon be enjoying. As for French and me, we were bundled to the teeth in rugs and blankets, shoulders hunched against the wind and snow. He flicked the whip over the horses' backs, and they pressed forward, the sleigh following smoothly after them.

French whooped and urged on the horses, and I had to agree it was a completely different experience than the hours spent in the brougham, lumbering over one mogul after another and sliding precariously around corners on two wheels. This ride was smooth and effortless in comparison; 'tis true the horses still had to struggle through the heavy snow, but at least they no longer had to drag the brougham through the drifts. I was just thinking how much faster and more efficiently we could now travel when there was an almighty thump, the sleigh skidded sideways in the road, and French fought the reins as the horses shied violently.

"What the devil . . ." he exclaimed.

"We must have hit a rock," I said, turning round in my seat to look for the culprit, but the snow lay smooth and unbroken except for the trail churned by the horses and the tracks of the sleigh's runners.

"It didn't feel like a rock," said French.

"How frequently do you drive a sleigh?"

"It's not my driving skills. Next spring there'll be a great bloody boulder in the middle of the road back there, mark my words."

He subsided into silence, his attention focused on the horses and trying to discern the road beneath the snow. I snuggled into the rugs and considered our situation. We were still miles from the coast, and the weather would likely have an effect on shipping as well as ground transportation. We might be fortunate enough to catch Ivanov and Oksana before they made Dover, but even if we didn't, they might find it difficult to locate a ship sailing for Calais in this weather, assuming, of course, that they were making for France. That seemed logical, given its proximity, but that was only a guess. It seemed to me that if we didn't intercept them before they landed on French soil, the game was up, despite French's brave words to the effect that he'd follow Ivanov to St. Petersburg if necessary. I for one would not be accompanying him if he did. After this experience, I couldn't bring myself to think about winter in Russia.

In fact, the vista that presented itself to my eyes seemed depressingly like what one would encounter if one were foolish enough to take a tour of Mother Russia. In an open sleigh. In the middle of the winter. A frozen wasteland of fields and low hills surrounded us, broken by copses of trees, their limbs black against the snowy pastures. Here and there, a thin line of smoke marked the existence of a lonely farmhouse or inn. The wind moaned and torrents of snow poured over us, accumulating rapidly on any exposed surface, including yours truly. Every five minutes I had to lean over to shake the snow off my hat or I'd become top heavy. It seemed as though we had already followed Ivanov into the heart of Russia.

I had thought myself into a funk, which is unusual for me, as being a madam requires a great deal of optimism and perseverance, for God knows, it's not an easy life, what with the interfering busybodies trying to rescue me from a life of moral turpitude, the heartless peelers and the witless bints scratching and clawing at each other like a roomful of cats. Perhaps it was just the effects of several nights without sleep, the numbing cold and a particularly vicious brandy at one of the inns along the way, but whatever the reason, I was feeling glum.

I thought French might be as well. After the initial exhilaration caused by our change in transport, he'd sat hunched over the reins in brooding silence, likely thinking the same uplifting thoughts as I, excluding the part about the busybodies, peelers and whores, of course. His thoughts were probably preoccupied with inferior ports, lackadaisical butlers and the Endicotts of the world.

If I wasn't careful, I could lapse into a full scale attack of self-pity, and as my mother used to say, my girl, you've no time for that. Right. I straightened my spine and stamped my feet briskly.

"What's our plan, French?"

"Plan?"

He'd been miles away, possibly composing a letter to his wine merchant or considering the fabric for a new suit. Well, I must admit that's unfair. He was probably thinking of affairs of state and such, as he seemed the dedicated type.

"The plan for what we do when we catch up to Ivanov and Oksana. How do you propose to stop them?"

"Don't you worry. I have a plan."

"Is it a state secret, or can you share it with me?"

He mumbled and flapped the reins.

"You don't have a plan, do you?" I said, aghast. "Do you mean we've driven all this way, in this weather, and you don't have any idea what to do when we run into the Russians?"

He looked at me irritably. "I don't have a plan because I don't yet know what we'll encounter when we find them. I'll decide then what we should do. What is this preoccupation of yours with plans? 'The best laid schemes,' etcetera, etcetera. I'm at my best when I'm freelancing."

Well, that had struck a nerve, which meant he had no plan at all. I think he really believed all that rot about freelancing and thinking on his feet. Thank God one of us was prepared. I'd yet to see the hard case who could say no to the business end of a British Bulldog. So I settled down (sullenly) to enjoy the sleigh ride, with the wind howling and whipping hard pellets of snow into my face and my feet slowly turning to ice. The sun had risen by then, but there was no warmth to it, its rays failing entirely to penetrate the heavy cloud cover and falling snow.

"I think our best hope is to follow them into Dover and snatch the case from them there," said French abruptly. I suppose he was trying to be conciliatory. "They'll have to arrange transport, which means they'll be out in the town, exposed to attack. We'll take the case and collect the two of them at the same time. They can spend a bit of time in gaol, contemplating the virtues of a democratic government."

"And Yusopov? Presumably Ivanov shared the information on British troop strength with him."

"I'd agree it's likely he did. Yet Yusopov will be at a disadvantage if we snatch Ivanov and Oksana. He'll have to send another agent out of the country with the news, or try to send it via diplomatic pouch. In either case, we'll have the embassy under surveillance and can interdict the messenger."

I contemplated the success to date in interdicting Russian agents with stolen information, but diplomatically refrained from comment.

"Wouldn't it be simpler just to make Yusopov disappear? You know, a dreadful accident with two whores and a swing, for example?"

French chuckled. "A useful idea. We'll see what Dizzy has to say about that."

"If you're planning a flimp, we should have brought that little blighter Vincent. He's the finest fingersmith I know."

"Yes, he'd be useful in this situation. But I couldn't countenance exposing a minor to such danger."

"I hate to disillusion you, but Vincent is about as innocent as a baby cobra."

French's stiff face cracked into a smile. "I don't doubt it. I'd just like to see that he lives to become a full-grown cobra. Here," he said, and handed me the reins.

"I've never driven a team in my life," I said, pulling sharply on one set of reins and dropping the other. The horses looked back at me with, I swear, disdain, if not loathing. They knew an amateur when they saw one.

"High time you learned, then. I need some rest. While I'm resting, I'll think of a plan."

I punched him in the arm, which made not the slightest impression as he was protected by several layers of blankets.

"Any advice on how to handle this sleigh?"

"Don't hit any rocks," he said, shut his eyes and promptly dozed off.

I was nervous as a whore in church, as they say, for the first half hour, constantly tugging at the reins and trying to direct the team one way or another until I finally figured out that they had done this a damned sight more often than I had, and I'd be better off just leaving them alone to find the best route. The only thing I had to be aware of was the horses' tendency to slow down unless I reminded them occasionally to keep up the pace with a flick of the whip across their rumps. Not unlike dealing with a bunch of tarts, come to think of it.

I'd settled into a nice little routine, with my mind elsewhere (on warm fires and dry clothes, to be exact), when I noticed a change in the sleigh's speed. I glanced up sharply and noticed that the horses had broken into a jog, something they'd been unable to do previously because of the depth of snow in the road. Now they were clearly following a broken trail through the drifts, one made by a coach and horses, and one made quite recently, as the falling snow had yet to fill the tracks, leaving only a soft sprinkling, like icing sugar, over the ruts from the coach. Was it Ivanov and Oksana and their Cossack guard? Who else would be out in this weather, traveling the route to the coast? It had to be our quarry.

I prodded French with my elbow, and he was instantly awake. "What is it?"

I pointed at the tracks with my whip.

"Ivanov," said French. I could swear he licked his lips.

"Time to make a plan, French."

He gave me a withering glance and relieved me of the reins and whip. He touched the horses lightly and they increased their pace a fraction, but it had been a few miles since we'd left the Green Man, and the pace and the distance had taken their toll. The nags were winded, straining at the tugs, and beginning to stagger. French noticed it, too.

"Let's hope we come to an inn soon. We need fresh horses."

This being England, where the national sport is drinking (I've never understood the chauvinistic urge to denigrate the Irish for their habits; in my book any John Bull was stiffish competition for any Paddy in the drinks department), we soon found one. The Golden Lion, this one was called, and it occupied a lonely knoll miles from anywhere. I was damned glad to see the rampant yellow lion on the sign and smell the wood smoke from the fire, as my feet and hands were cramped from the cold.

French pulled up into the yard, spraying snow and shouting for the stable boy. A sullen youth, chinless and vacant-eyed, came reluctantly out into the weather.

"Your finest horses, boy, and be quick about it." French chucked the reins to the young man, catapulted himself from the sleigh, and charged into the inn, bellowing for the landlord.

"Eh?" The stable boy scratched his head, dislodging his cap in the process, then spent a considerable amount of time locating the cap in the drifts and knocking the snow from it before replacing it on his head.

"Eh?" he repeated.

"Oh, for heaven's sake. Have you got any horses for hire?" I said.

"Oh. Aye. But they ain't the finest we got. Those went to some foreign blokes who just come through here."

"How long ago were they here?" I asked, but the concept of time clearly eluded the youngster. He scratched his head again, lost his cap again, and I sat through the pantomime for the second time.

"Never mind," I said. "Give us the best horses in the stable, quick as you can."

I followed French into the inn and found him in close conversation with the landlord. I sidled up to listen.

"Yup. They come through here not twenty minutes ago. Hired four horses, and paid in gold, they did. Most custom I've had in a week."

"Did they seem to be in a hurry?" asked French.

The landlord nestled an unshaven chin in one hand and searched the ceiling for an answer. After a lengthy pause (they weren't a sharpish lot at the Golden Lion), he said, "Why, no, they didn't seem to be. They didn't hang around, but they didn't seem pressed for time or such like."

French shot me a triumphant look. As long as our prey remained unaware they were being pursued, they would likely be moving at a slower speed, conserving their horses' energy rather than pushing the creatures in these brutal conditions.

"I need two horses," said French.

"The boy is harnessing them now," I said. "But Ivanov and Oksana took the four best; we'll have to make do with what we can get."

The landlord bristled. "Here, now. There's no call to run down my animals. Every horse I've got is top-drawer."

"I'm sure they are," said French soothingly. "How much?"

I left the two of them arguing over a price, while I availed myself of the facilities (primitive) and had a quick brandy (ghastly). Thus fortified, I joined French in the yard, where the stable boy was settling the breast collars around the animals' chests while French looked on in dismay.

The landlord's "top-drawer" horses were a bony, spavined pair, with coats coated in mud and matted tails. They looked like they'd just done a grueling run for the Royal Mail and now needed a good rest and a bucket of feed. Then they'd be ready for the glue factory.

"Ye gods," said French, and passed a weary hand over his eyes. "How are we supposed to catch Ivanov with these beasts?"

"Take heart," I said. "Do you really think Ivanov's horses are much better than this? And they've got to drag a coach with at least three people on board—Ivanov, Oksana, and the Cossack guard. I like our chances."

As if Mother Nature had decided to take sides in this chess match, the wind chose that moment to subside to a mournful whine, the skies lightened, and for the first time in eighteen hours, the snow slackened, until only a few flakes drifted past our faces. The horses huffed and whinnied and stamped their feet as if, despite appearances to the contrary, they were eager to join in the chase. The omens looked good, as they so often do just before disaster strikes, but of course we were unaware of what lay before us.

We climbed into the sleigh, adjusted our rugs, and French spoke encouragingly to the horses. God knows the poor nags needed heartening, for French had that mad look in his eye, as if the scent of Ivanov had reached his nostrils.

As we turned out of the stable yard and gathered speed, the sleigh bucked and slewed wildly. French grasped the reins and uttered a series of oaths.

"Must you hit every rock between London and Dover?" I asked, after I'd recovered my hat and fastened it firmly on my head.

"It's not as though I can see them under the snow," he said. "It's hard enough just staying on the road."

The horses did their damnedest to keep a lively pace, but they were exhausted and wobbly in the traces, their breath coming in laboured gasps. French was chomping at the bit, hunching forward on the edge of his seat and scanning the road ahead of us with the intensity of a ferret going down a rabbit hole, but he knew the horses were giving all they had, and we'd have to be satisfied with that.

We pottered along for a while, with French grousing continually about the lack of speed and me looking at the scenery, as there was little else to do. The countryside lay in frozen silence, broken only by the wheezing of the horses, the metallic jingling of their harnesses and the susurration of the sleigh's runners on the snow. The road wound through snowy fields and tangled thickets, crossed frozen streams, rambled through acres of apple orchards, skirted the steep sides of the valleys. The road was a single, sunken track through this area, often bounded by thick hedges that made French swear at the loss of visibility and grumble until we reached an opening where we could see across the fields to the thin black line of the road before us.

I was thinking it was rather pretty, in a country sort of way, but I'm a London girl through and through and found the lack of dirt and smoke, spectacle and noise, a bit unnerving. The open vistas and the intense silence made me edgy. It was then I felt French spring from his seat like a startled hare.

"Is it them? Can you see them?" I was infected with his excitement.

"Perhaps," he said. "Take the reins."

He thrust them into my hands as he said this, then in one agile movement bounded onto the seat beside me and, using my shoulder to balance, stared hard into the distance.

"What do you see?"

"It's a coach of some sort. It's gone into a copse, but there's a straight bit of road ahead and the coach should be coming out any minute."

His hand on my shoulder was quivering with energy.

"Well?" I said.

"Wait a minute. I think I see it. It's, it's . . ." His hand tightened on my shoulder so sharply that I gasped.

"It's a coach and four." He laughed aloud. "And there's a bloody great Cossack holding the reins. I can see his light blue hat from here. We're not a half mile behind them, India. Give us more speed."

I whipped the horses obligingly, but after a few steps at a half gallop, they settled back into a slow, painful jog. I'd gladly have used the whip on Oksana (I remember distinctly it was her who plumped for leaving Rowena and me in the embassy attic), but I couldn't bring myself to wallop these poor nags.

French dropped into the seat. "Bloody hell. They haven't got it in them, have they?"

"Slow and steady wins the race," I said, but I knew the horses didn't have the heart. "Look here, we've almost caught up with them with these two horses. As long as the Cossack doesn't catch on to the fact that we're following them, I believe we can stay within striking distance. And even if he does turn around and see us here, who's to say that we're not just a couple of innocent travelers, enjoying a sleigh ride now that the weather has cleared?"

We played a game of cat and mouse for the best part of an hour, with the Russians riding blithely along in front of us, carefully preserving their horses' strength, seemingly oblivious to the red sleigh that followed in their wake. French and I let the horses jog along slowly, but we made ground anyway, our horses not having to cut a new track in the drifted snow with each step but traveling in the ruts left by the Russians' horses. And we had the advantage in that the sleigh was light as a feather, compared to the coach, with three people on board and no doubt all the luggage needed in Paris or St. Petersburg or whatever city they'd chosen for their final destination.

Each time the coach wound out of sight behind some curve of the road, we found ourselves a little closer when it emerged again into view.

"If only we had fresh horses," French sighed. He glanced at me from under his brows. "Or less weight in the sleigh."

"Don't get any ideas, French. Without me, you're only one man without a plan. By the way, how's the plan coming?"

But I was not destined to hear French's plan (though I doubted seriously that one existed, even at that stage in the chase), for just then the coach approached a long hairpin curve in the road, which turned nearly back upon itself, leaving the occupants of the coach and the occupants of the sleigh staring at each other across five hundred feet of frozen hop vines.

The Cossack on the driver's seat glanced casually at us and

raised his whip to his fleece hat in greeting. Ivanov was seated at the window facing us, and as his head turned nonchalantly in our direction, both French and I looked away to avoid being seen. But it was too late. There was a shout from the coach, and the Cossack guard had swiveled in his seat, probably thinking his passenger was having a heart attack or had finally gone stark raving mad at being confined in that coach for so many hours. But Ivanov had his head and arm out the window, gesticulating at us and shouting up at the guard in Russian, his voice carrying across the field to us. The Cossack, responding no doubt to the shouted commands, laid the whip to his nags, and they surged forward against the drifted snow, struggling mightily.

French seized the reins from my hands and snapped the whip over our own horses' backs. I'll say this for them, they were game, but they were in no condition to play at Roman chariot races with the coach. They surged forward at French's urging and struggled to maintain a steady trot, but they were both winded and blowing hard, sides heaving, and I knew it was only a matter of time before they had to stop or drop dead in the traces.

"Listen, French," I said, clutching my hat with one hand and hanging on to the side of the sleigh with the other. "We can't maintain this pace and neither can they."

French's face was a mask of determination. "We're not slowing down, India. If the horses collapse, we'll walk. But now that I've got Ivanov in my sights, I'm not stopping unless I'm forced to do so."

It's not as though I am a member of the Royal Society for the Prevention of Cruelty to Animals, but I hated to watch these gallant brutes be pushed beyond their limits, all because a civil servant had demonstrated the questionable judgment of bringing secret documents to a whorehouse.

The coach vanished around a bend in the road, and French let out a roar of frustration. I thought it would be an impolitic time to mention equine welfare again and so I concentrated on not losing my hat and what French and I would say to one another when the horses died. And then there was the small matter of what would happen next with the Russkis. Surely we were drawing close to another inn, and they would have to stop there for fresh horses. We'd be pulling into the stable yard before they'd have the chance to harness the horses and bolt, and then what would we do? Well, the subject of plans would probably be as welcome as that of not whipping the nags, but since I might be called on to face Ivanov with a set of barkers in his hand, I had a vested interest in what might transpire.

"French," I said, as we came to the bend around which the coach had disappeared, "I really think—"

I was flung forward out of my seat and narrowly missed landing on the horses' backsides as they juddered to a halt in the road, heads tossing wildly, nostrils flaring, and snow spraying out from their skidding hooves. Beside me French lurched forward, his boots scrabbling for purchase on the sleigh floor, and the next thing I saw was French flying out of the sleigh, caroming off one of the horses, and landing in a drift of snow along the roadside. Poor bastard. I had assumed his role of government agent required certain demonstrations of agility and dexterity, but apparently not. Since I'd known him, French had spent an inordinate amount of time taking pratfalls in the snow. The thought that he'd been helped along on two occasions by yours truly did not trouble my conscience.

The horses were still stamping and plunging, and French came up spitting snow and profanities, so it took a moment before I understood the reason for our precipitate halt. The Russian coach stood directly in the roadway before us, and our horses, coming quickly around the bend in the road, had stopped only inches from the back of the coach.

My heart sank as Ivanov came striding through the snow, stroking his mustache and smirking broadly at French. He looked right at home, as though he was on his own estate in Russia, ready to sort out a particularly recalcitrant serf and enjoy it while he was at it. The Cossack driver was a step behind, and he looked to be a right rotter, with a pitted face and an evil scar tracing a red slash across his face. He was smirking, too. As expected, Ivanov held a pistol, leveled at French, and the Cossack had drawn his *shashka* and was eyeing me as though I was a particularly succulent roast beef ready for carving.

"Mr. French." Ivanov's voice was thick with satisfaction. Well, he could afford to be arrogant, as his rival was still thrashing about in the snow, trying to find his feet and cursing like a sailor. But at Ivanov's words, French lay still and glared up at him. I wouldn't have wanted to be on the receiving end of that scowl, but it fazed Ivanov not a bit.

"'Lo, Ivanov," said French, cool as you please. "Remind me to acquaint you with some of the rudiments of sound driving when you have the time."

Ivanov grinned mirthlessly. "So you play the prankster at a moment like this? What is that expression? Whistling past the graveyard? Perhaps this is some of the famous British sangfroid in the face of defeat? Eh? Is that it? Putting on a brave face for Miss Black, when you know very well you've lost the game?"

"The game isn't over, Ivanov."

"Really? Let's see now. I'm holding you at gunpoint, and at a word, the guard here will leave Miss Black with a scar to match his own. I don't think you have any countermoves left."

I shivered and did my best to look miserable (easily done in the frigid air) and frightened (no playacting required there), and gripped my purse as though I were some society ninny whose worst nightmare was to be separated from her rouge and a clean kerchief. My purse held those things, too, along with the Bulldog I was so fond of.

Ivanov cocked his head to one side and smiled triumphantly. "I've read the memorandum to the prime minister, prepared by your War Office. Believe me, if those idiots were staffing our military offices, I'd consider resigning my commission. But we would have dealt with the problem of bureaucratic incompetence by sending the imbeciles responsible for such inaccuracies off to a penal labour camp to contemplate their ineptitude."

French remained silent, but seemed to be considering the wisdom of making just such a suggestion to Dizzy, if he ever made it back to the prime minister's office.

"In any case," said Ivanov, "I now know that Disraeli has been running a bluff for the past few weeks. Not a wise move, with such lax security. Your security services need some seeing to, my friend. Those agents you placed around the embassy? Disgraceful. A child could have eluded them."

As Vincent had amply demonstrated that fact, it was difficult to argue the point. French didn't bother. With as much dignity as he could muster, he struggled to a sitting position, brushing the snow from his shoulders and pushing his black hair from his face. Ivanov took a step backward, keeping the pistol leveled at French's chest.

"If you've read the memorandum," said French, "then I'll have to kill you."

I thought this would send Ivanov into a paroxysm of laughter, but he only shrugged. "I thought you'd feel that way. But as you can see, my friend, I control the situation. And I've no intention of giving you the opportunity to kill me."

"I need be given nothing," said French, with contempt. And then the snow exploded as he reared up from his seated position and lashed out with one leg, catching Ivanov behind the knees and toppling him backward into the drifts. In an instant, French was on him like a mongoose on a snake, one hand gripping Ivanov's wrist, forcing Ivanov's revolver to the ground, and the other hand locked around Ivanov's throat.

The Cossack gave a guttural exclamation and started forward, but in a twinkling I had the Bulldog out of my purse and in my hand, and I obtained the Cossack's attention by swatting him on the ear with the revolver as he charged past me. He skidded to a halt and turned a thunderous visage in my direction, his face crimson with anger and that hideous scar now a white seam across his face. It was enough to scare the doughtiest of whores (and I'm not her). I briefly considered the consequences of abandoning French to his fate, but as I cast about for a bolt hole, it was all too evident that there was nowhere to run in this frozen wilderness. I'd have to stand and fight, even if the fellow coming toward me did look like an extra from *The Tragical History of Doctor Faustus*.

The guard let out a blood-curdling scream (he evidently did sound effects, as well) and raised his *shashka* over his head. A man's masculinity must be a fragile thing, seeing as how he tends to overreact when he's smacked by a woman. A little cuff on the ear from another man and the Cossack would probably have settled in to dispatch his attacker with an air of professional boredom. But let a member of the fairer sex count coup on his stern self, and the bloke was out of his mind. He took a slow, menacing step toward me, and licked his lips as if to show me how much he'd enjoy displaying his skill with that bloody great knife of his.

I waved the Bulldog in front of his face, just in case he hadn't realized that I'd boxed his ears with a .442 caliber pistol. That brought him up short for a minute, as he cogitated a bit on whether he could run me through before I could shoot him between the eyes. Evidently he liked his chances (most men do, when it comes to women, and that's a great advantage to us all, my dears), because he gave me another one of those evil smiles, gripped the *shashka* in both hands and charged.

Now, I've never killed a man in cold blood before. I didn't have time to consider whether there was any wiggle room in the sixth commandment, but I thought these might be considered extenuating circumstances by the Almighty. I don't usually concern myself overly much with moral issues anyway. So when that great Cossack oaf bore down on me with the clear intent of cleaving off my head like this year's Christmas goose, I held my ground, raised my revolver, took careful aim at the crossed bandoliers on his chest and pulled the trigger.

The .442-grain bullet spun him around like a child's top; the *shashka* went flying out of his hand to bury itself in a drift, and the Cossack crashed to the ground with the sound of a boulder rolling downhill. At the shot, every crow within a mile had risen into the air, and their raucous calling broke the heavy silence.

Out of the corner of my eye, I saw that Ivanov and French had ceased their wrestling match, stunned by the roar of the gunshot, which was still echoing in the cold air. French looked around wildly, and then, noticing a revolver in my hand and the absence of one large, scar-faced Cossack, renewed his efforts to subdue Ivanov. French had Ivanov's pistol hand pinned beneath his body and was trying to drive his thumb into the Russian major's eyes (not cricket, that, but who gives a damn?). Ivanov was twisting like an eel, trying to extract his pistol from under his body and fend off French's probing fingers at the same time. To tell the truth, this match wouldn't have attracted many of the touts; it looked strictly amateurish. Both men were encumbered by their heavy coats and gloves, and the snow made footing treacherous, which resulted in the two of them grappling and thrashing around, sending the snow flying, but neither gaining much of an advantage over the other. It looked like a schoolboy punch-up on the athletics field; the combatants would retire as soon as they'd run out of steam, perhaps bleeding from the nose or mouth, but mostly just sweating and out of breath.

A game changer was needed, namely me. I plunged through the snow toward the two men, which was no small feat in itself, as my skirts were soon encrusted with the icy stuff and heavy as lead. I halted a few feet from the two, who were still locked in an embrace, panting hard and faces squeezed with effort.

"Ivanov," I shouted, and pointed the Bulldog at him. "I've killed your Cossack. You may as well give up now."

Two heads popped into view, bearing similar expressions of incredulity. They must have thought I'd fired a warning shot. I do believe my stock rose dramatically with the two antagonists.

"You've killed Dmitri?" said Ivanov, wheezing asthmatically.

"Dead, by God," said French, with not a little admiration, I thought.

"That's right," I said. "A *shashka* is no match for a Webley. Something," I added witheringly to French, "I've been trying to get through that bloody thick skull of yours for some time. Now, Major, please release your grip on that pistol and stand up."

Very slowly, he complied. French took the gun from Ivanov's hand and backed away until a distance of several feet separated the two men. I'd have done the same thing; having seen Ivanov's panther-like ferocity at close quarters, I wouldn't get near the man either. All he needed was half a chance, and he'd be on you.

"It is you who now holds the whip hand," said Ivanov, with a graceful little bow to French as he acknowledged his defeat. He spread his arms open theatrically, baring his chest. "It remains only for you to shoot me, and the secrets of your bungling government will be safe."

"I doubt you would hesitate, Ivanov, but I draw the line at shooting an unarmed man," said French.

There's that damned public school indoctrination, always cropping up at the most inconvenient times.

"You'll return with us to London, where you will be our guest for an extended stay. It won't be Claridge's, but neither will it be a labour camp."

"That will cause some outrage among my Russian brethren."

"Not if they don't know about it. I rather think you'll set sail from Dover, Ivanov, but never land in Calais."

"You cannot hold a Russian major indefinitely, without charges. You British are renowned for your system of justice." Ivanov looked defiant.

"I wouldn't rely on that if I were you. If you're tried at all, it will be for espionage against the state. Not quite the same thing as shoplifting some cuff links. As it is, I would not be surprised if you were shunted off to some dreary castle in Scotland, until things die down and the knowledge you possess is no longer relevant."

"I am prepared to suffer what I must for the sake of my country," said Ivanov.

"Spoken like a true patriot," said French. I felt ill.

Then Ivanov grinned wolfishly. "But not this time, I think."

An arm encircled my throat and a body pressed close to mine. This in itself was not unduly alarming, but the small, cold circle of metal pushed against my temple was.

"Drop your weapon, India, or you shall share Dmitri's fate," said a voice I recognized.

Of course the alert reader (and, if I tell the truth, probably even the barely conscious reader) will have remembered that Oksana was an occupant of the coach. In my defense I can only say that I was so intent upon preventing the Cossack from taking off my head, or French's, that I had completely forgotten about Oksana's existence. Until she pressed a pistol to my head.

"Oksana," I said glumly. I slid a sideways glance and noted the look of grim triumph on her face. She was stylishly decked out in one of those stunning Russian fur hats and a full-length fur coat, both in the rare shade of jet known as "black diamond sable." I coveted them both instantly. Compared to her I looked wet and frumpy. I conceived, if it were possible, an even more intense dislike of the woman.

The barrel of the gun bored into my skull.

"Drop your gun, India. I won't ask again."

I didn't think she would. I let go of my Bulldog and watched it disappear into the churned snow at my feet.

"Now you, Mr. French. Please return the major's weapon to him."

French was looking at her with a bemused expression. "And if I don't comply with your request?"

I was afraid I knew the answer to that question.

"Then I shall have no choice but to shoot India in the head."

Usually, I adore being right, but not in this instance.

"I should then have sufficient time to shoot you," said French. "And then Ivanov."

I thought French seemed unduly optimistic about his mastery of the shooting arts, not to mention insufficiently concerned with the welfare of India Black.

"You have an unduly optimistic view of your skills, Mr. French," said Oksana, "but if you want to try your luck, I'll indulge you."

There was a longish pause . . . which stretched on interminably as French struggled visibly with his decision. I hardly dared breathe, what with Oksana's arm across my windpipe and French's evident desire to leave Ivanov by the road with a bullet hole in his cranium. Finally, after an unconscionably lengthy time (from my point of view), French sighed regretfully and tossed the pistol in the air so that when it returned to his hand, the grip now faced Ivanov. Reluctantly, French extended the weapon to Ivanov, who snatched it from his hand.

"For a moment, I wasn't sure what your decision would be," Ivanov laughed. "But as usual, you can count on an Englishman's sense of honour. I didn't think you'd allow Miss Black to die, even if she is a whore."

"She may be a whore," said French, "but she's a damned fine shot. Felled your Cossack guard in one go. I'd be careful about insulting her, if I were you."

Just what I was thinking.

Ivanov shrugged. "As she won't be getting her hands on a pistol anytime soon, I'm not worried. Now, we've wasted enough time here. There's a ship waiting for us at the coast. I do apologize, but I feel compelled to bind you both for the remainder of our journey."

Oksana held French and me at gunpoint while Ivanov conducted a hasty search of the coach. After a few moments, he'd scavenged an extra pair of leather reins, several lengths of rope, and a belt from the dead Cossack. At his instructions, we turned our backs to him, and he bound our hands, first French's and then mine.

"Into the coach with you, French. And please don't be so foolish as to try anything. The first victim of any impetuosity will be Miss Black. And we've already seen that you're unwilling to see her pretty face disfigured by a bullet to the temple."

French climbed into the coach and Ivanov followed him, shoving him into one of the seats and tying his feet together. Then it was my turn for the same treatment, with Ivanov roughly roping my feet together with the Cossack's belt and twisting the leather until the knots were tight. Then he propped me on the seat next to French and left the coach, summoning Oksana to him.

"I suppose I owe you my thanks for giving up that pistol," I whispered to French. "But by God, we're in some trouble now. What do you think they intend to do with us?"

"Your gratitude is unnecessary," said French gruffly. I think he was embarrassed.

"And as for your question, I don't think they'll do anything to us until they reach Dover and ensure their escape route to the continent is clear. We'll have our chance, then."

Every glass of water was half-full to French.

There was no time for further conversation as Ivanov and Oksana returned to the coach, dragging the dead driver. They opened the door to the coach and with a great deal of straining and cursing, managed to maneuver the body onto the floor, where it lay across our feet, which was deuced uncomfortable as the fellow weighed a bloody ton. The dead man's eyes were open, staring accusingly at me. I didn't feel any sympathy for the bloke. He'd have lopped off my head if given the chance and bragged about it afterward. My only concern was for my boots; I'd paid a pretty penny for them and couldn't bear the thought of the Cossack's blood staining them. I pried my feet out from under the body and rested them on the guard's legs.

Then it was time for the final humiliation. Ivanov stripped my muffler from my neck and, taking a knife from his pocket, cut it into small pieces.

"I need hardly remind you that we still have several miles to travel, and it will be necessary to change horses along the way. Obviously, I cannot allow you to raise an alarm at any of the inns, so you shall have to be gagged. Please open your mouth, Miss Black."

I sat mute, jaws clamped shut. No need to help the bastard do this, I reasoned.

Ivanov huffed impatiently. "Come, come. The alternative is to put a bullet in your head and bury you under the snow. We haven't much time; which will it be?"

Put like that, it wasn't a difficult decision. I opened my mouth, and Ivanov stuffed it full of woolen cloth. For good measure, he tied a length of the muffler around my face to hold in the gag. French succumbed to the same treatment with an air of imperious indifference, but I knew he was seething inside, as was I, and that the rest of our journey would be spent plotting our revenge.

TWELVE

We set off then, with Ivanov up top driving the coach and Oksana perched on the seat opposite us with her pistol pointed at us. I won't bore you with the details, for I don't like reminding myself of the hours we spent in that coach. If I'd thought the trip had been uncomfortable so far, from this point it was hellish. It wasn't pleasant, sharing a coach with a stiffening corpse, but that was the least of our worries.

With both hands and feet bound, French and I had no way to brace ourselves against the constant pitching and yawing of the coach. We jolted against the sides of the coach, and against each other, and against the sides of the coach again, and so on, for hours. Our plight amused Oksana, and I won't soon forget the sight of her sneering Slavic face as we ploughed through the drifts and bounced over the frozen ruts in the road. She sat across from us in her fine fur coat and hat, the gun in her hand never wavering, with her feet propped casually on the dead Dmitri.

After an hour of jouncing over the rough track, the coach halted, and I felt Ivanov spring from the driver's seat. The door opened and he looked in.

"Is everything satisfactory?" he asked Oksana.

She nodded, without removing her eyes from us. "The prisoners are cooperative, Vasily Kristoforovich."

"There's an inn just down the road. We'll be stopping there to change horses." Ivanov stared hard at French and then turned his steely gaze on me. "Listen to me, both of you. You will not make a sound while we are at the inn. You will not create a disturbance, or attempt in any way to alert the innkeeper to your presence. If you do, I'll shoot the innkeeper and any witnesses. Then I'll shoot you both, place your bodies in the building, and set it on fire. Is that clear?"

It was indeed. We could only nod silently. Well, I suppose it was too much to expect that we would have been untied and escorted into the inn to warm ourselves by the fire and have a bite to eat.

We complied with Ivanov's directions at the inn, and the change of horses was accomplished quickly. We could hear the rough voices of the innkeeper and his stable boy as they harnessed the fresh horses to the coach. It sounded very English and homely, and for a minute I almost lost my nerve and wished myself back safe in Lotus House, away from the cold and the dead Cossack and the exquisitely turned out Oksana. I could feel the sting of tears close to the surface, but I refused to give way. Then I recollected that I had had little to eat since dawn, my hands and feet were numb from lack of circulation, it was colder than the proverbial witch's tit, and French and I were being held prisoner by a ruthless Russian major and his bitch of an accomplice. No wonder I was feeling a bit down.

Cheered by the revelation that I did not in fact have a serious character flaw, I turned my thoughts to our predicament, and the prospects for extricating ourselves from it. We had a decent shot at escaping, I thought. The coach pulling into Dover would surely (please, God) arouse the interests of the British agents who had been alerted to watch the port for stray Russians. If the agents were worth their salt (perhaps an unreasonably sanguine view of their capabilities, given past performance), we could expect the coach to be stopped and ourselves freed. Provided Oksana didn't get trigger happy at the first alarm.

As that didn't bear thinking about, I moved on to ponder what might happen if the Russian arrival into the port escaped notice. They would surely take a ship to Calais as quickly as possible. What, I wondered, did they intend to do with us? Shoot us both and leave us to be found when the snow melted? French's disappearance would certainly cause alarm at the highest levels of government, and a search would be mounted immediately when it was known he had gone missing. The Russians could ill afford the diplomatic contretemps that would ensue if Ivanov were tied to our deaths (at least French's death, that is; I doubt anyone would give a toss about the odd tart being eliminated from the picture). Of course, you can't always count on the Russians giving a fig about public opinion. They're an odd lot, those Russkis, and just as inclined to poke a sleeping dog as let it lie.

Perhaps Ivanov was planning to take us with him, keeping us as hostages until he'd safely delivered the news of the state of the

British army on to St. Petersburg. Once that message was on its way, French and I no longer constituted any threat to Ivanov or Oksana. In fact, there would no longer be any need for French to kill Ivanov. I sat back with satisfaction, pleased with this script, not least because Ivanov was a sharp one, and he had probably figured out that once he'd sent the telegram, French, being the schoolboy he was, wouldn't think it honourable to kill him out of spite.

We jolted along for the best part of the day, changing horses frequently, as Ivanov pushed the creatures hard. Having found that French and I were on his trail, he seemed imbued with a sense of urgency, as though he feared that other agents might be after him, and we did not linger at any inn. Ivanov brought bread, meat, and brandy to Oksana, but she never alighted at any of the public houses to stretch her limbs or answer nature's call. The woman had a bladder of iron.

French and I spent the day trying to keep our balance as the coach lurched through the drifts, slamming into one another and trying to ignore Oksana's ruthless smile while she watched our acrobatics. I needed sleep, but it was impossible. With a mouthful of wool, I was desperately thirsty. Every time Oksana had a nip of her brandy, my throat contracted painfully. There'd been no food since early that morning, and my hands and feet were cold lumps of flesh. All in all, I wouldn't rate the Russians very highly as hosts for your next coach tour.

There wasn't anything to do but ruminate about the situation. I invented several exquisite forms of torture for Ivanov and Oksana to entertain myself and spent a good bit of time thinking of ways to relieve Oksana of her stunning coat and hat.

Near dusk, the coach slowed, and Oksana pulled back the curtain to look out the window. Then the coach tipped and swayed, and it was clear we had left the main road for a smaller track. French looked up sharply.

Oksana smiled. "As you have surmised, we will not be going to Dover. No doubt you were hoping for some assistance from your associates there. You will be disappointed."

Spoken in that gloomy Russian voice, it sounded like an announcement that the end of the world was nigh. Perhaps it was.

We creaked along slowly for an hour or more, until darkness had fallen. Then the coach came to a stop, and Oksana stirred.

"We have arrived," she announced.

Ivanov opened the door of the coach and peered in at us. Beyond his head, I could make out a few faint lights and hear the dull, insistent thump of the sea on the rocks. I could also hear voices. *English* voices. My heart quickened.

"Just a little longer, Miss Black, and we shall set out on the last leg of our journey. Hawkins!" The latter was a summons, for in a moment more heads blocked out the dim lights on the shore and I felt rough hands grasping my person, in ways I'd have made any other bloke pay for. Obviously, these particular Englishmen were in the pay of the Russians. An appeal to their patriotism would likely be futile.

I let out a strangled yelp, and Ivanov said sharply, "Careful there."

I was hauled unceremoniously from the coach and tossed over the shoulder of a giant ruffian, who smelled strongly of herring. He was also lame, with one leg shorter than the other, but he managed to carry me effortlessly, one arm swinging loose and the other clamped over the back of my legs. The only difficulty was that his halting gate caused me to slam into his back at every second step, which was deuced uncomfortable for me but didn't seem to affect my captor in the least. (As he appears at a later point in this narrative, I shall christen him "Bob.") My view was also somewhat constricted, being comprised primarily of the coarse cloth of his coat, but I could see from the corner of my eye that we were passing along an irregular track of shingle, between a number of small wooden shacks. Here and there, a lantern gleamed dully through a window. A fishing village, by the looks of it, though I'd wager that the chief source of revenue here was smuggling.

The roar of the sea grew louder, and my bearer's feet left shingle and trod onto a wooden pier, which swayed precariously under our weight. Waves lashed at the pilings, sending sprays of foam over us. Since night had fallen, the wind had risen sharply, and now I heard it moan through the rigging of a ship. It had started to sleet again, and the pellets stung my cheeks. I had been all for the scenario of being carried alive to France and left to find my way home to England after Ivanov had wired his news to St. Petersburg. I hadn't given much thought to the actual journey across the Channel. Until now. The prospect of such an excursion in this weather seemed rather dismal.

It grew dimmer when the fellow carrying me came alongside a boat tied to the pier. As it was dark and the boat bucking like a mustang, I couldn't discern many details, but first impressions did not inspire confidence. The planks and beams creaked audibly under the pressure of wind and water, and the mast seemed oddly pliant. Or perhaps it was just my point of view; it was difficult to make a careful observation when turned upside down.

My confidence ebbed further when the ruffian loosened a hatch cover and we descended a few steps into the main cabin of the boat. It was a dreary place, enlivened only by a single lamp that struggled to illuminate the gloom. I was carried down the narrowest of passageways, between a miniature galley and a small coal stove on one side and a set of two bunks, one on top of the other. The cabin smelled of damp wool, paraffin and dead fish. Despite the odor, my spirits rose at the sight of the stove. If the Russians had sprung for some coal, the passage to France might just be bearable. The blankets on the bunks looked tumbled and filthy, and probably hosted a whole colony of bedbugs, but even they looked tempting.

The fellow carrying me, however, passed through this luxury suite and into the "C" class accommodations. He wrenched open a door in the bulkhead, and we entered the forward cabin where he dumped me (rather harder than strictly necessary, I thought) onto a rough wooden floor. I heard the rasp of a match, and then a weak yellow glow filled the cabin as my captor lit a lantern fastened to the wall. He gave me a wide smile, filled with discoloured stumps of what had once been teeth, and stamped out.

I struggled to an upright position and surveyed my surroundings. Clearly, our vessel had seen better days. The cabin was tiny. I could have extended my arms (had they not still been tied behind my back) and touched both sides of the hull. The floor and walls were warped and damp, and the room smelled of previous cargoes, which had not included any tulips from Amsterdam. There was no furniture; the only fixture was the lantern on the wall. I was hoping at least for a stove, but there was none, and the air was frigid. The only entrance was the one we'd come through; there was not even a porthole to be opened for a breath of fresh air. Obviously, the Russians hadn't heard of the accommodations available on the P&O.

The door to the cabin opened and two men struggled through, carrying French by the shoulders and legs. He, too, was deposited on the floor with a thump, and then Oksana and Ivanov, carrying Bowser's case, entered the cabin, and they and the local brigands stood looking down at us, like so many entomologists observing two particularly interesting beetles. The two Englishmen who had carried in French were not the finest specimens of our fair race. The first was squat as a toad, with a cast in one eye and a hairy mole on his upper lip ("Beauty" seemed an appropriate moniker for this bloke). The second villain was short and wiry as a terrier, with a mouthful of green teeth, which he displayed by leering continuously at me. I dubbed him "Moss Mouth."

At an order from Ivanov, Beauty and Moss Mouth knelt and loosened the bonds on my feet and hands. The restoration of blood to these appendages was first a relief, and then excruciating. I had to bite my lip to keep from crying out. I set to work, chafing my hands and feet fiercely, trying to restore the circulation. Beside me, French was massaging his own wrists and glaring up at Ivanov. Mercifully, the two ruffians also removed our gags, and I laboured to produce some spittle, a difficult task after a day spent gnawing on my muffler.

"I gather we are to accompany you to France," French said hoarsely.

"I think you'll agree that it's much the wisest course of action," said Ivanov. "Once I've telegraphed the information from your War Office to my superiors, you'll be free to go. I'd leave you behind, but you're a dogged fellow, and I'm sure you'd find a way to prevent me sending that telegram." He looked around the cabin. "I'm sorry these conditions are so Spartan, but I'll see that you have something to eat and drink. We'll be casting off soon. And, please, no heroics. As you can see, there is only one way in and out of here, and it will be closely guarded."

He turned on his heel and departed through the doorway, followed by Oksana (still looking dazzling in that sable coat and hat), Moss Mouth and Beauty. The door shut behind them with a thud.

"Do you really think he'll let us go once we reach France?" I asked.

French shrugged. He was on his feet, prowling around the cabin, examining every nook and cranny.

The door cracked open and the two men returned, with Beauty carrying a small bundle and Moss Mouth sporting a revolver, which he pointed at French.

"'Gainst the wall there, guv," he said, waving the gun to illustrate his point.

French moved obediently to the wall and Moss Mouth placed his bundle on the floor. He shut the door firmly and a key grated in the lock.

French resumed his search of the cabin. I scooted across the floor to the bundle and examined its contents. A greasy packet contained meat, though I was hard pressed to identify it as beef, pork or lamb. I hoped it was one of those; the alternatives were too frightful to consider. Our thoughtful hosts had included a loaf of stale bread, beginning to turn green at the corners, and a bottle of brackish water. I drank it anyway and was not surprised to find that it tasted like ambrosia.

I held out the bottle to French. "Drink?"

He stalked over and took a long swallow. "What I wouldn't give for a large brandy," he said.

"I'd settle for a stove. I'm beginning to think I'll never be warm again."

French was exploring the parcel, poking the meat gingerly. After some consideration, he tore off a small bit and held it to his nose.

"You're not going to eat that, are you?"

"I've eaten worse," he said, and then, after a pause, "I think." He chucked the bite in his mouth, chewed and swallowed. "Not bad. Not entirely certain what it is, but it's not bad."

He pulled off another chunk and handed it to me. "Here, eat this. You'll need your strength."

"For what? Cooling my heels until Ivanov decides to let us go free? Not that that will be difficult to do in this weather."

French was scraping the mold from the loaf of bread. "He's not going to get the chance to send that message. We're breaking out of this cabin and taking over the ship."

I snorted. Not the least bit ladylike, but etiquette had gone by the wayside on this trip. "And how do you expect to do that? For one thing, the door is locked. And Ivanov said it would be guarded."

He looked at me in exasperation. "India, I have had some training in extricating myself from just such circumstances as these. The lock and the guard are minor inconveniences."

"And then? There are five of them out there waiting for us. And have you forgotten that Oksana and Ivanov both have guns? And while I'm thinking of it, shouldn't you have a dagger down your boot or something? You are the most ill-prepared secret agent I've ever met." A slight exaggeration, as French was the first secret agent I'd met (and, I hoped, the last).

"I don't carry a dagger," French bridled. "Rather messy, you know. You have to get in close to use it, and inevitably there's a great deal of blood." He pulled up his trouser leg and fished in his boot. "But I do have this," he said, pulling out an impressive cannon of a handgun. "The Webley .577 Boxer revolver. It will blow a hole right through you."

I gasped. "You've had that with you the entire time we've been chasing Ivanov? Why didn't you use it on him when we ran into him with the sleigh?"

Irritably, French stuffed the pistol back in his boot. "Because, if you recall, I had Ivanov's pistol in my hand at that time. There wasn't any need to pull this out and wave it around."

"You should have shot the bastard then," I said, still miffed that French had been holding out on me.

"There was the small problem of Oksana holding a pistol to your head."

"Oh," I said, somewhat chastened.

We heard the key rasp in the lock and the door swung open. Moss Mouth and Beauty were back, this time carrying a rather larger bundle. They tossed it carelessly into the middle of the cabin and retreated through the door, careful to keep their distance from us, though Moss Mouth bestowed a radiant smile upon me as he left.

"What the hell is this?" said French.

The bundle groaned and stirred, sending shards of ice tinkling to the floor.

"Bloody hell," breathed French. "Vincent."

He was on his feet in an instant, clucking like a mother hen over Vincent's prone body, brushing away the ice and snow that had accumulated on the boy, and then taking off his overcoat and tucking it around Vincent's body, which made me sigh in exasperation. Would the man never learn? His beautiful coat, of finely spun wool and with a gorgeous astrakhan collar, would have to go on the fire as soon as Vincent got through with it. French seemed oblivious to the fate of his coat. He was patting Vincent's cheek and murmuring softly to the boy.

"The boy's half-frozen. India, give me your cloak," French ordered.

Damn and blast. "Er, you're sure he needs it?"

"Give it here," French snapped. "You don't want the boy to die, do you?"

Well, I could hardly answer that, could I? I handed over the cloak, without enthusiasm. Another perfectly good item of clothing for the bonfire. French spread it over Vincent, then sprang to his feet, strode to the door and slammed his fist against it, making the warped wood jump.

"Ivanov!" he shouted.

In a moment Moss Mouth opened the door cautiously, with pistol in hand. "Wot d'ya want?"

"We need brandy for the boy," said French. "Quick as you can."

"I'll check with the guv'ner." The door slammed shut.

In a moment it opened again. "Stand back, you." A bottle of brandy rolled across the sloping cabin floor. French seized it and knelt beside Vincent. He cradled the boy's head in his arm and opened Vincent's mouth, tilting the bottle up and sending a good portion of the contents down Vincent's throat. I could only hope, for French's sake, that the cold had killed the vermin that routinely shared Vincent's clothes with him.

Vincent regained consciousness in a spasm of coughing and retching. He blinked several times and then looked up into French's face.

"There ya are, guv," he said weakly.

"Don't talk, Vincent," French shushed him. "Here, have some more brandy."

You don't have to offer liquor twice to Vincent. He took a healthy jolt and shuddered visibly.

"That 'its the spot, it does. I was near froze through. Ain't a fit night for man nor beast out there."

He managed to sit up, hugging French's coat and my cloak closely about him. His face and hands, which had had a bluish tinge, were beginning to return to a normal colour (though it was difficult to be certain, given the layer of grime).

"Lord, what a gallop I've 'ad," he said.

"How in the world did you get here?" asked French.

"Why, I 'opped on the back of your wagon and then that damned sleigh."

That explained the way the sleigh had bucked and skidded when we'd left the last two inns. Vincent had thrown himself upon the runners.

"And when you two got yourselves nicked by them Russians, I rode on the back of their coach all the way here. I wuz tryin' to sneak around, ever so quiet, until I could find a way to let you out, but I wuz so cold I could 'ardly move, and one o' them bastards caught me by the scruff of the neck and tossed me in 'ere with you."

"You followed us all the way from London, riding out in the open?" I was shocked. Shocked and impressed. It was a damned sight more than I would have done.

Vincent nodded. "Any more of that brandy?"

He took another slug (no other word for it), then French and I took turns trying the local favorite. It turned out to be a fine French cognac, the spoils, no doubt, of some smuggling operation.

"Is that meat?" asked Vincent.

"Of a sort," I said, and handed him the packet and the loaf of bread. He fell on it like a starving hound.

"Why the devil didn't you make an appearance when Ivanov and French were duking it out on the road to Dover?" I demanded. "We could have used your help then."

"It was clear you two weren't goin' to be able to take that Ivanov bloke and that Russian bitch. I figured I should 'ang back, sorta like a reserve column, you know? Ready to rush in when you needed me."

I opened my mouth to dispute Vincent's assessment of French's and my capabilities, but it occurred to me that he had pegged it exactly, and I decided to let his observations go unremarked.

The three of us sat on the floor then, sharing the last of the brandy, and huddled together for warmth, with me praying fervently that the lice and fleas had decided to migrate to the aft cabin, where there was a warm stove and plump Russians to feast upon. We had nearly finished our picnic when we heard shouts and clattering from the deck, the cabin floor tipped ominously, and the rattle of the anchor being raised penetrated the thin hull. We were on our way to France, on a clapped-out wreck of a boat during one of the worst winter storms I could recall. The three of us looked at each other, and a heavy silence settled around us as we contemplated the journey ahead.

Vincent had the final swallow from the bottle, brushed a crumb from his mouth with a genteel swipe and said, "Right, then. Wot's the plan?"

"We're hijacking the ship," I said. "And as we're leaving port, shouldn't we get moving?"

Vincent's eyes gleamed. "'Ijackin', eh? Just like them pirate fellers. This'll be a treat. What 'ave we got for weapons? Oh," he said, patting his pockets. "'Fore I forget, India, here's this for you." He extracted my Bulldog from his trousers and handed it to me.

"Vincent, you're a treasure," I cried.

"I dried it the best I could. 'Ope it still works. That was good shootin', the way you gunned down that big Russian bloke. Remind me not to steal no more cigars from ya."

French took the pistol from him and opened the cylinder, peering down the barrel and taking out each bullet and examining them one by one. "There's no snow compacted in the barrel. It's wet through, though. We'll see if we can dry it further. With luck, it'll shoot when you need it. If not, well, you can at least threaten someone with it."

"French has a .577 Boxer," I said waspishly. "He's been carrying it around, saving it for a rainy day."

"Wot am I goin' to use?" asked Vincent.

French fumbled in his boot and produced a dirk.

"Here," I said indignantly. "You said you didn't carry a dagger. Close quarters. Too much blood. Etcetera, etcetera."

"One of the things I find most charming about you, India, is your certainty that you're entitled to know everything. A good agent always keeps something in reserve."

"What have you got in reserve now? A derringer in your unmentionables?" That stumped him, as I knew it would.

He ignored me, handing the dirk to Vincent. "I trust you know how to use one of these?"

Vincent took it nonchalantly and hefted it in his hand, testing it for weight and balance. "From the cradle," he said. "Just tell me whose throat to slit."

"I'm hoping we won't have to slit anyone's throat," said French. Vincent looked disappointed.

"You're a bloodthirsty little hooligan," I said.

French rose to his feet and made his way unsteadily to the door. We were in open water now, well away from the protection of the coastline, for the boat was climbing steeply over waves, then crashing down into the troughs with a shudder. I felt the first stirrings of nausea and hoped it wouldn't get worse. I noticed Vincent had begun to look peaked, and even French was pale beneath his dark complexion. He jiggled the handle of the door cautiously, careful not to make any noise, but I doubt a battering ram could have been heard above the shriek of the wind and the groaning of the ship.

He returned to our little group and sank down into a sitting position.

"I expect Ivanov and Oksana are in the aft cabin, out of the weather. There may also be a guard on the door."

"Then 'ow do we get out of 'ere?" asked Vincent, running his thumb down the length of the dirk's blade, testing the edge.

"I'm afraid, Vincent, that you'll have to die."

We took our stations. Vincent lay huddled beneath French's coat and my cloak, cradling the dirk in one hand and ready to throw off his coverings as soon as he got the signal from French. I hovered over him like an attending nurse (though I was careful not to actually touch the boy; even the thought of escape wasn't strong enough to overcome my aversion to Vincent's filth). Tucked into the folds of my skirt, my hand was wrapped around the Bulldog's grip. French had wiped down all the surfaces of the gun, dried the bullets and replaced them for me. I only hoped that if I pulled the trigger, I wouldn't lose a hand. French had stuffed the big Boxer into the pocket of his jacket, where it made a bulge that a blind man couldn't have missed.

He looked us over critically, and I was reminded of the first time we had met, on the night Vincent and I had been trying to dispose of Bowser's body. Less than a week ago, I'd been innocently minding my own business, haranguing bints, flattering lusty old goats and haggling with tradesmen. Since the day of Bowser's death, my world had turned upside down. I'd endured kidnapping (by the prime minister, no less), performed a naughty routine for a Russian count and been held hostage at the Russian embassy. I'd nearly killed myself (and French) trying to steal Bowser's case from William Gladstone's hotel room, ridden in an open sleigh through some hellish weather, been kidnapped again (at least it was the Russkis this time, and not my own countrymen) and was now on my way to France. Say what you will about the experience, at least I hadn't been bored.

French nodded at Vincent. "Are you ready?"

"Ready."

"Don't forget to groan, lad. Remember, you're on the verge of death."

"Righto."

"India?"

"Oh, get on with it, will you? We must be halfway to Calais by now."

French hammered on the door. "Ivanov? Are you out there?"

Ivanov's voice came, muffled and suspicious, through the door. "What do you want?"

"It's the boy. He's not responding. It's too cold in here." There was a hint of hysteria in French's voice, which I thought was a nice touch, if a bit overdone. Somehow one could never think of French as getting hysterical about anything.

Silence. Then Ivanov spoke. "I'll give you another bottle of brandy."

"He needs to warm up by the stove, Ivanov," French shouted. "Look, you plan to let us go after you've sent the telegram. You don't want to ruin things now by letting an English boy die on your watch, do you?"

I heard the Russian equivalent of "Bloody hell," then the key turned in the lock.

"Step to the other side of the cabin, French."

French obeyed, making sure his boots clumped heavily across the floorboard.

The door cracked open and Ivanov peered in. "What's wrong with the boy?"

"He's frozen," I said. "He can't get warm in this cabin. He needs a fire."

I nudged Vincent and he groaned piteously.

"I'm afraid he'll die," I said, doing my best to sound tearful and shaken.

Vincent let out another moan, this one more hideous than the last.

Ivanov edged through the doorway. He carried his pistol in one hand, taking care to aim it at French. He'd regret that, in a moment.

Beyond him I could see Oksana reclining on the lower berth,

Bowser's case tucked into the crook of her arm. She was watching us carefully, and her pistol lay near at hand.

"Stay against the wall, French," Ivanov ordered. He stepped gingerly into the room, coming to stand over Vincent and me. Vincent looked up at him with the face of an angel dying slowly of the plague.

"I'm so cold," he said, shivering for effect. "Please 'elp me, mister."

Ivanov bent closer.

"Now, Vincent," said French.

At French's words, Ivanov whipped back his head and sprang to his feet. But Vincent was faster. He flung off the coat and cloak and the dirk was at Ivanov's throat in an instant.

"Drop that barker," hissed Vincent, "or so 'elp me, I'll slit your gullet."

After that, things began to happen at a rapid pace. Oksana was rising from the bunk, groping for her pistol. I stepped around Ivanov and made it to her side in three quick strides. Her mouth was already opening to sound the alarm. It was my turn to jam a revolver into her temple.

"Say anything and you're a dead Russian bitch," I whispered.

She closed her mouth, but the vicious little hellcat wasn't ready to give in. (I console myself with the thought that she was warm and comfortable and her reaction time much quicker than mine, being as I had as much dexterity as a block of ice, which I closely resembled at this point in the narrative.) Oksana made a motion with her hand, as though she were going to toss her pistol onto the bunk on which she had been lying, but instead she flung up her arm and walloped me in the head with the gun. I had just enough time to raise my own arm in defense, but she still caught me a stinging blow across the head. I staggered back against the galley, dropping the Bulldog. Across the cabin from me, Oksana was lifting her gun, taking aim at my forehead. She did not look best pleased.

There wasn't much time; I launched myself at her just as she fired. There's nothing quite like the idea of being shot in the face to provide an extra burst of adrenaline to a person, especially if that person relies on her looks for her living, as I do. I ducked my head and felt a sharp blow to my shoulder, a split second before I buried it in her rib cage and upended her onto the lower bunk. The pain was excruciating and I let out a howl. The pistol flew from Oksana's hand, striking the cabin wall and caroming onto the floor. Now the odds were even again, except for that searing pain in my shoulder. I presumed I'd been shot, but it didn't bear thinking of at the moment, as the Russian she-spy had her arms around my throat and was doing her best to throttle me.

I heard footsteps pounding on the deck overhead, and French cursing a blue streak. He grabbed Vincent by the collar and yanked him upright, all the while training the Boxer on Ivanov's head.

"Find a way to secure that hatchway," French roared, and shoved Vincent into the main cabin. He rocketed past Oksana and me, sparing me a sympathetic glance as he passed by, but he was intent on following French's order. Ungrateful little bugger. After all I'd done for him, I'd at least have expected he'd find a convenient length of wood and club Oksana on the head on his way to bar the door. But, I concede, it did make sense to bar the entry into the cabin of the three ruffians topside, until we'd subdued the Russians.

You wouldn't think a diet of fish eggs and vodka would produce a race of Amazon women, but it felt like I was grappling with one now. Oksana was astride me on the bunk, fingers buried in the soft skin of my throat, her face just inches from mine and aflame with bloodlust. Her mood wasn't improved by the fact that we were being flung from side to side by the action of the waves, and since her hands were occupied at the moment, she had no way to keep from periodically crashing into the wall of the cabin. Her teeth were gritted with the effort of trying to keep her balance and strangle me at the same time.

I could see Vincent from the corner of my eye, desperately searching the cabin for some way of preventing Ivanov's hired thugs from opening the hatch and charging down the steps into the cabin.

French was shouting instructions from the forward cabin while he held Ivanov at gunpoint.

"Find a rope, Vincent. Tie it to the handle and then to that block there."

Vincent dove under the berth beneath me and emerged in a moment with a coil of hemp under one arm. He scuttled across the cabin like a frantic crab and was reaching for the handle of the hatch when it burst open, sending him flying into the corner. He slammed into the wall and slid slowly to the cabin floor, still clutching the rope and scrabbling through his pockets for French's dirk.

The first fellow through the door was Bob, the bloke who had carried me aboard. He took in the scene in the cabin in a glance. He obviously decided that Oksana had the upper hand at the moment (and how right he was) and that a filthy brat constituted no threat, for he turned a murderous gaze on French and launched himself directly at him. Bob's lame foot was a bit of an impediment though, giving him the slow and lurching gate of a wounded rhino. French evaded him by merely stepping to one side like a Spanish bullfighter, clipping Bob at the base of the neck with the Boxer as he lumbered past, sending him crashing to the floor in a tangle of arms and legs.

But that moment's distraction was enough for Ivanov. He unleashed a haymaker at French, which caught French just under the jaw and sent him reeling backward into Bob, who had scrambled to his feet and was anxious to extract some revenge on the poncy bastard who had thumped him smartly. He grabbed French's arm and swung him around so that they were face-to-face. Bob drew back his fist, smiling hideously and intent upon delivering a knockout blow, but French dissuaded him by shoving the Boxer up one of his nostrils. These local hoodlums certainly aren't up to London scratch: one of our bad boys from the metropolis would have noticed French still had his pistol in his hand before he tried to engage in fisticuffs.

Ivanov closed on French from behind like a panther closing on his prey. One arm encircled French's neck, and the other grasped French's wrist, just above the hand that held the Boxer. French twisted violently, trying to escape Ivanov's grip, but the Russian's clasp was like iron. It occurred to Bob (wonderfully bright, he was) that *now* would be an opportune time to strike the poncy bastard, since someone else had dealt with the issue of the Boxer. He advanced on French with that same idiotic grin, hand bunched into a fist the size of a ham.

As Bob cocked back his arm, French leaned backward into Ivanov, raised his booted feet and planted them squarely in the stomach of the oncoming villain. Using Bob as leverage he shoved off, sending the Englishman flying and Ivanov tumbling over onto his back followed shortly by the full weight of French smashing down on his sternum. Even with the screaming of the wind and the creaks and thumps of the ship under sail, I heard Ivanov's breath gush out of his body like the sound of a blacksmith's bellows. French staggered to his feet and withdrew to the doorway, where he leaned against the doorjamb, rubbing his jaw.

More footsteps clumped overhead. They paused at the open hatch.

Over the wind, a voice called out tentatively, "Oi, guv! Wot's goin' on down there?" Moss Mouth.

French looked at Ivanov and Bob and held his finger to his lips.

I had my own trouble at the moment. Oksana had momentarily slackened her attempt at shuffling me off this mortal coil while we both observed the battle between Ivanov and French, but with Ivanov now subdued she redoubled her efforts, gouging her thumbs into my trachea. I clawed at Oksana's hair and got a good handful, heaving with all my strength. I felt the roots give away and Oksana shrieked. She glared down at me, and her biceps bunched beneath the fabric of her coat. Her grip on my throat tightened and suddenly the air felt colder and the light in the cabin began to fade. I needed to do something quickly, or I was dead.

I squirmed until my hands were between our bodies. I clasped them together and brought them up as forcefully as I could (given my limited air supply and the now sharp, insistent pain in my shoulder), driving the knuckles of my clenched hands into Oksana's chin. I felt her teeth click together, and her head snapped back. Her grip on my throat loosened, and I took the opportunity to follow up with a fist to her jaw. It was still a bit feeble, given my condition, but she fell backward, moaning loudly. I shoved at her limp body, pulled my legs out from under her and fell off the bunk, rasping for air and searching for my revolver.

At the sound of Oksana's shriek Moss Mouth decided he had better get below and join the fracas or potentially lose his thirty pieces of silver. He swung down through the open hatchway, a ship's hook clenched in his fist. His eyes widened as he took in the strange little tableau we presented: French with a cocked pistol, Ivanov still flat on the floor, gasping for breath, a sheepish Bob clutching his stomach, an unconscious woman in the lower berth, and Vincent . . . Vincent with a length of timber that connected with Moss Mouth's forehead with the sound of a melon being dropped from a second-floor window. The ruffian crumpled limply to the floor without a sound.

"Presumably," said French, "we won't be disturbed again. Someone has to remain on deck to steer the boat."

I took the opportunity to collect Oksana's pistol, and then searched the floor for my Bulldog. I finally found it in the dark recesses under the lower berth, wedged between a pile of rope and a soft canvas bag. I heard nothing from the lower berth and I congratulated myself on putting Oksana out of commission. I stumbled to my feet, panting like a winded stag, and cautiously approached the bunk. Oksana lay in a crumpled heap, snuffling gently. Just to make sure she wasn't playing doggo, I poked her warily with the barrel of the Bulldog. She didn't move.

I let myself breathe then, feeling a stabbing pain cascade down my arm from my shoulder. I looked at my hand and noticed a thin line of blood snaking between my fingers and dripping onto the cabin floor. My throat felt raw when I swallowed, and my head throbbed where Oksana had clobbered me with her pistol.

Ivanov had managed to raise himself to a sitting position, though he was still gasping for air and his face had a distinctly greenish tinge. "Well done, India," he said sardonically.

Vincent whooped and performed an Indian war dance, his eyes alight with the thrill of the fight. "Blimey, India! I couldn't tell who was gonna come out on top. You two were goin' at it like two cats in a bag. I thought she 'ad ya down fer sure and certain, but you got a punch like a prizefighter." He looked proud enough to burst.

"We watched nearly the entire entertainment," said Ivanov, looking dispassionately at Oksana. "I must say, I believe Count Yusopov would have enjoyed it immensely."

"It's right down his alley," I agreed. I glared at my cohorts. "I suppose it was asking too much for either of you to lend me some assistance in subduing Oksana?"

"I'da shot her," said Vincent, "but all I had was this ole dagger and I didn't want to take the chance of gettin' you instead of 'er." He jerked his head in French's direction. "'E coulda shot her, though, if 'e 'ad felt like it."

French smiled. "I didn't think there was any need, India. You seemed quite capable of handling this by yourself. Now," he said briskly, ignoring my glacial stare, "let's tie these four up and attend to that wound of yours."

French handed me his Boxer and instructed me to keep an eye on our captives (an unnecessary instruction, but men can't seem to resist pointing out the obvious to a woman).

One advantage to taking prisoners on a boat is that there is plenty of rope about. In a twinkling, French and Vincent had secured our prisoners, with Vincent looping the rope in place and French tightening all the knots. I was pleased to see Ivanov wince when French pulled his bindings into place. Bob and Moss Mouth had their turn next, with Moss Mouth glaring murderously at Vincent (still chafed about that blow to the head, I suppose), and Bob submitting with good grace. I think it had dawned on him that if he were bound, he needn't be topside during this weather, and there was a neat little stove down here in the cabin, putting out a fair amount of heat.

When the prisoners were trussed tightly, French said, "I'm going up on deck to check our position and inform the last of this bunch that we're turning around and heading back to England." He gave me a concerned glance. "Will you be all right for a few minutes more?"

"Of course I will," I said. No need for French to know that my body had just turned into blancmange and my knees were rattling like castanets.

"It's bloody cold in here, Vincent," I said. "Put some coal on that fire, will you?"

Vincent took one look at my face and hastened to comply with my request, adding coal and stoking the fire until a nice blaze began to burn. He dragged a heavy coil of rope to the stove, arranging it into a sort of nest for me, covering it with one of the blankets from the berth. I sank down gratefully, huddling as close to the stove as I could, but never taking my eyes from our Russian friends and their English accomplices, who were crammed together in a sitting position on the lower bunk.

Vincent sat down next to me. In the fight, he'd somehow acquired Ivanov's revolvers, and he held them cradled in his lap with a finger on each trigger. The adrenaline from the brouhaha had worn off. His face looked pale and drawn. As the stove began to draw and the cabin to grow warmer, his eyes grew heavy and his head began to droop. I felt a twinge of sympathy for the boy; he'd done something that no pampered upper-class brat would have attempted, braving snow and cold and danger, and for what? A government that didn't give a damn about the likes of him. The thought made me irritable (or perhaps it was the twinge of sympathy I'd felt, a wholly unusual and not entirely comfortable emotion for me).

"Do stay awake, Vincent," I snapped. "If you fall asleep, one of those pistols may discharge. One gunshot wound per trip, that's my limit."

Vincent's eyes jerked open. "Sorry, India," he mumbled. But his eyes were already closing again before the words had left his mouth.

THIRTEEN

I watched as he fell into a deep slumber, then reached over and gently removed the pistols from his lap, placing them on the floor beside me within easy reach. I glanced at our prisoners. Bob had fallen asleep, snoring loudly with his mouth open. Moss Mouth was awake, leering at me again with a peaty grin. Ivanov meditated silently, eyes on the floor. I got a start when I got to Oksana. She was awake, staring balefully at me. I had never been the recipient of such a murderous look in my life, which is saying something when one works amongst the tarts of London. She had lost her hat in our scuffle, but she still wore the sable coat. I wished I'd had the forethought to strip it off her before French had tied her up.

"I see I have injured your shoulder," she hissed. "I only wish it had been your head I had hit."

"I pity you, Oksana. You're a bad shot and you have a glass jaw. I'll bet the Russian government will think twice about sending out such an incompetent spy in the future. Perhaps you'll have time to polish up your pugilistic skills in the labour camp, fighting for scraps of food, and so forth. Probably won't give you a pistol to practice with, though."

Ooh. That got her. She swelled up like a toad, cheeks twitching with indignation.

"You will pay for your cheek," she snarled.

"Undoubtedly, but I don't think the debt collector will be you."

She subsided into silence then, which was just as well. Baiting her had been a bit of fun, but I was beginning to feel rather tired. I wished French would come back soon and keep an eye on our inmates while I had a well-deserved rest. Speaking of French, where was he? He'd been gone quite a while, and come to think of it, I hadn't noticed any slackening of our forward motion, nor had we come about to alter our course. In other words, we still appeared to be headed to Calais.

The weather was growing worse, as well. The wind was blowing across the swell, and our little vessel was wallowing from wave to wave, buffeted on all sides by the turgid water. The beams creaked and the hull groaned, and above these noises I could hear the wind shrieking through the shrouds.

French had probably threatened Beauty with a fish knife, or something equally alarming, and Beauty had responded by tossing French overboard. I was just struggling to my feet with the intention of going on deck when the hatch popped open and French staggered into the cabin, soaked to the skin and cursing violently.

"Hellfire and damnation," he said, coming over to crouch by the stove and shake the sleet from his hair and eyebrows. "It's blowing a gale out there. The sleet is piling up on the deck and the wind is ferocious."

"What about Beauty?" I asked.

French looked at me quizzically. "It's a damned odd time to discuss aesthetic issues, India."

I shook my head impatiently. "No, no. That's what I call the bloke at the wheel. The other two are Moss Mouth and Bob."

"Ah. I see. Well, Beauty, whose name is Hawkins, by the way, is quite happy to answer to a new master, namely me."

"Was he difficult to persuade?"

"Oh, no. I merely promised not to prosecute him and his friends here for treason against the state. And, I offered him double what Ivanov was paying them. I don't think he gave a toss about the first inducement, but the second convinced him to change his allegiance."

"You're *paying* him?" I asked incredulously.

"Can you sail a boat, India?"

"No."

"Neither can I. And as talented as Vincent is, I doubt he has much experience at it, either. We need these men. In fact, I'm about to let one of them go free to help Hawkins. Otherwise, we'll have to man the sails."

Moss Mouth was listening intently. "Did I hear you say you'd pay double what this Russian feller is payin'?"

"Interested?" asked French.

"I'll sign up. Untie me and I'll 'elp 'Awkins get us into port."

"Triple," said Ivanov, "if you disarm these people and deliver us as planned."

"Triple?" said Moss Mouth incredulously. "'Ell's bells."

"I'll pay you three times what we agreed," Ivanov reiterated.

Moss Mouth looked at French. "Whaddya say to that, mister?"

French pulled up his trouser leg and delved into his boot, bringing forth a blackjack. Without a word, he crossed the cabin to Ivanov and cuffed him smartly behind the ear. Ivanov's eyes rolled upward and he toppled slowly sideways into Oksana's lap.

"You brute," she said. "You will pay for that."

"I didn't know you had a blackjack," I said peevishly.

French ignored my comment and held the blackjack in front of Moss Mouth's face. "I don't think he'll be able pay you if he's out cold."

"I reckon not," said Moss Mouth nervously.

"I also think we will be lucky not to lose a crew member overboard in such weather. So don't get greedy, mate. Remember, pigs get fat, and hogs get slaughtered. I'm going to untie you and send you topside. You and Hawkins are going to sail us into port. Your former employer here," French inclined his head at Ivanov, "is going to be sitting in an English gaol soon. He won't be leaving it for some time, and he certainly won't be paying you anything. Now, get up on deck and get us back to England, before I change my mind about the money and the charges of treason."

Moss Mouth nodded submissively, but I wouldn't trust the fellow an inch, and I suspected French felt the same way. But we were in a pickle, with no way home unless these ruffians took us. We'd have to take our chances and stay vigilant. I sighed. There'd be no sleep for me until we reached land.

French patted down Moss Mouth. Then, satisfied that he had no hidden weapons, French cut the ropes that bound him and sent him out through the companionway into the storm. French shut the hatch behind him and came to sit by me again.

"Now, then. Let's see to that shoulder of yours."

"It's stopped bleeding. It'll be fine until we get back to England."

He leaned closer to me, ostensibly studying the wound in my shoulder, but he had something to say. He put his lips near my ear. "We're not turning around and heading back to England. At least, not yet. The wind won't allow us to make landfall anywhere on the southeast coast. We're going on to Calais. We'll have to wait out the storm in port there, and then return to Dover."

He plucked at the fabric of my dress, now stuck to the bullet wound with dried blood. I sucked in my breath.

"Damn and blast!"

He snatched his hand away. "Did that hurt?"

"Not nearly as badly as the news you just gave me. Are you sure Hawkins is telling you the truth?"

"As I'm not a sailor, I can't say for certain. But I do know it's beastly out there. Hawkins is struggling to keep on course for France. I don't think he's faking that look of terror I saw on his face. We'll be lucky if we don't get blown down into the Atlantic."

His expression softened as he took in my disheveled appearance. "Regrets, India?"

"Just that I didn't take that fur coat off that Russian slut when I had the chance."

French laughed. "You've been drooling over that coat since you first laid eyes on it."

"*And* the hat. That ensemble would make quite a splash in the neighborhood."

"Then you shall have them. If not Oksana's, then a hat and coat of your own just like them."

"That's generous of you."

"It's the least Her Majesty's government can do for you."

I agreed. French pocketed his Boxer and commenced work on my shoulder. The wound was not deep, but the bullet had carved a shallow furrow along the top of my shoulder. French found a bottle of the same brackish water we'd shared earlier and sponged out the laceration, tut-tutting over the threads from my dress that needed extracting. It was deuced hard work to get them out, as they had dried to the wound, and the ship was rolling and pitching to such an extent that it was difficult to keep a steady hand. French did his best under the circumstances, though by the time he'd finished sponging off the blood, I looked as though I'd been left outside in the rain and my shoulder was throbbing like the devil.

He pulled his shirttail from his trousers and ripped off a portion to bind the wound. I bit my lip and endured the pain as he manipulated my arm; there was nothing else to do, except contemplate a suitable form of revenge for Oksana. When French had finished, he sat back on his heels and examined his work with a critical eye.

"You need an antiseptic on that, as well as a proper dressing, but that should get you safely into harbor. We'll find you a doctor in France."

"Thank you," I said stiffly.

"You're welcome," he replied formally.

His hand still rested on my shoulder. His gaze was locked on my face. His grey eyes, usually as cold and hard as stone, had softened and looked slightly out of focus. He looked decidedly un-French-like.

"You're not going to vomit on me, are you, French?" I edged away from him, along the rough planks of the cabin floor. "Are you seasick? Do you need a drink of brandy?"

His eyes snapped into focus and he shook his head irritably. "Oh, do shut up India. I'm not ill and I'm not going to vomit on you," he said. "Though it could hardly do any more damage to that dress of yours if I did."

"It's not my fault Oksana shot me. If you hadn't been playing about with Ivanov and Bob, you might have lent me a hand and shot her before she shot me."

"And left a bloody great hole in that coat you're so fond of?" He rose briskly and stomped toward the hatch. "I'm going up top to watch Hawkins and, and, what do you call that other fellow?"

"Moss Mouth," I said. "On account of his teeth."

"Ah. Moss Mouth. I'll try to remember that. You'll be all right down here by yourself?"

"Yes, fine. See if you can't get those two whipped into shape and get us to France as quickly as possible."

"I'll relay your orders, India. Any instructions for Poseidon?" He threw me a sarcastic salute and opening the hatch, ducked his head and exited into the driving sleet.

I have complained previously about the various difficulties I'd endured since Bowser had had the gall to die in my brothel, but none of these experiences can compare with what I encountered on that journey to France. Our vessel might just have been seaworthy in the calmest of waters, but in the tempest that raged around us, it had all the durability of a raft made of sticks. The hull shuddered as the boat climbed the waves, then shuddered again as it plunged into the troughs, only to lurch ominously toward the bottom of the sea as a towering swell closed over the bow. The hatch was closed, but each time a deluge descended on the bow, the water came foaming through around its edges, and in no time at all the floor was awash with cold seawater.

As the water began to creep in, I stood hastily and woke Vincent. He resisted me for a moment, muttering in his sleep, so I had to grab his shoulder and give him a good shake. He was on his feet in a flash, hair standing on end and his eyes wild.

"Wot? Wot is it?" he demanded, finding Ivanov's pistols and waving them frantically.

"Water," I shouted. "The sea is coming in. We'll be drenched if we don't move."

The tide had begun to slosh around my boots. I pointed to the upper berth.

"Up there," I shouted over the roar of the storm.

We clambered up, stepping on Ivanov (still unconscious, so he didn't feel a thing), Oksana (I certainly hoped she did; I'd done my best to plant my boot heel in her thigh as I climbed), and Bob, who had finally been jolted awake by the ship's motion and was looking very worried indeed, something which did little to dispel the hard knot of anxiety in my stomach.

"Blimey," said Vincent. "Wot a gale. How long do you reckon before we get to Dover?"

I shared the information about our inability to make an English port and the decision to continue on to France. Beneath the layer of grime, his face turned pale.

"God 'elp us," he said.

I'm not the sort of person who counts on the Almighty to answer desperate summons, calm the waters or part the seas, as though he's got nothing better to do with his time than rescue humans from their own reckless stupidity, but I will admit to having a quick word with the Old Chap, though of course I did nothing so foolish as to promise to change my ways or go to chapel on Sunday. He wouldn't have believed me if I had.

So Vincent and I sat on the top bunk, watching the water gurgle and foam on the floor below, and listening to the beams and planks of the hull creak and groan. It sounded like the old tub was coming apart, and any minute I expected the hull to spring open and the ocean to come gushing in, but to her credit she ploughed on through the seas. Every few minutes, Vincent or I would lean over to make sure that Oksana, Ivanov and Bob were still where they ought to be. Other than that amusement, there wasn't much to occupy our time, except for uttering the odd curse or prayer when the ship hit a particularly rough patch or the wind rose to a howl. I was reminded of what Sam Johnson had said about sailing: it was like being in jail with a chance of drowning. I believe the old boy was on to something there.

Over the next several hours, Vincent and I took turns dozing. It was deuced uncomfortable, with the wet blankets and the wind probing the spaces between the planks, but after several nights with little or no sleep, I had no trouble dropping off. Waking posed no difficulties either, as approximately thirty seconds after I fell into a slumber, a wave would hit us broadside. The boat would screech as she keeled over and I'd awake with a start, grasping for a handhold and cursing all boats, Russians, Bowser, the Sublime Porte and the English Channel.

There wasn't a sound from the lower berth. I peeked over the edge from time to time. Ivanov was lounging with his back against the hull, his feet propped on the bunk. Evidently the frigid water sloshing around his ankles had finally roused him to wakefulness. Oksana's face was pinched and wan. She too had her feet in the bunk, bracing herself against the movement of the ship. Bob had evidently decided that if he went back to sleep, he'd wake up from this nightmare, for he was cocked to one side, snoring gently.

Time passed slowly. Eventually, Vincent could stand it no longer.

"I'm goin' to see French," he announced, "and find out wot's goin' on."

"Is that wise? You could lose your footing or get blown overboard. Can you swim?"

He gave me a disgusted look. "Don't you worry about me. I can look after meself. Wot about you? Can you 'andle these brigands alone?"

"I think I'm capable. I did manage while you were sleeping."

He grunted, jumped down from the bunk and disappeared through the hatch.

"India?" It was Ivanov.

I craned my neck over the edge of the bunk and looked down at him.

"What is it?"

"I wonder if I could trouble you for a drink of water. I've developed quite a nasty headache."

"Shouldn't wonder. French gave you a good wallop." I added callously, "And, sorry, no water for you until we get to port."

"Well, then. Perhaps you'll satisfy my curiosity instead. I've been pondering your involvement in this affair, and I can't fathom why in the world you're here in the middle of all this."

I didn't really have an answer for that. I know, I know. Earlier, I blathered on about my love of adventure and the stubborn streak that made me finish whatever I started, but after this cruise, I wasn't sure I believed that anymore. To tell the truth, if I'd been offered a ride home on the nearest magic carpet, I'd have taken it then and there, and to hell with Bowser's case, the state of the British Army and the road to India. Consequently, with nothing snappy to say, I remained silent.

"I suspect it may have something to do with Mister French," mused Ivanov. "Most women would find him attractive, don't you think?"

"Until they made his acquaintance," I said.

Ivanov chuckled. "You mustn't protest, India. It merely confirms my suspicion that you're here because of him."

I felt a reply rising in my throat but I bit it back. It was insufferable, listening to this arrogant bastard try to goad me into doing something stupid, which, clearly, was what he intended.

"Mister French certainly does influence me, Ivanov, but not in the way you assume. For example, if he weren't here to prevent it, I'd have killed you and Oksana by now and thrown your bodies overboard. French is too much the gentleman to murder you in cold blood."

"I wouldn't bank on his being a gentleman once this is over. As soon as you are no longer of use to him, you'll be nothing more than what you were when this started: a whore. I rather think Mister French values his social standing too much to associate with a trollop."

"That nettle doesn't sting, Ivanov. I know who and what I am, and if I wanted to be something different, I would. And I must say, you disappoint me. This attempt to dissuade me from any amorous notions I might have about French will only work if I *have* any romantic attachments to the man. I shall be happy to see the back of him when this affair is settled. Happier, even, than I will be to see the back of *you*."

"I doubt that, my dear. I've grown rather fond of you over the past few days. You have shown considerable skills and resources. You would be of great interest to the tsar."

"Are you trying to recruit me?" The thought was ludicrous, but I did have to restrain myself from inquiring whether I'd be issued a sable coat and hat.

"Why not? You would be perfectly situated at Lotus House. We know many young men who are rising through the ranks of the military and politics frequent your brothel. You would be well-placed to provide us with information, and we would be willing to pay you a great deal of money."

I had to hand it to the man. Bound hand and foot, facing a lengthy sentence in an English gaol (if he didn't drown first), and he was still trying to winkle his way out of this. Nobody does arrogance like the Russians; the English aristocracy isn't even playing in the same league.

I was about to ask about the benefits of being the tsar's agent (My own knout? A borscht allowance?) and speculating on the size of the pension when the hatch flew open and Vincent, along with an enormous quantity of seawater, hurtled into the cabin. His clothes clung to him and his hair was plastered to his head. I had to look twice, but after several minutes out in that squall, the driving rain appeared to have scrubbed most of the grime from his face. He looked almost . . . clean.

"Land 'o!" he said, grinning maniacally. "We c'n see France. French says to untie that other smuggler bloke and come on deck. It'll be all 'ands to the pump, 'e says."

At the word "land," I'd jumped from the upper bunk and landed with a splash next to Ivanov.

He grinned sourly. "The journey is almost over, but the game is not. Don't forget that."

I gave him a pitying look. "If I were headed to one of our English prisons, I'd be surly, too."

Oksana had sunk into the depths of her sable coat, which, given its prolonged exposure to the damp air and seawater, was looking a little worse for the wear. She resembled a giant rat, peering out at me from the wet fur with hard, beady eyes.

Vincent used French's dirk to cut through Bob's bindings, while I verified that Ivanov and Oksana were in no danger of loosening theirs. Then Vincent shoved Bob ahead of him through the hatch, with the dirk pressed into the small of his back, and I followed them up onto the deck.

It was still dark, and the rain and sleet slanted sideways, propelled by a stiff wind. My vision was partially obscured, but the atmosphere had grown lighter, and far away to the east a thin mauve line had appeared on the horizon, heralding the arrival of dawn. But even more heartening were the tiny pinpricks of light that shone in the darkness just ahead of us. We had reached land. Well, I should hasten to amend that statement; we were in sight of land. There's a vast difference between seeing the dark bulk of the earth, and actually arriving in a snug harbor, as any sailor can tell you. Especially in weather like this. It would be hard going to maneuver this decrepit tub into port.

But it was still *land,* and my heart lightened at the thought (even though it was France). I don't care much for the Frogs. They're still preening themselves over the revolution (where average people behaved like savages from the Dark Continent) and Napoleon's victories (he was a Corsican, for God's sake, and half his troops were foreign mercenaries), and they are insufferably supercilious to boot. I said that no one could do arrogance like the Russians, but I do believe the French are a close second. Not to mention that their drains are the worst in Europe; all that cheese and garlic, you know. But I digress.

We found French manning the wheel, straining to hold the ship steady in the crosswinds. I staggered over to him, struggling to stay on my feet on the wet, pitching deck. I had to grasp whatever handhold I could find, a rope here, a rail there, all the while praying I wouldn't end up in the drink.

Hawkins was struggling to tie down a flapping line, and Moss Mouth was nowhere to be seen. I mouthed a question at French, and he lifted his head to the mast, where Moss Mouth was standing on a yardarm, desperately trying to gather in a piece of sailcloth that was whipping about in the wind, threatening to dislodge him from his perch. French grabbed Bob by the arm and shouted instructions in his ear, and in a flash Bob was clambering up the rigging to join Moss Mouth.

"I thought you said you couldn't sail," I shouted in French's ear.

He gripped the wheel. "I can't. But I'm more damned useful down here than up there in the shrouds. How are the captives?"

"Ivanov has asked me to join the Russian intelligence services."

For some reason, French found this uproariously funny. He flung back his head and let out a roar of laughter. "What did you say?"

"We were just about to negotiate the compensation when Vincent came along and fetched me."

"Well done, Vincent," French said. He was still smiling.

The horizon was growing brighter, and I could clearly see the outline of the French coast: a low, dark grey bulk against the lighter grey of the sky. For the first time in days, I sensed our luck changing for the better. The wind had subsided just in the few minutes I'd been on deck, and the rain and sleet were slackening as well. That luminosity on the eastern horizon meant that we would see the sun today. Now we had only to make port.

"That's Calais ahead of us," said French, pointing to the northeast of our position. My heart caught in my throat. At last, a town. A town where I would find dry clothes, fine French cognac and a hot meal. Say what you will about the French, they do know how to put on a feed. My mouth watered at the thought of a warm baguette slathered in butter.

I won't bore you with the details of how we got that little vessel off the storm wracked ocean and into port. As a matter of fact, I couldn't tell you the details, for to me the mizzen staysail looks the same as the mizzen topmast staysail, which looks nearly identical to the mizzen topgallant staysail. And then of course there's the mizzen sail, the mizzen topsail and the mizzen topgallant. Nomenclature designed by men, certainly, for even the silliest of women would have named them all differently so there'd be no confusion in the middle of a gale.

"*Raise the mizzen topmast staysail!*"

"*Eh? Did you say the mizzen topgallant staysail, Cap'n?*"

"*No, you bloody idiot. Raise the mizzen topmast staysail.*"

"*Oh. The mizzen topsail. Righto, sir.*"

"*No, no, no! I said, the mizzen topmast staysail, you ignorant ass!*"

You see my point, I'm sure. But once again, I digress.

I was rather enjoying myself on deck, not having to do any work but keep a revolver aimed at the nearest of our three deckhands and breathing the fresh, invigorating air. I did notice eventually, however, that instead of heading directly into Calais, we seemed to be edging obliquely in toward the coast, at an angle calculated to land us just south of the town itself.

"Why aren't we headed for Calais?" I asked French, watching as a very accessible quay slid away behind us.

"We can't very well dock in the municipal port with two Russian spies tied up in the cabin. We have to keep their existence a secret from the French authorities. Hawkins says there's a village not far from Calais. We'll land there. You and I will keep watch over our guests. We can't afford to let those three Englishmen off the ship. They might alert the authorities, though I doubt it. It's more likely they would reconsider Ivanov's offer to triple their pay, and try to release him. I don't trust them any more than I trust Ivanov or Oksana."

"And what then?"

"I'll send Vincent into Calais to find our agent there. He'll arrange transport back to England for us."

"What about these English bastards? Are you really going to pay them?"

"Certainly. Provided they keep their end of the bargain and don't try to cut my throat, I shall keep mine. We wouldn't have survived that storm without them. I won't lose any sleep tonight worrying about the morality of a few pounds to a few brigands."

The sun had risen over the horizon as we rode a strong swell toward a tiny French fishing village. The occupants were stirring; I could see thin lines of smoke rising from the chimneys of the cottages, and a few men were moving about on an ancient stone wharf.

"We'll attract attention to ourselves here," I pointed out.

"Yes, but this village is much like the one we left from. Smuggling, not fishing, is how most of these families earn their livelihood. We'll have no trouble from them. Or so Hawkins says," he added.

Bob and Moss Mouth were scrambling among the rigging, loosening ropes and tucking up sails. Hawkins came to the wheel and touched his forelock.

"Beggin' pardon, sir, but I best take over from 'ere. Tyin' up can be a bit dicey."

French surrendered the wheel and perched on the rail surrounding the deck.

Despite the fact that I'd been kidnapped and held hostage by these men, I had to admire the dexterity and skill of Bob, Hawkins and Moss Mouth. They adroitly negotiated the winds and currents, until our craft glided gently alongside the pier, where Moss Mouth jumped agilely ashore and secured us with a few nonchalant turns of the rope.

"Back aboard," said French to him. "India, how are your linguistic skills?"

"I can provide a reference from my customers," I said. "But if you want to know whether I speak French, I can acquire food and drink for us."

He shot me an amused glance and fished a handful of coins from his pocket.

"After we have something to eat, I'll send Vincent on to Calais." He offered me his hand, and I crawled out of the boat and onto shore. My legs were wobbly and at first I waddled around like a pregnant goose, but after a few steps, I found my land legs and strode off in search of food.

I suppose the inhabitants of that little village were accustomed to foreigners pitching up on their shore, for an exorbitant amount of coin soon produced a fine ham, a block of cheese, a rather mean portion of butter, several loaves of bread, and three bottles of brandy, one each for Vincent, French and me. There were no questions asked (which indeed I couldn't have answered anyway, as my French was limited to pointing to my open mouth and looking piteous), and no one seemed the least bit curious about us. No doubt they expected us to unload our cargo and disappear when night came. To ask questions would only invite trouble. My kind of people.

We had a sumptuous repast on the deck. It was still bloody cold, with the wind blowing steadily, but the rain and sleet had abated for the moment, though menacing clouds on the horizon signaled that the storm had yet to blow itself out. I preferred to be on deck; the cabin below was wet, cold, and miserable, and the company left a great deal to be desired.

After we'd eaten, French summoned Vincent, and they huddled together in the bow, with French whispering instructions to Vincent and Vincent nodding frequently. French gave Vincent a pat on the back, handed him some money, and Vincent scurried onto the quay.

"See ya soon, India. Don't shoot anybody 'til I get back," he said.

Cheeky sod.

"Mind you be quick about this, or I'll shoot you."

"You do 'alf scare me," he said, and was out of sight before I could reply.

Our repast (particularly the brandy) had taken some of the chill off, but the wind was playing up again, singing through the rigging and sending cold shivers down my spine. To the east, a line of dark clouds reared up from the French countryside. Our three English buccaneers shared the deck with us, lined up opposite us against the rail while French kept a wary eye and a cocked pistol on them.

Hawkins lit a pipe and squinted at the sky. "We'll have another squall 'ere, just any minute now. There's rain in them clouds," he said.

French motioned to Moss Mouth. "Go below and bring up two blankets. Is there any foul weather gear aboard?"

Moss Mouth laughed. "If there were, mate, I'da been wearin' it by now."

"Fetch the blankets, then."

Moss Mouth complied, returning with two damp squares of wool that smelled like they'd been used to wrap fish and chips.

"Drop them on deck, please," said French, and Moss Mouth dumped the blankets unceremoniously at his feet. At French's direction, he returned to join his friends along the rail.

French handed me a blanket with a wry smile. "Make yourself comfortable, India. Unless you'd rather go below."

"I think not," I said, envisioning Ivanov's surly countenance and Oksana's sour face. "I'd rather sit out the storm up here. After all, I can't get much wetter or colder."

"How 'bout us, guv? It's bloody cold up 'ere," said Moss Mouth. "My fingers are so frozen, they're liable to break."

"Just a little longer, lads, and soon you'll be sitting in a warm, cozy cabin, on your way back to England."

"Don't forget the chink," said Moss Mouth, ogling me lecherously. "Them English whores don't give it away for free."

"You'll get your money," said French.

"And the thanks of a grateful nation," I added.

The sky had darkened abruptly, signaling the advent of the storm. Heavy clouds roiled the heavens, and thunder rumbled ominously overhead. The halyards were slapping the mast and our little craft began to rock. A few fat drops spattered on the deck, and I covered my head with the blanket, just as the deluge began. Rain lashed the deck, stinging any exposed skin. I gathered the blanket tightly around me and resigned myself to once more being wet, cold and unkempt. A comb and some rouge wouldn't have gone amiss just then.

French had draped the blanket around his shoulders, but he sat with his head uncovered, his black hair whipping in the wind and water cascading down his face. His Boxer remained steady in his hand, pointed at the smugglers. I had my Bulldog at the ready, but the three looked so utterly miserable, shoulders hunched against the driving rain and their heads buried in their hands, that I didn't think they could summon the strength or the will to attack us.

I must really learn to avoid these sorts of categorical statements, for just as I was reassuring myself that French and I had nothing to fear from these brigands, a shot rang out from the cabin below. Three heads popped up simultaneously.

French was on his feet in an instant, making for the hatch and shouting over his shoulder, "Watch those men, India!"

I whipped my revolver from the folds of my blanket and aimed it at Moss Mouth. "Don't move an inch, you maggot," I said to him. "I've already killed one man on this journey, and it won't bother me to add to the total."

French had the hatch cover off and was standing to one side of the opening, peering cautiously down into the gloom.

"Ivanov," he shouted over the roar of the wind.

Oksana's face appeared, tearstained and wild-eyed. "The major has shot himself."

"Excellent," I snapped. "That will save a bullet."

"But what am I to do?" Oksana implored. "I cannot stay here with Vasily Kristoforovich's body."

We were back to where we started, with Oksana (f/n/a Arabella) pitching a fit over sharing a room with a corpse. She'd get no sympathy from me this time.

"Leave him where he lies," I said to French.

I thought for a moment that French's better instincts (you know, that public school rot about damsels in distress, respect for fallen adversaries, etcetera, etcetera) would prevail and he would trundle down into the cabin and lay Ivanov out like a fallen soldier who'd perished in battle, offering words of solace to Oksana. But for once I was wrong about the man.

"Hand up the case, Oksana," he said in a hard voice. "And stay below."

"On the contrary, I think we will come up. I very much need to breathe some fresh air," said a voice that bore a remarkable resemblance to that of the deceased Vasily Kristoforovich Ivanov. And then a second gunshot rang out.

French pitched backward, his Boxer flying from his hand and skittering over the deck toward Moss Mouth. The smuggler's dexterity among the rigging had been noticeable, and he was no less light on his feet now. He bounded up quick as a cat and leapt for the gun. There was no time to think, much less shout something ineffectual like "Stop or I'll shoot," so I took aim, prayed that the Bulldog was still serviceable and pulled the trigger. There was a satisfying explosion of sound and the delightful smell of cordite, and when the smoke had cleared, I was pleased (for once) to see Moss Mouth staring at me open-mouthed, clutching the bloody claw that had been his hand. Dammit, I'd missed. I'd meant to kill him. Moss Mouth began to bawl like a motherless calf, a most irritating sound under such stressful circumstances.

I swung round to see Hawkins and Bob shifting nervously, clearly undecided about what to do next. Take on the crazy woman who'd just amputated their compadre's hand? Go to the assistance of the nob who had taken Ivanov's bullet? Which side to choose?

"I'm paying three times what I offered you," roared Ivanov, storming up through the hatch with Oksana in tow. That decided the matter for Bob and Hawkins. Bob launched himself at me in a flying tackle, which given his lame foot, he executed with all the speed and agility of a walrus climbing onto an ice floe. I had to hand it to him; the fellow had spirit, but he wasn't the brightest candle in the chandelier. Here he was charging at me while I held a pistol in my hand, pointed in his direction. If he had any doubts about what I could do with it, he could glance to his left and see Moss Mouth still writhing on the deck, clutching his hand. I sighed. Bob was so stupid, it seemed a shame to kill him. Then I thought about him shouldering me like a sack of flour and carrying me aboard ship. I considered that he'd had no idea, and had probably cared not one iota, what fate Ivanov had chosen for me when he tossed me into the forward cabin. Perhaps it was better to remove Bob from stud service, after all. I pulled the trigger.

Not surprisingly, Bob's forward advance was checked (severely) by the big .442 slug. The bullet caught him in the shoulder and sent him spinning backward at a dizzying rate, until his feet tangled in a coil of rope and he crashed to the deck.

In the few seconds it had taken me to knock two miscreants from the pitch, Ivanov had reached the deck, and I found myself looking down the barrel of the revolver in his hand. Tucked under his other arm was Bowser's black leather case. By this time, I was heartily sick of that thing.

I expected to see Ivanov's imperious smile, but his visage was as terrible as that of a Spartan commander who'd just gotten word of the latest Helot revolt. Oksana was a step behind him, looking exultant despite her wet fur coat and drooping hat. I had the urge to hand her a mirror.

Ivanov paused to look at the fallen French. I followed his gaze. What I saw shocked me into immobility.

French lay sprawled on deck, his coat flung open and a dark red stain spreading slowly across the front of his white shirt. His face was turned toward me, and his eyes locked on mine. He was struggling to breathe, his chest heaving with the effort. He opened his mouth to speak, but I heard only the rasp of his breath in his throat. His hands clawed spastically at the waistband of his trousers. Well, you never can tell what a fellow will do when he's dying, but that seemed rather out of character for the straitlaced French. I had to avert my eyes.

"Such a shame, is it not? I find it personally repugnant to kill a worthy opponent. There are so few in this match that we play," said Ivanov, nudging French's boot with his own.

Things were looking deuced difficult for French. Any minute, Vincent might arrive with French's men from Calais, but a minute from now might be too late. I needed to do something, and quickly.

"Why not put a bullet in his head and end his suffering, then?"

Ivanov looked up sharply, the corners of his mouth turning up in grim smile. "By God, you're a cold one, India Black. Are you sure you wouldn't like to join us in the service of the tsar? I think you'd go far." Oksana made a retching noise.

Ivanov wasn't the only one staring at me. Out of the corner of my eye, I noticed that French had stopped twitching and was looking daggers at me. So the poncy cove wasn't about to go the way of all earth just yet. Clever fellow, but what did he expect me to do? Divert Ivanov's attention long enough for French to stagger to his feet and slash the Russian's throat with a fingernail? That would leave Oksana and Hawkins for me to deal with, but given the alacrity with which I had dispatched Moss Mouth and Bob, I thought the odds were in my favor. Well, if French wasn't dying, then perhaps I could keep Ivanov distracted with a little conversation, though words have never been my strong suit. I'm a woman of action, myself. Where was Dizzy when you needed him? He'd have nattered away until Ivanov's eyes glazed with boredom and he fell asleep. But as Dizzy wasn't here at the moment, it was down to me.

I was searching for some suitable topic for discussion when Ivanov preempted my efforts.

"Seize this woman," he said to Hawkins, waving his pistol in my direction. Hawkins was a dab hand at following directions. I heard three quick steps across the deck, and then his arms snaked around my body from behind and grasped me tightly.

I repeat my observations about the quality of your rustic rascals versus the finer rogues to be found in the Smoke. Any London thug knows never to snatch someone from behind. The first thing a child of the streets learns is how to escape the clutches of peelers, pederasts and preachers. I merely bent over abruptly at the waist, and Hawkins, still clinging to me, was pulled off his feet. I could hear the toes of his boots scraping the deck as I twisted abruptly and fell heavily to one side. We crashed to the deck, with Hawkins's arm trapped beneath my body. I heard the sound of a stick being snapped in half, and then Hawkins was sitting up, holding his elbow and gnashing his teeth in pain.

Ivanov rolled his eyes and Oksana shook her head, lips pressed together like a maiden schoolteacher watching the antics of some unruly boys. I could sympathize; it was damned difficult to get good help these days.

French had managed to right himself, and he was digging industriously in his trousers. I thought he'd been shot in the chest, but maybe he'd struck his head when he had fallen; how else to explain this bizarre behavior?

Those were my thoughts at the time, and I'm not ashamed to admit that I was certain the man had lost his mind. Why else would he be arranging his package at a time like this? But to give French his due, he had one more trick up his sleeve, or down his pants, as it were.

His hand emerged from his clothing, holding one of the finest of American inventions: the Remington .41 rimfire derringer. A bullet fired from one of those little pocket pistols was so slow you could actually see it moving through the air. The firepower was so negligible, that if you fired at something more than twenty feet away, the bullet was likely to bounce off the target. But if your quarry was near to hand (for example, across the table from you), he had no chance of surviving a well-placed shot. That's why the Remington was so popular with cardsharps in the western United States; it was deadly when fired from a few feet. It was, in short, the dog's bollocks when it came to close-range killing, and Ivanov was a scant two feet from French.

"Ivanov," French said hoarsely. I, of course, would have shot the bastard in the back, but French was too much the gentleman for that.

The Russian caught the warning in French's voice and turned slowly. Ivanov's intentions were clear; his hand was already extending in French's direction, the revolver cocked and ready, when French fired. There was a good deal of black smoke and a detonation that rang like a thunderclap. The bullet clouted Ivanov high in the chest, sending him reeling toward the side of the ship. Oksana cried out and reached for him, but Ivanov had lurched into the railing and was already falling, pitching headfirst into the water, Bowser's black case striking the railing as he went over and springing open. I heard the splash of Ivanov's body and saw water cascade into view, as a sheaf of white papers bearing the crest of Her Majesty's government took flight on the wind, swirling away into the dawn light like a flock of seagulls on the wing.

I rushed to the railing and stared down into the water. Ivanov was floating facedown, arms outstretched, his body bobbing on the waves.

"Well done, French," I cried. "You've killed the bugger." Now for the bad news. "Though I'm afraid Bowser's memo is gone, scattered on the wind."

"At the moment," French said huskily, "I couldn't care less. At least it's out of Russian hands."

The mention of Russian hands reminded me that Oksana was still on the loose. I expected to see her on deck, but when I turned, she had fled.

French pointed at the dock with an unsteady hand. "She hared off that way, right after I shot Ivanov. Go after her. And take my Boxer. It'll do more damage when you shoot her."

Well, I suppose even gentleman have their boundaries, and I suppose being shot like a dog by Ivanov had pushed French over his.

I grabbed the Boxer from the deck, where it lay after Moss Mouth's ill-fated attempt to gain possession, clambered up onto the dock and sprinted after the fleeing Russian spy. In the growing light I could just see her ahead of me, running unsteadily in the direction of Calais, that glorious sable coat (for so it still was, though damp with seawater) and hat rippling in the pale light.

"Stop, Oksana," I called. "You'll never get away. I'm right behind you." I sucked in a deep breath at the conclusion of this monologue and resolved to keep my shouted instructions to a minimum, at least while giving chase. It took all my energy just to stagger along.

Oksana was still clipping along, stealing a glance now and then over her shoulder at me. I wasn't in the best of condition, what with the cold, sleet, snow, rain and seawater I'd endured, not to mention a minor gunshot wound to the shoulder (it was throbbing like the devil right now), and I could see that Oksana was soon going to outpace me. I gave it a final push, summoning what little reserves of strength I had left. Oksana had reached the end of the dock now and was making her way up a small incline, along a graveled road. I lurched to a stop, dropped to one knee to steady myself and wrapped both hands around the Boxer.

"Oksana," I shouted. She paused to look back, as I had hoped she would. Idiot. I would have kept hoofing along, perhaps adding some evasive procedures for good measure. Anyone with any sense knows how difficult it is to hit a moving target with a revolver, especially at a distance. No wonder Ivanov wanted some fresh blood among the tsar's agents.

I pulled the trigger, and the Boxer roared. I am accustomed to the powerful kick of my Bulldog, but the .577 caliber packs a punch like nothing I've ever experienced. My arms flew skyward and the concussion knocked me arse over teakettle. I lay on my back in the dirt and looked at the gun in my hand, stunned at the impact. I'd have to spend some time practicing if I wanted to shoot one of these cannons with any skill at all.

I climbed to my feet, joints creaking and my shoulder quivering with pain, and I scanned the road ahead of me. Bloody hell. Just before the crest of the incline, a crumpled form lay in the road. Aches and pains forgotten, I dashed up the hill, still clutching the Boxer in one hand and holding my skirts up with the other. (Note to self: purchase trousers for next spy adventure.)

I stopped a good distance away and approached Oksana's body cautiously. She was a sly puss, and I wasn't about to get within reach of her claws. She looked oddly flat lying there, as if the very substance of life had been drained from her, leaving only a husk beneath the rippling fur of her coat. She'd been a ruddy large girl, as lots of Russians are, and her death tableau seemed strangely unreal. When I drew near, I saw my error. I had not felled Oksana with one shot from the Boxer. I had, in fact, only bagged myself a very nice sable coat, made in Russia, and in perfect condition, if one did not count the neat round bullet hole in the hem.

I started up immediately, climbed to the crest of the hill and searched the road that stretched out before me. Far, far ahead of me, I saw a tiny figure, still racing along, due to arrive soon in Calais. While I'd been recovering from the hammer blow of the Boxer and creeping up on a dead fur coat, Oksana had been making tracks. I'd never catch her now. I wanted to weep. But I didn't.

EPILOGUE

So we had failed. I had hoped that French's men, led by Vincent, might encounter Oksana on their way out to the fishing village, but they had not. She had slipped into the warren of small shops, taverns and boarding houses that surrounded the port of Calais and disappeared from sight. French's men kept watch over the telegraph office in the Place d'Armes for several days, but no one answering her description appeared. No doubt the Russians had their own agents in Calais, and they had spirited her away at the first opportunity.

The British agents in Calais proved extremely efficient at repatriating our friends Bob, Hawkins and Moss Mouth to an English gaol, after cursory medical attention and lengthy interrogations. As expected, the three knew nothing more than that they were to receive a tidy sum for ferrying the two Russians to France and had they known that French, Vincent and I were employed on Her Majesty's business, would of course have accorded us every courtesy. Their interrogators, being English, met this bald-faced lie with a raised eyebrow and polite disbelief. It did not absolve the three smugglers from their misdeeds, and they are now enjoying the hospitality of Her Majesty's government.

French and I were showered with attention, with the finest French doctors (smelling of garlic, but what can one do?) poking and prodding us, cleaning our wounds and bandaging us with enough linen to start a hotel supply company. Luckily, those Russians are damned poor shots. Oksana had grazed my shoulder at close range, and Ivanov had had a perfect opportunity to pump a bullet into French's heart but missed by a wide margin. Vincent explained the former error by pointing out that Oksana was a woman and what did you expect? (Earning a kick from me, which you'll no doubt agree he deserved.) And the latter by postulating that Ivanov had been in the cavalry and "'twas better with a sword." Possibly, he was correct.

French was soon feeling well enough to castigate me for suggesting that Ivanov put him down like a dog suffering from canine distemper.

"It was such a shocking statement that it distracted Ivanov's attention while you fished out that derringer." I did not point out that when I'd made the suggestion to Ivanov, I'd had no idea that French had a derringer in his unmentionables.

I plunged on. "Speaking of that derringer, why didn't you tell me you had it stuffed down your underwear? And how in the world do you manage to secrete such an armory on your person without clanking like a medieval knight in armor when you walk?"

"The derringer wasn't stuffed in my underwear," he said scornfully. It's awfully easy to get a rise out of a secret agent: just disparage their tradecraft. "I have holsters specially made for the guns and a scabbard in my boot for the dirk."

Even more disappointing than Oksana's escape was our failure to recover Ivanov's body. By the time French's agents arrived with Vincent, the tide had turned and the Russian was no longer bobbing alongside the boat. French's men took one look at his white face and bloody shirt and decided that his life was more important than hiring a flotilla to search for a dead Russian spy. Our men in France kept an ear to the ground, waiting for word of any unidentified bodies washing ashore, but none were found. The conventional wisdom was that Ivanov had satiated the appetite of some predatory fishes, but the smart money (including mine) was on Ivanov's survival. He was a hard bastard to kill.

That left two Russian spies unaccounted for, and thus it came as no surprise that word of Britain's troop strength (or lack thereof) eventually arrived in St. Petersburg. Whether it was Oksana or Ivanov (and my money's on that slick bastard) who managed to convey the contents of Bowser's memo to the tsar, we never learned. French was all for affecting the disappearance of my close friend, Count Yusopov, to prevent him sending on the word of the contents of Bowser's memo, but after much hemming and hawing, Dizzy decided not to eliminate the tsar's chief military agent in Britain, fearing, no doubt, a midnight visit at his country home by a Terek Cossack.

Rather unpredictably, however, the news of Britain's military weakness seemed to have little effect on Russian military strategy. I held my breath for the next few months, expecting those Slavic bastards to mobilize their army immediately and quick march to Constantinople, taunting Dizzy along the way and daring him to stop them. I anticipated a plea for enlistment in the British forces to stop the Slavic bastards and was a tad disappointed when it never materialized; a military campaign would have brought scores of randy young bucks to London and increased trade at Lotus House.

It seemed that even with the knowledge that the British were ill prepared to fight, the Russians were loath to do so themselves. They muddled around a bit during the spring of 1877, trying to find a diplomatic solution to the dispute between their Serbian friends and the dreaded Turks. But by April of that year, it had become clear that the Serbs were incapable of taking on the Sublime Porte (no surprise to anyone who knew the state of the Serbian army, except, apparently, the Serbs), and so the Russians declared war on the Ottoman Empire.

Though the Russians knew that Britain could do little with its small army to prevent an invasion of the Porte, they failed to realize that the Turks had a bloody large army that might object to an infringement of Ottoman territorial sovereignty. Over the next few months, the two armies clashed sporadically, marching and countermarching across rivers and over dry, dusty plains, climbing mountain passes, besieging each other in grim little outposts that no one had ever heard of and never would hear of again, and generally kicking up dust and keeping Europe on edge. I'm giving you the condensed version of events here, of course, for who is really interested in a few grubby fracases between the Turks and the Serbs and Russians? I suppose if I were a peasant with a half-dozen sheep that ended up feeding the Turks or a grove of olive trees that served as firewood for the Serbs, I might give a damn, but as it is, I'm just not interested. I've got my hands full with the bints here at Lotus House. But I digress.

After several months, neither Russia nor the Sublime Porte had achieved anything in the way of decisive victories. True, the Russians had advanced into the Ottoman Empire, causing a lot of hand-wringing and brow wiping in Constantinople (not to mention London), but the Ottoman armies always found a way to deal their Russian counterparts a stinging blow, as if to remind them that they were a long way from home, by God, and the party wasn't over yet. Finally, the Turks offered terms, and the Russians accepted. The parties signed a treaty at San Stefano (a squalid village a hundred miles from Constantinople, where the Russians had halted their advance), and the heads of the European governments sighed collectively in relief.

Until they learned that by the provisions of the treaty, the tsar had acquired parts of Armenia and Georgia (they say you should never look a gift horse in the mouth, but I say good luck to the Russians; they'll have their hands full with those blokes and be deuced lucky if they hold on to those territories). This extension of the Russian empire did not go down well with London, Paris and Berlin, especially when it became clear that the Russians had no intention of actually complying with the treaty and laying down arms. Instead, they headed for Constantinople, hoping, apparently, that no one would notice.

Dizzy was apoplectic. He promptly sent a British fleet to sail through the Dardanelles as a warning to the Russians not to advance any farther, and he reinforced the message by sending Indian troops to Cyprus, just a short sail away from the tsar's army. Russia, having thought the matter over and concluded that Armenia and Georgia were pretty nice consolation prizes, finally turned its troops toward home.

There's more of course, but I won't bore you with all the details. Suffice it to say that like so many things in life, I (and Vincent and French, of course) had expended a great deal of energy (and nearly lost our lives, to boot) in what turned out to be a futile enterprise that accomplished nothing. It's a funny old world; while we were chasing Ivanov and Oksana all over England and across the Channel, nothing seemed more important than getting our hands on Bowser's case. But as soon as the Russians had won and Ivanov (I'm still betting it was that sly devil) had slipped away to tell the tsar how exposed Britain was, it didn't seem to matter at all. Knowing Britain's troop strength probably confirmed Russia's decision to invade the Ottoman Empire, but I'm convinced they would have done so anyway, to protect their close cousins, the Serbs (a loyalty that's bound to lead to more trouble, you wait and see). And Dizzy managed a respectable showing, anyway, with our fleet plying the waters of the Mediterranean and the dusky lads from the subcontinent filing off the ships and into encampment on Cyprus, weapons at the ready.

The world had a few more surprises in store. Gladstone became prime minister again, not once, but *three* times. I never did like the old prig, but the British public tended to rally round him from time to time. I hear Vicky wasn't overly fond of the man, either. That's the only thing I've ever liked about that woman.

Dizzy lived until 1881, a year after Gladstone became PM for the second time. I suspect it was that news that killed him. Despite his queer ways, I liked the old queen. He was just as much an outsider as I am, looked down upon by many for his Jewish lineage (irrelevant, as far as I'm concerned) and for his outlandish dress (well, even I have to admit he was a bit daft in that regard). Still, I'll always have a special place in my heart for him.

Endicott continues to serve in various positions in government, which continues to prove unfortunate for those forced to work with him.

Charles Calthorp still prowls the streets of London, like his idol Gladstone, looking for souls to save (and if the souls belong to buxom young tarts, so much the better).

Peter Penbras continues to expose shocking stories of governmental ineptitude. He is never without material.

Rowena Adderly still plies her trade at the Silver Thistle. She hasn't given up on breaching the walls of my petticoats, and I haven't given up resisting her siege.

And Vincent? Suffice it to say that exposure to the influence of French was not enough to render him into a clean, presentable, Christian young gentleman. In short, Vincent remains Vincent.

I don't know how he brooked it, but after Dizzy's term as PM ended, French served the Grand Old Man. I know this for a fact, as French and I were destined to share a few more adventures together. And no, I haven't discovered French's Christian name. Of course, it would be easy enough to do; a brief trip to the British Library should reveal the information. But where's the fun in that?

As for my sable coat and hat, I doubt that I shall ever see it delivered to Lotus House. Apparently, some clerk in the office of the exchequer took one look at French's expenses incurred during our escapade and fainted dead away. When he'd regained consciousness, he took a red pencil and began slashing through the itemized list like a man possessed. Unfortunately, my hat and coat were victims of his bureaucratic mania.

You might think I'd be bitter, after an experience like that. But I'm a cynic, and so the fact that I failed to change the world with my adventure didn't dishearten me in the least. By the time

I was back at Lotus House, comfortably ensconced in my study, counting the day's receipts and using a chisel to break up one of Mrs. Drinkwater's ginger biscuits, I'd recovered my equanimity. Besides, this affair proved to be just the first of many such, when I have found the British government at my doorstep humbly asking for my assistance in extricating them from some predicament. And in most cases, I've graciously agreed to help.

In fact, I've rendered my assistance so frequently that I'm contemplating having cards printed up. Nothing flash, you understand. Something discreet, but elegant. Jet-black ink on cream vellum, perhaps. "India Black: Consultant to the British Prime Minister on Affairs Foreign and Domestic." Who knows, I might even induce that great lump Vicky to grant me the royal warrant for Lotus House, and I can post a brass plaque by the front door: "Lotus House: Purveyor of Sluts by Appointment to Her Royal Majesty." Now, wouldn't that be something?